Other Books by L.L. Bartlett

The Jeff Resnick Mysteries
Murder On The Mind
Dead In Red
Room At The Inn
Cheated By Death
Bound By Suggestion
Dark Waters

Short Stories
When The Spirit Moves You
Bah! Humbug

Abused: A Daughter's Story

Writing as Lorraine Bartlett

The Tales of Telenia (Fantasy)
Threshold
Journey
Treachery

The Victoria Square Mysteries
A Crafty Killing
The Walled Flower
One Hot Murder
Recipes To Die For: A Victoria Square Cookbook

Short Stories
We're So Sorry, Uncle Albert
Blue Christmas
An Unconditional Love
Love Heals
Prisoner of Love

Writing as Lorna Barrett

The Booktown Mysteries
    Murder Is Binding
    Bookmarked For Death
    Bookplate Special
    Chapter & Hearse
    Sentenced To Death
    Murder On The Half Shelf
    Not The Killing Type
    Book Clubbed

A JEFF RESNICK MYSTERY

DARK WATERS

by L.L. Bartlett

Polaris Press

Polaris Press
P.O. Box 230
N. Greece, NY 14515

Acknowledgments

My thanks go to Leann Sweeney for her advice and for sharing her knowledge on a number of subjects, and to my first reader, Dru Ann Love. I struggled with a title for this book, but my friend Jennifer Stanley (aka Ellery Adams) suggested Dark Waters, which was perfect. Many thanks to Pat Ryan Graphics for my beautiful cover; and to Frankly Graphics for formatting the trade paperback edition.

ONE

The air encircling me was alive, icy pinpricks of energy penetrating every inch of my body and soul. The wind whipped through my hair as I spiraled higher, higher, racing through inky darkness, drawn to a blinding white light that pulsed like a beating heart.

Below me yawned a black, fathomless abyss—the end of everything.

My gaze swung back to the light, filling me with increasing trepidation. Did the light hold salvation or damnation?

Confusion swelled within me. This was wrong, very, very wrong. My panic escalated until it was almost unbearable.

The light above me swelled with sickening speed, getting larger, becoming a super nova that exploded in a dazzling flash of deadly radiation. It ripped me apart, leaving me nothing but billions of scattered molecules destined to float through the vast cosmic nothingness.

Alone.

Forever.

Someone grabbed me under the arms, pulling—yanking—me away from the light.

Back to safety.

Back to life.

A voice.

Calling my name.

Bringing me back from the brink.

Warm fingers encircled my wrist, grounding me in reality.

"He's breathing better now," said the same voice, one I knew well and trusted.

I opened my eyes and saw my brother Richard's concerned face above me and thought, with great annoyance, *Now what?*

My eyes slid shut and I did a physical assessment. My back hurt—like I'd been whacked by a plank. My right hand throbbed in time with my heartbeat, the palm stung.

Stung?

Oh, yeah. I'd been talking to Richard's wife, Brenda, not paying attention as I deadheaded annuals in the window boxes. I'd grabbed a buzzing bee instead of a withered pansy. I'd stared at my hand and watched in shock as the sting quickly reddened and transformed from a speck to a welt. Then I was sweating and cold on that hot, early fall afternoon. The world wobbled, the sky tilting as I'd fallen off the bottom rung of the stepladder.

"Jeffy?" It was Brenda this time, her voice worried.

I opened my eyes again and looked around me, avoiding their worried gazes, and looked down. The creamy, hand-crocheted cashmere afghan from their living room had been tossed across my chest. Dappled sunlight wavered through the oak leaves above me. A cushion of cool grass lay beneath me.

Physically, I was quickly recovering. Mentally, I was as embarrassed as hell.

"I didn't know you were allergic to bee stings," Richard said.

"Neither did I," I croaked. My throat still felt constricted. "How much do I owe you for services rendered?"

"House calls don't come cheap," my physician brother said, distracted, as he packed up his gear.

"Since we're in your backyard, you didn't have far to

go."

"Lucky for you," he said. "Are you feeling better?"

Surprisingly, "Yeah."

"Well, you scared the hell out of me," a very pregnant Brenda said, sounding annoyed. "And now we're going to be late."

She wasn't unconcerned for my welfare—one look in her deep-brown eyes told me that. But she had other things on her mind on that particular afternoon.

I glanced at my watch. Her sister Evelyn's plane was due in less than thirty minutes.

"You'd better go without me," Richard said, brushing the knees of his grass-stained, beige Dockers. "Jeff shouldn't be left alone just yet."

"I'm fine," I insisted, and what's more, I pretty much was.

"Not bad," Brenda agreed, "considering you nearly died five minutes ago."

I struggled to my feet. "You're exaggerating. I just had the wind knocked out of me when I hit the ground." In fact, the only outward sign of my ordeal was the puffy skin on the palm of my right hand.

Brenda gathered up her purse, cell phone, and car keys from the grass nearby. Richard helped her to her feet. She gave me a quick hug, and I soaked in her relief for me and growing anxiety for what else was to come.

"I'm sorry, Brenda."

"Hush up," she said, gave my cheek a quick peck, then turned to give Richard a proper kiss before she headed for the dark Mercedes parked in the drive.

We watched as she backed out, and then headed toward Main Street.

I bent to pick up my pruning shears. "I'm sorry I messed up her day."

"It's probably better that she goes alone."

"I'd better finish—"

Richard put a hand out to stop me. "No more gardening today. And not until we get you tested for allergies."

"I feel fine," I protested.

He grabbed the bushel basket of culled, dead blossoms I'd been working to fill. "Come on, let's go inside."

Richard headed for the driveway, but I lagged behind and shaded my eyes as I looked up at the bright sun overhead. It wasn't half as piercing as the light in my ... dream? Vision?

Not nearly as scary, either.

The beveled leaded glass windows of Richard's study acted like prisms, thanks to the late afternoon sun coming through them. The antique grandfather clock ticked loudly, measuring out the hours in a steady rhythm.

"It was weird," I said and popped the antihistamine into my mouth, swallowing it with a sip of the tepid water Richard had given me. I sank back into the cool leather wing chair in his study.

"Sounds like a classic near-death experience," Richard commented dryly, and sampled his Scotch. He sat perched on the edge of his big mahogany desk, which dominated the north end of the room. It didn't seem fair that he got Scotch when I was the one who'd had the traumatic experience.

"Yeah, but I thought you were supposed to find peace and comfort in the light, welcomed by your long-dead relatives, yada, yada, yada. If that's a sample of what's to come, I'm not going."

He smiled wryly, and then sobered. "Seriously, Jeff, you went into anaphylactic shock. The way your hand swelled means this isn't the first time you've been stung. Next time, you could die."

I ignored his probable death sentence. "Well, I don't

remember it ever happening before." It was lame, but an honest answer. Since I got mugged some eighteen months before, suffering a fractured skull and what the attending quack blithely called a "little brain damage," there was a lot from my past that I didn't remember. And the injury had not only left me with often crippling headaches, but damnably annoying empathic abilities. Some people called me psychic. I called myself unfortunate.

"You ought to get started on allergy shots right away to desensitize you. Otherwise, no more gardening."

"Allergy shots? Those are for snot-nosed—" did *I* fit the description? "—wimps."

"Being allergic does not make you a wimp. Not getting the shots makes you criminally stupid."

"Then hand me a dunce cap."

"I hope you're not serious," Richard said.

"Couldn't you give them to me? Or maybe Brenda?"

Richard frowned. "You're not afraid, are you?"

"It's not fear of injections it's—" God, I didn't want to discuss this. I looked away. "I just don't like needles."

"I don't think we're talking needles. I think you're talking trust."

I couldn't meet his gaze, but, yeah, he was right. After what I'd been through these last couple of years, there were only two people on the planet I trusted implicitly: Richard and Brenda. I loved Maggie, my lady of nearly eighteen months, but after she'd dumped me earlier that summer—before the guy she thought she loved turned out to be a class A heel—I wasn't sure I could ever fully trust her again, though I was more than willing to try.

"I've got things to do," I said, getting up from the chair.

"Oh, no," Richard said, pushing me back down again. "Not after what happened out in the yard. You may not be out of the woods yet, and I want to keep an eye on you. It's possible the symptoms could reoccur. You can stay in your old room tonight. Then tomorrow we'll find you an allergist."

I let out a breath. I trusted Richard. I trusted his medical judgment where I might not trust others. "Okay."

Thundering footsteps on the parquet floor echoed outside in the hall. We both shot looks at the grandfather clock across the room. Brenda had been gone less than an hour.

"She's here," Brenda called as she approached, her voice unusually high. She stopped in the study doorway. "The flight came in early, and Evelyn brought a surprise."

"Uh-oh," Richard muttered, his face going slack. He was on his feet, meeting Brenda halfway. An elegant, older black lady joined Brenda just inside the door. Impeccably dressed in a dark suit and a dove-gray blouse, her short straightened hair was streaked with strands of white. Evelyn Mason looked every inch a high school principal, albeit newly retired: damned intimidating.

"Evelyn," Richard said, sounding pleased. He gave her a quick kiss on the cheek, then hugged her.

"It's good to see you again, Richard," she said stiffly—and without sincerity.

"And here's the surprise," Brenda said. "This is Da-Marr, Evelyn's nephew."

I stood, my calves pressed against the chair to keep me upright, trepidation settling over me like a smothering cloak once more.

A young black man stood in the doorway. Dressed in dark, baggy pants and an equally baggy white shirt, his head was covered in a pink do rag, and heavy gold hoop earrings hung from both ears. He reached out and shook hands with Richard.

"Hey, man. I heard a lot about you." He looked past Richard to me.

My gut tightened.

"Evelyn, Da-Marr, this is my brother, Jeff Resnick,"

Richard said.

My gaze met Da-Marr's.

My mind flashed to the cold March night some eighteen months before.

The baseball bat came at me.

My arm shot up in a defensive move. The bone cracked—a compound fracture—sending skyrockets of pain up my arm.

The bat swung toward me again, whanged into my skull.

I fell to my knees on the cold, wet concrete.

My cheek slammed onto the icy cement.

I tried to raise myself.

The bat smashed against my temple.

My universe went black.

Richard caught my arm and kept me from keeling over.

Heart pounding, the breath caught in my throat—I couldn't get enough air. Pin prickles of ebony danced before my eyes.

Richard shoved me back into my chair, pushing my head down to my knees. Blood roared in my ears. "Breathe," he ordered, grasping my wrist to take my racing pulse. "You're going to an allergist tomorrow. No arguments."

But it wasn't anaphylaxis that had my guts tied in knots.

It was pure and simple terror.

TWO

Richard raised his wineglass. "To Betsy Ruth."

"To Betsy Ruth," they all echoed, and all but Brenda, who was drinking ice water, raised their glasses. After a ceremonial sip, the real business of passing plates and platters of steaming food around the big dining room table began.

The catering van had arrived half an hour early. Richard generously tipped the deliveryman while Brenda and Jeff scrambled to add another place setting to the table. Evelyn helped dish up in the kitchen, and everyone took a bowl or platter into the formal dining room.

"Betsy Ruth," Da-Marr repeated with the hint of a sneer. "That's a old fashioned name for a twenty-first century chick. You oughta name this girl something more hip. Tashawna's a lot prettier. More fitting."

Brenda glanced at Richard, braving a smile. They'd both known that their interracial marriage was a sore spot with some of Brenda's relatives, but Richard hadn't expected the subject to surface quite so soon.

"Actually, it's Elizabeth Ruth," he clarified, "after Jeff's and my mother, and Brenda's twin sister."

Da-Marr looked at Evelyn. "The one that died?"

Evelyn nodded.

Da-Marr served himself several slices of prime rib. "You always get dinner catered?"

"Not usually," Richard admitted. "But with the baby

coming, it didn't seem right that Brenda should have to cook for a crowd."

"Luckily the portions are huge," she said, sounding nervous. "It was such a nice surprise for you to bring Da-Marr, Evie."

"I didn't realize Richard's brother was still living here. I thought he would've been out on his own a long time ago." Evelyn leveled a reproachful glance at Jeff.

Silence followed that rebuke.

Richard took a breath and smiled, determined to keep the conversational tone light. "Jeff doesn't live with us. He has an apartment over the garage."

Jeff said nothing, adding a minuscule portion of green beans to his nearly empty plate.

"It's good for Da-Marr to see new places—how other people live. I thought he could help Richard with yard work or something while we're here," Evelyn continued.

"Uh, that's my job," Jeff said; it was the first time he'd spoken since their guests had arrived.

Brenda cleared her throat. "How nice of you to think of us. I hope you won't be bored, Da-Marr. We lead a pretty quiet life."

That wasn't entirely true since Jeff had reentered their lives, but Richard wasn't about to dispute it just then. "Are you between jobs right now?" he asked Da-Marr.

"Da-Marr's going to college next semester," Evelyn answered for him.

"Just Philly Community College," Da-Marr said. "I got my GED over the summer. I can't make no money with just a GED and Aunt Evelyn's got me some scholarships lined up. After, I might transfer to Pitt or Penn State."

"What will you major in?" Brenda asked.

"I dunno. Maybe Criminal Justice."

Jeff glared at the Da-Marr, mouth open, his expression incredulous.

"Da-Marr could be a lawyer one day," Evelyn chimed in.

"I dunno," the kid said again, reaching for another helping of potatoes. "I haven't made up my mind yet."

Cutlery clattered on bone china as the conversation waned. Richard filled the gap by topping off wine glasses.

Jeff's glance had dipped back to the table. It was his turn to clear his throat. "We're, uh ... supposed to take delivery of the boat tomorrow, Rich."

"Boat?" Da-Marr asked, looking up from his plate.

Richard smiled. "Brenda calls it my 'folly.' We bought it at a government auction."

Evelyn glowered at Brenda. "We?"

"Jeff and me," Richard clarified.

"Since when does the government sell boats?" Evelyn asked.

"After they confiscate them from drug runners," Brenda explained.

"Drug runners?" Da-Marr asked, his interest piqued.

"Zero tolerance," she explained. "It's just a toy. Richard will never have time for it, but I wasn't about to let him waste more tens of thousands of dollars on a new one."

"What kind of boat are you talking about?" Evelyn asked, her voice filled with reproach.

Richard reached behind him for his wallet. He took out a folded photograph and handed it to her. "It's a Slipstream 9000—a forty-six footer."

Evelyn let out a horrified sigh. "Oh, my."

"Lemme see," Da-Marr said, reaching to take the picture from her. His eyes grew round. "You know how to drive one of these things?"

Richard shrugged. "Not yet. But we've already taken boating safety courses. Jeff found all the specs online so we know how it operates, how fast she'll go. Now we just need a bit of experience on the water. It should be a piece of cake."

Brenda snorted.

Richard threw a look at Jeff, but he seemed preoccupied, staring at his plate.

"Are we all going to retrieve this—this boat?" Evelyn asked, her tone conveying her lack of enthusiasm for joining the adventure.

"I wasn't planning on it," Brenda said and buttered her roll.

"Maybe you'd like to come along, Da-Marr," Richard said.

Jeff's head snapped up, his eyes wide, the muscles along his jaw taut.

"Sure, sounds cool." Da-Marr shoveled a large piece of meat into his mouth.

Jeff looked at Richard. "We only have two life jackets."

"We can get more," Richard said.

"I don't need no life jacket," Da-Marr said.

"Can you swim?" Brenda asked.

"Ya think the boat is gonna sink?"

"The Niagara River has a strong current. Better safe than sorry," Richard said.

"You'd probably die of hypothermia first," Jeff muttered into his wineglass.

Da-Marr turned on him. "Wha'd you say?"

Jeff lowered his glass. "The water's cold—about sixty-five degrees this time of year. If you fell in, you'd likely suffer hypothermia. That can kill you." It almost sounded like a threat.

"How would you know?"

"I nearly died from hypothermia a year ago."

"I thought you got mugged."

"This happened after that." Jeff's icy stare could have drilled a hole through solid granite. Da-Marr met it with equal disdain.

"I might not be available," Jeff added. "I've got to be at work at noon."

"That's no problem. The Slipstream salesman is supposed to meet us at nine. We'll still have time to give her a trial run."

Jeff stared at Da-Marr and then shrugged.

Brenda cleared her throat and forced a smile. "Anybody ready for dessert?"

Jeffy was in rare form tonight," Brenda said, pulling back the spread on the king-sized bed.

Richard grabbed the other side to help her. It was damage control time. "I think what happened to him this afternoon rattled him more than he cares to admit. And you know how he feels about the prospect of consulting yet another physician. After his experience last spring, he's paranoid to—"

"Oh, come on, you know damn well his accident had nothing to do with that."

Richard straightened, deciding to play dumb. "What are you talking about?"

She let out a breath, her face tight with anger. "Da-Marr."

Oh, hell. "Okay, so they didn't hit it off. Why are you so upset?"

"Isn't it obvious?"

Richard hesitated. "No."

She let out another harsh breath. "Da-Marr's a young, black man."

Maybe bluffing was the better part of valor. "So?"

"So, what type of male do you suppose beat Jeffy with a baseball bat?"

"He never said."

"Did he need to?" she challenged.

Richard said nothing.

"When Da-Marr walked in, Jeffy looked at him as if he was responsible for that beating. That's unfair. That's—

that's positively racist! And I never would have thought that Jeffy—"

"Brenda, calm down," Richard whispered. "Our guests will hear you."

She pursed her lips, her fists clenched at her side, breathing loudly though her nose.

Richard crossed to her side of the bed and took her in his arms, but she stood rigid in his embrace. "Come on, sit down," he said, pulling her down on the bed. "Think about it logically. Jeff was traumatized by the mugging. It changed his entire life, and not for the better. It's not surprising he still has unresolved issues around it. He doesn't come into contact with young people, black or white, on a regular basis. And the fact he fell off the ladder an hour before he met Da-Marr could've brought back all the angst he still hasn't dealt with."

"And never will," Brenda said bitterly.

Richard sighed. "You may be right. But you can't take his reactions personally."

"Da-Marr is a guest in *my* home, and I won't stand for anyone—not even Jeffy—insulting a guest. And did he have to bring up the boat in front of Evelyn?"

"We are taking possession tomorrow."

"Yes, but talking about it seems like we're flaunting your wealth. I don't want Evelyn going home to tell my whole family how uppity and pretentious we are."

"Are we?"

"I don't think so, but I can't predict how our good fortune appears to others. And I still don't understand why you feel you need such an extravagant toy."

"We had a great time on Tom and Olivia's boat this summer. I thought it might be fun to tool around the lake on a boat of our own."

"Not with a baby in tow."

"Lots of people take their kids out on boats."

"Kids, not infants."

"Betsy won't be an infant by summer."

"No, she'll be toddling around, fall off, drown—"

"Now who's paranoid?" She wouldn't look at him. "Brenda, what are you really angry about?"

She blinked back tears. "I just told you."

He shook his head. "There's something else bothering you. Now, what is it?"

She looked away. "Nothing. I just—" She wouldn't look at him, her lower lip trembling, her eyes now overflowing with tears. When she spoke, there was a catch in her voice. "What if Jeffy is so prejudiced against African-Americans he can't accept our baby because she's not white?"

Richard cupped her chin, turning her face toward him. "Well, for one thing, she won't be a teenaged boy. And a toothless baby in diapers isn't all that threatening."

Brenda's mouth dropped open; she glared at him. Then her anger dissolved into a giggle. "You have incredible power over me, Dr. Alpert."

Richard shrugged, struggling to keep a straight face. "It's a gift. Look, you know Jeff loves you. He'll love the baby. I don't think you have anything to worry about."

She gave a grudging nod, but her eyes were still troubled.

"If it'll make you feel better, I'll talk to him about it in the morning," Richard promised.

"What about now? He's only downstairs in Curtis's old room."

"Ha! He waited for us to come up here, then snuck off to his own place. He's probably the worst patient I've ever seen when it comes to following orders."

"Do you think he'll be all right?" she asked.

Richard smiled. Trust Brenda to worry about Jeff even when she was angry with him. "Yes. You've had a busy day, too. You ought to get some sleep. It's only another five days until the baby arrives."

"If she comes on time."

He helped her into bed, crouched beside her, pulled up the covers, and kissed her lips. "Go to sleep."

She pouted, but said, "At least I always follow doctor's orders."

A swell of tenderness welled within him. "Like hell you do."

THREE

The baseball bat smashed onto my raised arm, breaking my ulna. My knees buckled and slammed into the wet concrete sidewalk. The bat arced over me and clipped my shoulder. It came at my head again, fracturing the squamous part of my skull.

Blackness engulfed me, leaving me suspended in an inky void.

I was caught in a whirlwind, cold air freezing each and every cell in my body, engulfing my soul. With no way out, I was powerless against the sucking wind that spun me higher, higher into the vortex.

I awoke with a start, gasping, heart pounding, and sweat covered. Two scary dreams had merged into one experience. I rolled onto my back and stared at the darkened ceiling above me. The clock read six fifty-nine. It was way too early to get up, but I was pretty sure I wouldn't be able to get back to sleep.

I threw back the covers and grabbed my blue velour robe, tied the belt around my waist, and headed for the galley kitchen and the coffeepot. Morning noises brought my cat Herschel flying around the corner and skidding to a halt in front of his bowl with a smart "Yow!"

"Yeah, yeah, I'll get to you," I rumbled, and drew water from the tap, filling the carafe and attending to the coffee first. While it brewed, Herschel feasted on turkey and giblets cat food. I'd sniffed it before putting the bowl down on the floor. Disgusting.

I tried not to think about the nightmare, instead turning my thoughts to the Slipstream 9000. I parked my cup on the coffee table, sat down on the couch, and grabbed the color pictures and text I'd printed off the Internet.

Richard had called it "our" boat, not that I'd contributed a nickel. We'd only been aboard her the one time just before the auction. I can pick up bad vibes like tuning into a radio station. Richard was concerned that something sinister had happened on the boat before or during its seizure and he'd asked me to play human divining rod. We both felt much better when I'd picked up nothing out of the ordinary, and Richard easily outbid the competition.

Too bad the boating season in Western New York had officially ended on Labor Day. The marina Richard had chosen on Grand Island had a derelict feel to it now that most of the boats had been mothballed for the winter. Ours would be going into the water for a few days of test drives before it, too, would be stored until spring.

The thought of another long, cold winter depressed me. My gaze swung to the framed picture of Maggie on my end table. We'd had a rough, strained summer as we'd tried to heal the wound of her infidelity. It had only scabbed over during the summer, but we'd been taking it slow, afraid to trust one another. Things had been getting better until about two weeks ago. I'd been busy at work, and presumably so had she. I'd called a few times, leaving messages, but she hadn't returned my calls. I wondered if I should just show up on her doorstep, but decided not to intrude. I should have asked Brenda, Maggie's best friend, what was up but now it was out of the question. Her hostility quotient the night before had been off the chart and I had an inkling why, but wasn't eager to push it.

I felt the need to vent my feelings about what had happened that day—the near-death experience and the tumult I'd relived when I'd laid eyes on Da-Marr—but I wasn't sure Maggie would be receptive to that crap. And I was afraid to mention it again to Richard—and definitely not Brenda.

No, I'd have to deal with this myself or find someone else to confide in.

But who?

Heavy dew covered the grass the next morning. Richard looked out the kitchen window to examine the day and saw Jeff kneeling in front of the south flower garden, weeding.

Anger coursed through him and he grabbed his coffee cup and headed outside.

"What do you think you're doing?" he called as he approached his brother.

"I'm weeding. What do you think I'm doing?"

"I told you not to."

"And I'm doing whatever the hell I please, which is to keep this garden looking its best for Brenda. Besides, I'm wearing gardening gloves. Nothing's going to sting me."

"Says you."

"Says me," Jeff agreed.

Richard felt angry enough to pour the remains of his coffee over Jeff's head. He had a few more choice words to deliver but didn't have the opportunity when Jeff stood, picking up the basket and heading for the garage. He tossed the weeds and dried blossoms onto the compost heap and entered the garage, putting the basket and gloves away.

"Why did you have go and invite *him* along?"

Richard eyed his brother's rigid back. No need to identify who 'he' was. It was so unlike Jeff to be petulant. He stood here like a stone statue, his face hidden—turned to the back of the garage. Jeff so seldom showed emotion that Richard almost welcomed the outburst. It made his brother seem more ... human.

"What kind of host would I be not to include a guest?"

Jeff rounded on him. "*You* didn't invite him to stay with us, and neither did Brenda."

"Yeah, well he's here now. And he's part of Brenda's family."

"No, he's not. He's related to her sister's brother-in-law, not her sister."

"Then he's part of Evelyn's family—which is the same thing to Brenda."

Jeff withdrew keys from his pocket, clicked the fob and unlocked the Mercedes. He picked up the new, still plastic-encased life jackets and tossed them into the car's trunk, slamming the lid.

"What is your problem with this kid?" Richard pressed.

Jeff's breaths came out in short gaps—like an asthmatic's, but he didn't answer.

"Brenda says you were mugged by black men. That you're unfairly projecting that experience on Da-Marr."

Still no answer.

"Were the guys who mugged you black?"

Jeff swallowed, looked away, biting his lip before answering. "Yes."

Richard exhaled harshly. "You can't condemn an entire race because of one incident."

Jeff said nothing; he still wouldn't face Richard.

"Brenda's worried you won't love the baby because of the mugging."

Jeff looked up, his gaze piercing. "Cherry pie?"

Richard frowned. "What?"

"That's how I think of Betsy Ruth. It's my pet name

for her."

"If you say so."

Jeff shook his head, the hint of a smile gracing his lips. "You haven't got a clue. You don't know." A silly grin brightened his features. "I already know her. What she'll be like—who she'll be. Trust me, this little girl will be the best thing that's happened to all of us."

An unreasonable surge of jealously swelled through Richard. Was Jeff spouting bullshit, or through his emphatic sensibilities—his own brand of extra sensory perception—had he already connected with the unborn baby? The idea both thrilled and repelled Richard.

"Brenda will never have to worry about me and this kid. I couldn't love her more if she were my own." He took a breath. "I guess I better have a talk with Brenda."

"It wouldn't hurt."

"Okay, later." His gaze strayed toward the house. "You'd better go get your ... friend."

But that wasn't necessary. The back door to the house opened and Da-Marr stepped out, looking like a caricature of a rapper, with his earrings and do rag. Not the typical denizen of Sundowner's Marina.

"You guys get up way too early," Da-Marr complained.

"Jeff's got to be at work at noon," Richard reminded him.

"You don't have to come with us," Jeff said, rather snidely.

"I ain't stayin' here to listen to those women talk baby shit all day, either."

"You might want to bring a jacket," Richard said. "It'll be cold out on the water."

"I don't need no coat," Da-Marr asserted.

"Suit yourself," Richard said.

"Hey, man, I gotta sit up front. I get carsick. You don't want me blowing chunks in the back of your pretty car."

Richard glanced at Jeff, willing him to submit.

"Why don't I just stay home and finish the gardening?" he grated.

"Why don't you just shut up and get in the car," Richard said, plunking his coffee mug on a shelf on the wall.

They all piled into the Mercedes. "Buckle up," Richard told Da-Marr, and was surprised when the young man complied. Jeff slumped down in the back seat, scowling like an angry child, and even Richard could sense the anger emanating from him. It was going to be an uncomfortable twenty-minute drive.

Somehow, I managed to survive the trip across town for Sundowner's Marina on the southeast shore of Grand Island. Da-Marr took control of the radio and blasted hip-hop, and Richard didn't stop him. I grabbed a tissue from the box Brenda keeps on the backseat and stuffed my ears, which probably saved me from one of my skull-pounding headaches.

The marina's parking lot was nearly empty. Not many people had come out to brave the gray day, choppy water, and gusty winds. Huddled in my jacket, I followed Richard down the dock to slip forty-seven, where we met up with Jerry Hasper, a local Slipstream salesman Richard had contracted to give us a quick-and-dirty overview on the ins and outs of boat ownership. I'd practically memorized the information I'd downloaded from the Internet, but reading and practical experience were two different things.

We stood on the dock staring at Richard's beautiful new-to-us boat. The boat still bore the last owner's moniker, "Easy Breezin'" in black vinyl letters on the stern.

"Damn, we need to come up with a new name," Richard said, gazing at the sleek, white fiberglass beauty.

"We've got all winter to do that," I told him.

"Hot Mama—that's what I'd call it," Da-Marr said.

I ground my molars together. And I'd choose to call it anything *but* that. Why did this friggin' kid think we needed his opinion on anything, let alone the name of *our* boat?

"Come on," Jerry said, "let's go aboard."

Easy Breezin' was one hell of a beautiful lady. With three sumptuous staterooms, cherry wood cabinetry throughout, and two heads, she had a tiny but elegant galley kitchen with Corian counters and a raised dinette. The area known as the salon was L-shaped with an ivory leather couch to port and matching barrel chairs to starboard. The whole area was enclosed by tinted sliding glass doors to the outdoor deck. Up top, the bridge deck was equipped with not only every boating mechanism known to man, but had conformable banquette seating for six, with a fridge and a wet bar that could host a pretty damn fine happy hour. The boat even had a washer and dryer. Easy Breezin' had everything a man could want in a luxury yacht, and boy did I wish it was mine. That it now belonged to Richard was the next best thing.

For the next ninety minutes, Jerry took us through the ins and outs of boat ownership. From the tour of the engine room below—with two Volvo diesel engines—to the ins and outs of disembarking and docking, to battening down the hatches at night, he showed us how everything aboard operated, including the quiet flush toilets and the electronic anchor winch.

Da-Marr hung out in the salon, out of the wind, and was silent through most of the debriefing—bored out of his skull. But his eyes were shiny with delight when Richard turned the helm over to him—before he invited me to drive the boat. I kept my mouth shut, but my resentment toward the kid inched up another notch. Why did a stranger deserve more regard than Richard's own flesh and blood? The thought made me feel petty, and my resentment toward Da-Marr cranked even higher.

"Wish the guys back home could see me now," Da-Marr shouted, and hooted with glee from the helm.

"The kid's really enjoying himself," a smiling Richard commented from the banquette.

At least one of us was having a good time. I sat at the other end of the couch, watching our wake and wishing I was anywhere else. It was stupid to let the kid's presence get to me. And I still hadn't figured out what I was going to say to Brenda the next time I saw her.

"Do you want a turn at the controls?" Richard asked.

Fuck yes! "No," I grumbled instead.

"Come on, Jeff. Stop acting like you've got a stick up your ass."

I glared at him. "Who says I don't have a stick up my ass?"

Richard didn't comment.

"We're getting close to the end of the island," I said as soon as I could see the North Grand Island Bridge up in the distance. There's a point in the Niagara River where boat navigation is forbidden. Next up—none other than Niagara Falls.

Richard turned back to the controls. "We'd better turn back for the marina," he hollered to Da-Marr.

"Come on, man, I'm just getting used to this beauty."

"Sorry, but Jeff's got to go to work."

"What about you?" he yelled back.

"Not today."

"Tell him to call in sick."

I glared at Richard. "Tell him to go fuck himself."

"Jeff!" Richard chided.

Richard crossed the deck, nudged Da-Marr aside, and turned the boat around.

I never did get my turn at the wheel.

When we reached the dock, Da-Marr rose from his

seat. "That was awesome. Better than driving a car past eighty." And did he do that on a regular basis? "Hey, Richard. Got a buck so I can get me a Coke?"

"Sure," Richard said and thumbed through his wallet, giving Da-Marr a handful of dollars.

"Thanks, man." Da-Marr jumped onto the dock.

"Don't go far," Richard cautioned. "We need to get going."

Da-Marr gave him a backward wave and started off toward the vending machines at the front of the dock.

"Perfect timing," I said. "He left us all the work."

Richard said nothing as he buttoned up everything inside, while I tossed out the bumpers and tied up the boat. If we'd actually known what we were doing, it would have taken a lot less time. I kept looking at my watch, wondering if I should call my boss and tell him I'd be late for work. My usual shift was at night—but Tom had a doctor's appointment, and Dave, the other full-time bartender, wasn't able to cover that day. They'd cut me slack so many times I'd have been a real bastard not to have agreed to help out.

Finally finished with our chores, Richard and I strolled up the dock looking for Da-Marr, but he was nowhere in sight. "Where the hell has he gone to?" I asked.

"He can't have gone far," Richard said reasonably, but we spent the next fifteen minutes wandering around the marina calling the kid's name with no results.

"Brenda is going to kill me if I lose him," Richard groused. He looked all around the area. "Do you think he could have gone back to the car?"

"Maybe. Why don't you go look. If he's there, blast the horn a few times to let me know. I'll keep looking around here."

"Right," he said, and we split up.

I went back to Easy Breezin', but Da-Marr hadn't gone

back there. I stopped in and asked the marina manager, but he said he hadn't seen the kid since we'd first arrived. I was ready to abandon the search when I saw Da-Marr step onto the dock from one of the few boats that were still in their slips.

"What the hell do you think you're doing?" I demanded.

"Checking out the competition. They got nothing on Richard's boat."

"You could get arrested for trespassing."

"Bullshit."

An urban kid in a very white marina? What planet did this kid live on?

"Come on. Let's go."

Since Richard hadn't had good luck at the car, he met us half way down the dock where Da-Marr gave him the same song and dance routine about checking out the other boats.

"I met the guy at the Coke machine. He wanted to show off his boat. I was just leavin' when pussy showed up."

If I'd been close enough, I'd have kicked that son of a bitch in the balls.

"Please don't do it again. If something happened, you might be falsely accused," Richard said reasonably.

"Hey, I'm from the city. I can take care of myself," Da-Marr bluffed and took off for the car.

"Famous last words," I grumbled, and glanced at my watch. I had fifteen minutes to get to the Whole Nine Yards. I estimated I'd be at least fifteen minutes late.

Richard hadn't moved. "What is your problem?"

"I'm going to be fucking late for work because of that asshole."

Richard shoved his index finger in my face, his expression livid. "You will *not* insult my houseguest and you *will* behave like an adult.

Damn, Da-Marr. At that moment I felt sure I could kill the little bastard.

I looked away and stalked off in the direction of the parking lot.

Da-Marr was already sitting in the passenger seat, looking triumphant as I climbed into the Mercedes' back seat. Richard got in and started the engine. "So you made a friend?" he said as he steered out of the parking lot.

"I guess," Da-Marr muttered. "The guy said the boat belonged to his father. I don't go round askin' people for proof." He reached over and switched on the radio once again, cranking up the volume.

I saw Richard look back at me via the rearview mirror.

If what Da-Marr said was true, then I looked like a jerk for tattling. But what if he was lying? There was no way I could prove it, so I kept my mouth shut. I looked at my watch and fumed. I pulled out my cell phone to call the bar. "Can you turn that down," I shouted.

Instead, Da-Marr pressed the button and the decibel level rose exponentially.

Richard reached over and hit the off switch. "Jeff's got to make a call," he said reasonably, but Da-Marr glanced over his shoulder and glared at me.

As I punched up the number for the bar, I had a feeling I was going to pay for the exchange that had just taken place.

But how?

The wheels on Jeff's car spun madly as it launched like a rocket down the drive and turned right onto LeBrun Road. Richard sighed—angry, and yet sympathetic at the emotion that had precipitated the childish act of defiance.

He shoved the keys to his own car into his pocket and stood staring at the now-empty drive, hesitant to return to the warmth of the house and the cold reception he was likely to receive from at least one person in residence.

It was with great reluctance that he entered the house and dawdled as he hung up his jacket on one of the pegs in the home's expansive butler's pantry. He could hear voices in the kitchen: one domineering and one almost quavering. God, his feet felt heavy as he plodded into what was supposed to be the heart of his home.

"I'm back," he called cheerfully as he entered the kitchen. Brenda sat at her usual seat at the maple table, looking small despite her swollen belly, while a commanding Evelyn stood in front of the stove, stirring something in a big stainless steel pot. "Something smells good."

"Evie's making bean soup. It's our grandmother's recipe," Brenda said, her voice sounding unnaturally high. That only happened when she was stressed—really stressed. It wasn't like her, either. He met her gaze, about to ask if she was okay, but her penetrating—almost imploring—gaze told him not to inquire.

"How did things go at the marina?" Brenda asked instead.

"Fine."

Her eyes narrowed. She knew. She always knew when he stretched the truth.

"It's a great boat. We'll have a lot of good times on it."

"It seems like an unnecessary extravagance," Evelyn said gravely. "Frivolous," she added.

"Da-Marr said he got to drive it," Brenda said, her cheerful tone sounding forced.

"That he did," Richard said, his eyes wandering to the cabinet where he kept the single malt Scotch. Evelyn would not approve of him pouring a shot this early in the day—but about now he felt as though he could use one. Was there a chance he could sneak off to his study to grab a neat glass of the store he kept there?

"I'm just about ready to serve," Evelyn said, as though reading his mind. "If you'll call Da-Marr, I'll dish up.

Brenda made to stand, but Evelyn leveled her right index finger at her younger sister. "Stay where you are. I'll take care of everything. I'm used to doing that in this family," she said, eyeing them both over the top of her glasses.

Richard bit his tongue to keep from speaking. His gaze shifted to Brenda, who looked about to cry. Oh, how he wished they could be alone to share in what was supposed to be one of the most joyful times of their lives, the birth of their daughter. Jeff coming into their lives had been terribly stressful, but ultimately a rewarding experience. He had to hope that Brenda reconnecting with her oldest sibling would ultimately prove as gratifying. Still, Jeff had never sought to impose his opinions on them ... probably because he was half a generation younger than Evelyn and felt no sense of entitlement.

"I'll find Da-Marr and then we can eat," Richard said and forced a smile.

Evelyn's laser-like gaze seemed to cut through him, and he escaped the kitchen.

Da-Marr was not in the living room. Richard was about to head up the stairs to check out the guest room when he heard a noise from down the hall—from his study. He turned and headed in that direction.

Da-Marr sat in the leather chair behind his desk, hunched over the computer. The sight made Richard's heart sink. He did not like anyone messing with his computer. If Da-Marr felt comfortable commandeering the car radio, what would he do to the computer?

"Lunch is served."

"I'm not hungry," Da-Marr said, not taking his eyes from the computer screen. "You ever think of getting a tablet 'stead of a desktop?"

"I've got one … somewhere," Richard added vaguely. "Let me borrow it."

So he could mess that up, too? On the other hand, Richard figured it might be less of a hassle to let the kid use it—even if he lost or broke it.

"I'll look for it after lunch. You'd better come to the kitchen. You know Evelyn doesn't take no for an answer."

Da-Marr closed the browser and rose from the chair. "Ain't that the truth."

Richard fought the urge to check the computer's history and instead followed the kid back to the kitchen. During the short time he'd been gone, Evelyn had set the table and was waiting for them, looking stern. "I was about to call you both."

"We're here now, Aunt Evelyn," Da-Marr said sweetly, and leaned in to kiss her on the cheek. It was the first time Richard had seen Evelyn smile since she'd arrived.

"Now sit down. The soup's getting cold. Da-Marr sat in Richard's customary seat, but a look from Brenda told Richard he would have to be satisfied with another chair at the table.

Anything to maintain a sense of peace and harmony, he thought. Still, as he grabbed the napkin at his place setting and shook it out over his lap, he wondered if he'd be able to get back to the computer before Da-Marr could get there, and hoped the history would still be available to check.

FOUR

I made it to the bar twenty minutes late. Luckily, my boss, Tom, had called his doctor's office to find they were running half an hour behind. He got there in time for his appointment. Just in time. Still, I felt like a shit for having caused his blood pressure to rise. The poor man already suffered from white coat syndrome, and driving across town like a maniac to get there on time hadn't helped.

I'd worked off most of my angry mood by the time the dinner doldrums rolled around. I didn't often work double shifts, and trade was slow, meaning it would be a long evening.

A few of the regulars arrived about seven, and it wasn't long afterward that I looked up to see my former high school acquaintance and now sort-of friend, Sam Nielsen, enter The Whole Nine Yards. Sam had been an acquaintance of mine back at Amherst High School. He was the editor of the school newspaper, and I was its photographer. I wouldn't call us friends now, but we had an understanding when it came to certain potentially newsworthy subjects. I brought him tips and he shared information. Thanks to me, a couple of times he'd actually broken stories before the local TV news crews even knew what was happening.

He was dressed in jeans and a bomber jacket, still wearing a work tie, and holding onto something tucked under his right arm. He sat down at the bar and I wandered over to stand before him.

"What are you doing here on a Monday evening?"

He set whatever he'd been holding onto the seat next to him and rested his arms on the bar. "Just thought I'd drop by to see how you're doing."

"A lie if ever I heard one. What can I get you?"

"A Molson Canadian—in a dirty glass."

"No can do. The health department would close us down."

"How's a guy supposed to look tough?"

I eyed the jacket. "Work out more at the gym?"

He shrugged. "Then how about a Molson in a bottle."

I turned for the cooler and grabbed one, setting it front of him. "What else brought you here tonight?"

Sam reached to his right and grabbed what looked like a big Kraft envelope but turned out to be four of them. He moved his beer aside and spread them out before him on the bar. Each was sealed, with no writing to indicate what was inside. "I was hoping you could help me choose my next big exposé."

"How?"

"Each of these envelopes has my notes for what could be a hot story. I'm just not sure which to work on."

"And what am I supposed to do; read the notes and chose?"

Sam shook his head. "Nothing that complicated. Just pick them up and tell me if you get any of your funny vibes."

"Funny they aren't," I said sourly.

"Humor me," he said and grabbed his bottle of beer, taking a swig.

I stared down at the plain brown envelopes. None of them called to me.

"Touch them—one at a time," he encouraged me.

I looked around the bar, but no one was paying attention to us. I picked up the first envelope and held it with fingers from both hands. I waited, not knowing what—if anything—to expect. Sam's gaze was riveted on my face.

"So?" he challenged.

"I'm not getting a damn thing," I said just loud enough for him to hear.

"Try another one."

I set down the first envelope and picked up another, which seemed to make my fingertips tingle. Something flashed in my mind—but too quickly for me to make sense of it.

Sam's eyebrows went up and he looked expectant. "That got a rise out of you."

"You could tell?"

"Yeah, your eyes went real wide."

I glared at him and put the envelope down, then picked up the next. Like the first, I got no funny feelings. In fact, nothing at all. I put it down and picked up the last one and got a jolt like an electric shock. I dropped the envelope on the bar.

"Whoa—what happened?"

"I'd say I found your next story," I said, eyeing the envelope warily.

Sam scooped up the other three envelopes and set them aside on the empty stool once more. "Pick it up again."

"No."

"Why? Are you chicken?"

"Yes."

"Oh, go on," he chided, taking another swig of his beer.

Instead of picking up the envelope, I placed the tip of my index finger on it. No jolt, but a familiar—unwelcome—face flashed before my mind's eye: Da-Marr.

I pulled back my finger.

"You don't look happy. What did you see?"

"What's in this envelope?" I said, looking down at the offensive thing.

Sam picked it up and tore open the top, taking out a wad of hand written and typed notes that had been paper clipped together. He scanned the top page, which had several yellow Post-It notes attached. "Ah, Jack Morrow."

"The financier Jack Morrow? Who was recently murdered? The one who was on trial for masterminding a Ponzi scheme, as well as racketeering and tax fraud?" I asked.

Sam nodded. "One and the same."

What in God's name could Jack Morrow, a shady financier and Buffalo native, have to do with Da-Marr, who hailed from Philadelphia and had never—to my knowledge—left that city until he'd arrived on Richard's doorstep the day before?

"So, what kind of vibes did you get?" he asked again.

"It doesn't make sense to me."

"What?" he persisted.

"I saw a kid's face."

"He's got a son and a daughter."

"How old?"

He shrugged. "Twenties. Maybe thirties. I'm not sure. I haven't done much research on him yet."

"Then who wrote the stories for the paper during the trial and after the murder?"

"Alison Kiefer."

"Can't say I've heard of her."

"You will. She's vying for my job."

"So that's why you want a hot story."

He took a swig of his beer, looking grim. "You got it."

Was Sam really worried about losing his job to the competition? Newspapers all over the country seemed to be hemorrhaging staff, and more and more of them were carrying stories from the Associated Press and other news agencies. I admit I didn't pay that much attention to the local section of the daily rag. I preferred to read the comics, the editorials, and the letters to the editor.

Sam shoved the envelope toward me once again. "Why don't you read the summary? Maybe you'll get some additional insight."

I wanted to touch those papers like I wanted to grow a third leg—yet I did it anyway. An unpleasant sensation bubbled up within me as I read the terse paragraphs. Jack Morrow was bad news, and yet I couldn't quite connect the sensations I experienced with anything specific I was learning about him.

I set the papers back on the bar and pushed them toward Sam. "Your notes alone aren't enough. If you want more, you've got to give me something the guy touched. Maybe take me some place he used to go. And I'm not even sure that will give me anything you can use in an article. What is it you want to write about, anyway?"

"I'm not looking to find his killer. But before the cops arrested him, Morrow cashed in a lot of his securities. He had millions of dollars in assets that the regulators were never able to trace. I want to be the one who can lead them to his hidden fortune."

"And you expect me to be able to find them for you?"

"Yeah, if you can."

"Would you like me to gift wrap the moon and give that to you, too?"

Sam grinned. "I wouldn't turn it down."

"And what if I *could* help you with all that? What would I get out of it?"

Sam sobered. "Morrow cheated a lot of people out of their life savings. You lost just about everything when you were mugged and they robbed your home. Wouldn't you like to help others who suffered a similar fate?"

Yeah, but I wasn't about to be suckered in so easily. "Except that I was physically robbed. A lot of Morrow's marks were just greedy, making risky investments because they let the guy blow smoke up their asses—promising them whatever they wanted to hear. The guy had to have some kind of charisma to pull that off with so many people."

"That he did. But can you blame people with kids who've got substantial college debt—or people who were looking to have a carefree retirement? It's human nature to want as much as you can get."

And Sam wanted to cement his job and reputation by nailing a story and looking like a hero. He had a slew of awards to his credit, but he was still worried about staying on top. If he felt this way in his late thirties, what was the next decade likely to bring? And how could I turn him down? He'd saved my ass by loaning me his gun not six months before. It had saved me, Richard, and Maggie, and he'd asked no questions when the gun wasn't returned.

"What do you want me to do?" I asked, resigned.

His mouth quirked into a smile. He knew he had me right where he wanted me. "I haven't figured that out yet, but now that I know you're on board, I'll think about it and get back to you." He took another sip of his beer. "So, anything interesting going on in your life?"

I shrugged. "Richard bought a boat." God, my life was so friggin' boring the most exciting thing going on didn't even have much to do with me.

Sam's eyes lit up.

"A Slipstream 9000," I went on.

He nodded, impressed. "Not the top of the line, but not far from it, either. Kinda late in the season, isn't it?"

"He picked it up for a song at a government sale. And how do you know so much about boats?"

"Who do you think writes the yearly feature on the subject for the Buffalo News?"

"Have you got a boat?"

"Yeah, and not nearly as nice. I sure hope you're

going to invite me onboard sometime."

"I haven't even driven the damn thing," I said, still smarting from the morning's non-adventure. "We've got the week to play with it before it goes into storage for the winter."

He shook his head. "The summer is far too short for those of us who enjoy the water."

"I don't swim and I don't fish—but I'm not immune to the pleasure of a sunset cruise with a beer in my hand, either."

"Well, don't count on it happening this week. The forecast is for cold, rain, and wind for the next few days. But believe me, on a frigid winter's night you'll be counting the days until the fair weather hits late next spring. If nothing else, it gives you hope," he said, tipped back his bottle and drained it.

"So now that you have a story to work on, what's next on your agenda?"

"Interviews. Would you be interested in coming along on a few of them?"

"What for? Do you want me to act as a human lie detector or something?"

"It couldn't hurt."

"I dunno. There's a lot going on right now." Then again, tagging along with Sam might give me an excuse to avoid the company at Richard's house. Again, I shrugged. "Call me," I said, leaving the acceptance of the invitation open.

"I'll do that." Sam grabbed his wallet, left a five on the bar, and gathered his envelopes. "Talk to you soon."

I watched him leave, and then picked up the money, put it in the till, and gave myself the change as a tip. I had a feeling that chump change would be a small price for Sam to pay for whatever we learned about Jack Morrow, since I had a feeling that that information wasn't going to be good.

I grabbed a damp rag and wiped down the bar, think-ing about the envelope that had given me a jolt. Why had I thought about Da-Marr when touching it?

Jack Morrow had been a felon. Was Da-Marr destined to walk a similar path?

At that moment, I didn't doubt it.

FIVE

Autumn had settled itself upon Western New York. The days were already getting a lot shorter. The lackluster sun came up at 7:18, but Richard found himself up hours before that. He'd slipped out of bed, leaving his sleeping wife, dressed, and tip-toed down to the kitchen where he'd read every section of the *Buffalo News* and was on his third cup of coffee when the phone rang. Everyone else in the house was still sound asleep, so he practically broke the Olympic long jump record to snatch the landline before it could ring again.

"Hello?"

"Richard Alpert?"

"Speaking."

"This is Frank Murray, manager of Sundowner's Marina. I'm sorry to disturb you so early, but I thought you should know that we've had some trouble here at the marina. Vandalism."

"My boat's been vandalized?"

"I'm afraid so. The lock on the sliding glass door was broken, and someone got inside and trashed the salon. The seats have been slashed—with all the stuffing taken out of them—likewise all the life jackets. Every cupboard was emptied, too, their contents smashed and scattered."

Richard swallowed hard. "How many other boats were ransacked?" he asked, his voice tight.

"Just yours, sir. I'm terribly sorry. We do have a security guard, but he didn't see anything or anyone unusual. We'll check our video cameras to see if they captured anything suspicious and turn it over to the police. You did have insurance on the boat, right?"

"Yeah, it's fully insured," Richard said, feeling sick at heart.

"Will you be coming in to assess the damage?"

"Yeah. I'll get there as soon as I can."

"We've called the police and they said they'd send someone over as soon as possible. I'm really sorry about this, sir. We haven't had any vandalism in quite some time."

"Yeah. Thanks for calling."

Richard hung up the phone, stared into his cooling coffee, and wondered if Jeff would be up to going with him. He didn't think he wanted to do it alone, and he sure as hell didn't want Brenda to find out about it—at least not while Evelyn was in residence. He could almost hear her not-so-subtle rebuke. Brenda had too much on her mind to worry about his folly. And right now, that's just what owning the boat looked like.

*A **dark** silhouette blocked my path.*

"Hey, dude, got some spare change?" The hefty teen stepped into the lamplight, grabbed my jacket, jolting me.

Another figure emerged from the darkened doorway of a closed deli. This one held a baseball bat. "Give us your money."

The big guy grabbed my arm in a vise grip.

I handed over what I had.

It wasn't enough.

The smaller one whacked the bat against his open palm. "Reggie wants to teach you a lesson."

In one swift move, I kicked the little guy in the nuts. He went down hard.

His bigger friend snatched the bat, heading for me like a killing machine.

My arm went up to shield my head. The bat came down and cracked my ulna.

Before I could do more than wail in pain, the bat slammed into my shoulder, knocking me to my knees.

The bat arced high once more and crashed into my temple. I tried to raise myself as solid ash connected with my skull once more.

And then like an explosion, everything was obliterated by a blinding white light, and once again I felt myself spiraling upward into the cold dark sky, away from this life, away from everything I knew and loved … forever and ever and ever.

I'd been awake for a full seventy-six minutes, staring at the ceiling, waiting for sleep to come again and had been sorely disappointed. My cat, Herschel, grunted in his sleep and nestled closer to my chest. It was the same damn dream—nightmare—that haunted me. First the mugging—always in greater detail than the last time—then the vision of spiraling into scalding white light. It bothered me that the light wasn't welcoming. That instead of salvation it offered obliteration. And how the hell did I know that?

I'd never been much of a churchgoer. I'd left that to my guilt-ridden alcoholic mother. She'd trudged off to mass three or four times a week, seeking peace but never finding it. I had no use for the institution. It was nothing more than a place of empty rituals. Sit, stand, kneel, reel off prayers in a monotone before I could get the hell out of there and back to my basketball or classic Trek reruns.

That said, it was the dreams that made me decide that it might be a good idea to talk to someone who might have insight on such things. For some reason I still can't fathom, a part of me needed to hear a theologian's assessment, if only to rule out that what I'd experienced was indeed a religious experience.

Before I could ponder much more, the phone rang.

Ten minutes later, a rather frantic Richard stood on my doorstep holding a large take-out coffee.

Twenty minutes after that, I'd drunk the last of Tim Horton's best brew as we stood on the dock at Sundowner's Marina and peered into the ruined salon of Richard's beautiful boat.

"Who could have done this?" he asked, "and don't you dare say Da-Marr. He was with us at the house last night—flipping channels until I thought Brenda would go insane."

"I've got a bad feeling whoever did this is someone even more sinister than Da-Marr—and that's saying something."

Richard studied my face. "What do you mean?"

"Until you get the title, we have no idea who owned this boat, but we do know it was seized for criminal activity—be it tax evasion or some other unsavory act."

"And you think someone believes there's buried treasure on this boat?"

"I don't, but somebody must. I mean, none of the other boats was vandalized. That means someone was targeting you—or at least your boat."

Richard sighed. "Insurance will take care of the damage, but that's not the point."

"Do you think you can get a claims adjuster out here today? Otherwise this baby is going into mothballs without us getting a chance to see what she's really got."

"What she's obviously got is a reputation. And not a good one at that." He stared at the ruin, looking depressed. "Have you got any ideas?"

"I'd love to just jump inside and give it the old touch test—to see if I can pick up any residual vibes—but that's not a good idea until after the cops take a look and test for fingerprints. My guess is they'll find nothing." The fact that they hadn't already made it to the marina, meant they'd had other more important incidents to deal with.

Richard shook his head, looking heartsick.

"I take it you haven't said anything to Brenda."

"You're damn right I haven't. And don't you say anything, either. I'm worried about her. This was not the time to have guests arrive, and she's doing too much trying to make Evelyn happy. A lost cause, if you ask me," he muttered.

I wasn't about to offer an opinion on that subject.

I don't know what story he'd fed Brenda to explain his absence, and I didn't want to know in case she grilled me later—that way I could plead innocent.

I patted him on the shoulder. "Look, I'll give my friend Sam a call. I spoke to him last night and it turns out he's a boat aficionado and he's got connections. He might have some ideas."

Richard nodded. "Thanks." He turned and headed back up the dock for the marina manager's office.

I pulled out my cell phone and hit Sam's number, which was on speed dial. Unfortunately, I got his voice mail, but I told him the short version of what had happened, and gave him the boat's registration number. I may have stressed that the boat had previously belonged to a drug dealer. I asked him to call me, reminding him I was open to accompanying him on the interviews, and left my number, hoping our conversation the evening before might give him the incentive to dig a little for my—well, Richard's—benefit.

After that, I caught up with Richard, who was waiting in the front parking lot for the cops to show up. He'd get a lot further with his insurance company if he had a police report to back him up. And knowing Richard, he'd probably already made a call to his insurance agent. The company appreciated his business and I was sure he would make it worth their while to send an adjustor out before the end of the day. Well-heeled clients had done the same for me when I worked in the insurance business. Knicks game tickets, restaurant vouchers—not that I'd asked for or expected them, but it had made them feel better, and keeping the customer satisfied—even ordinary Joes—had its own rewards.

I clapped Richard on the shoulder but didn't say anything. He seemed grateful for even that small gesture. We'd get through this. But something niggled the back of my brain, telling me that whoever had vandalized the boat hadn't found what he was looking for.

Not yet, at least.

SIX

Richard pulled up the driveway and found Da-Marr in front of the garage door, down on one knee beside the guts of the old lawnmower, which had been spread out across the asphalt.

Now what?

Richard switched off the engine, grabbed his keys, and got out of the car. "What's going on?" he asked, trying to sound jovial.

Da-Marr looked up, disgusted. "This thing is a piece of shit. You know that?"

"We don't use it. I have a lawn service come and cut the lawn every week."

"Yeah, well tell that to Aunt Evelyn. She told me to get out here and cut the grass, but this thing hasn't been started in years. I cleaned it up, but this spark plug needs to be replaced. It ain't firing right and I know you don't got no gap gauge."

"A what?" Richard asked, puzzled.

"See?" Da-Marr challenged. He straightened. "If Brenda will loan me her car, I'll go get a new one—and a gallon of gas—and get this grass in shape."

"But I already told you—"

"And I told *you* what Aunt Evelyn said."

He certainly had. Richard was also glad the kid hadn't asked to borrow the Mercedes. He didn't even like Brenda driving it, and he knew she was careful. Well, most of the time.

Da-Marr went back to work, reassembling the engine, and Richard headed for the house. He hesitated before opening the door. He couldn't pick up bad vibes like Jeff could, but it seemed like a cloud of tension had settled over his home. He wished he had an excuse to escape, but the hospital board wasn't meeting for another two weeks, and he was caught up with the paperwork the volunteer job entailed.

Once inside, he hung up his jacket and entered the kitchen. Evelyn sat at the table with a hardcover book open before her. "Good morning," she said with what sounded like disapproval.

"It's getting close to noon now," he answered with a nervous smile. "Is Brenda around?"

"She felt tired, so I made her go lie down."

Like Brenda couldn't have figured that out herself.

"I think I'll just head on up and check on her."

"Don't wake her," Evelyn ordered.

Richard forced a smile and made a hasty exit.

He trudged up the stairs and quietly opened the door to their bedroom. Brenda wasn't in bed, but she sat by the window with her feet up on the hassock and her e-reader in hand. "Hi."

"Hi, yourself," she said and switched off the device.

"Evelyn said she told you to take a nap."

"If I were to lie down without you here, I'd never get back up again," she said tersely.

"It's only a few more days."

"It seems like an eternity right now."

Richard moved closer and sat on the side of the bed. "Want to go to Ramon's for lunch? They say spicy food can jumpstart labor."

"If I believed that, I'd drive us there in a heartbeat." Brenda frowned and shook her head. "I don't want to move from this spot. I could happily stay here for the rest of the day, but if I don't come to lunch when called, there'll be consequences."

"This visit isn't turning out the way you thought it would."

Brenda looked down at the reader in her hand. "No."

He reached over to take her other hand. Her fingers clasped his, but then abruptly she disentangled them and sat up straighter. "The insurance company called while you were out."

"Oh?" he asked, wary.

"When were you going to tell me about the boat?"

"Tell you what?"

She leveled an angry gaze at him.

"You mean … the little problem down at the marina?"

"Vandalism isn't a *little* problem."

"They weren't supposed to call the landline. I asked them to call my cell phone."

"Well, they didn't."

"How pissed off are you?" he asked, dreading the answer.

"Pretty pissed off," she admitted, but then she sighed, the anger draining from her face. "How bad is it?"

"Mostly cosmetic," he said. "I'd already thought about updating the carpets and upholstery, and now you can choose what you'd like."

"I'm not setting foot on that boat."

"Ever?"

She shrugged. "I never said that. But—" she looked down at herself. "Not today. And not this week. And since you've already arranged to have it put into storage...." She let the sentence trail off, but then her expression hardened once again and, for a split second, she reminded him of her unforgiving older sister. "You *did* arrange to have it put into storage, didn't you?"

"Yes, I did."

"I assume you took Jeffy with you this morning?"

"He may have been there with me."

"You didn't have to go in separate cars; or did you think I wouldn't notice?"

"He had somewhere else to go afterward."

"He seems to have found a lot to do the past couple of days. Are we ever going to see him again?"

"You know he had to work a double shift yesterday."

"So what's he doing today?"

Richard shrugged. "I don't know. Something with that reporter friend of his, I guess."

"No good can come of that," Brenda muttered.

Richard made no comment. Since Jeff was on the top of Brenda's shit list, he decided to change the subject. "Da-Marr wants to borrow your car."

"What for?"

"Evelyn wants him to cut the grass, but first he's attempting to fix that old lawnmower in the garage."

"The one we were going to throw out?"

He nodded.

Brenda shrugged. "I don't care. My keys are hanging up on the rack in the kitchen. He's welcome to them." She looked over at him and scowled. "You don't want him to drive my car?"

"Hey, it's your car," he said.

"Yes, it is," she reaffirmed. "Why are you worried about it?"

"He doesn't know the area. How's he going to find a place that sells spark plugs?"

"Oh, I don't know—the yellow pages perhaps?"

"Brenda!" It was unmistakably Evelyn. She pounded on the door. "It's almost time for lunch."

"I'll be down in a few minutes," Brenda called, and then sighed. "Maybe for dinner we could do take-out from Ramon's."

"And what if Evelyn doesn't like hot spicy food?"

Richard asked, and helped her to stand.

"I'll broach the subject at lunch. Go on ahead, I'll be right down," she said, heading for the bathroom.

There hadn't been a sign that lunch was in the offing when Richard had passed through the kitchen not ten minutes before, but when he returned the table was set and Evelyn had set out an assortment of cold cuts, bread, and condiments buffet style on the counter.

As Brenda had suggested, Da-Marr had his nose in the yellow pages. "Is Brenda gonna loan me her car?" he asked idly.

"Yeah. The keys are up on the rack." He pointed.

Da-Marr looked up, and a sly, kind of creepy smile settled on his lips. "Does it got GPS?"

Richard nodded.

"Good." He slammed the phone book shut and turned to grab a plate.

"No you don't," Evelyn chided. "Not until you wash those greasy hands. Do it now."

"Yes, Aunt Evelyn," Da-Marr muttered, and turned to the sink.

She turned her gaze on Richard. "You're next."

"Yes, Evelyn," he said meekly, and waited his turn.

He would ask Ramón to use habanero or nagas chilies to spice up their dinner.

Betsy Ruth—get here fast and save us all!

After I left the marina, I had no intention of going back to Richard's house where I might be forced to suffer through another meal with his houseguests. I had my own agenda to follow and drove right past LeBrun Road.

I'd never been inside this particular church some four blocks from Richard's house, although I'd stood outside it for a time during Matt Sumner's funeral some eighteen months before. This time there was no guard at the door, and I climbed the steps and walked right through the front entrance.

I gazed at the darkened, unfamiliar place, trying to get my bearings. Despite the empty pews, the space vibrated with a sense of sorrow. A funeral must have taken place earlier in the day.

Two confessional booths stood at the rear of the cavernous space. Not ornate, just brown boxes that reminded me of old telephone booths in seedy old hotels.

I pulled open the door, sat down on the slip of a bench. I didn't see a silhouette on the other side of the screen.

I sat there for a long time, waiting, thinking—about the dreams, about the white light that wanted to suck me into the afterlife … something I didn't even believe in. I thought about what I might say—how I'd phrase it—trying out different scenarios. At last, someone knocked on the door of my confessional.

"Do you need help, sir?"

I opened the door a crack wider and saw the dog collar of an elderly, white-haired priest. "Yeah, I came for confession."

He laughed. "Son, you're a decade or so too late for that."

"How so?"

"We don't do that anymore. Now we have what's called the rite of reconciliation."

"Isn't that just my luck?" I asked. He stood there, expectantly, while I thought about it for a minute. "Father, could we pretend the church hasn't moved on? I could use a little spiritual guidance."

"It's highly unusual—" he started.

"Please, sir?"

The man frowned, the wrinkles on his face almost doubling. At last, he sighed. "Very well." He closed the door of my cubicle and I heard him open the one next to me, sit down, and close the door.

The panel went up. It was show time.

"Bless me, father, for I have sinned." My voice sounded rusty from lack of use. My mind scrambled for the words that were supposed to come next, but I drew a blank.

"How long has it been since your last confession?" prompted the disembodied voice from behind the screen.

I let out a breath. "Twenty-three years."

Silence.

What the hell was I doing here? How could this priest help me? A man who'd lived a sheltered life away from the world's temptations.

"Go on," the voice said at last.

"I'm not sure why I came here. I'm not sure I believe. That I ever believed."

"Perhaps you came to find your faith. In these troubled times, faith is tested on a daily basis."

"I consider myself a good person, but bad things have happened to me."

"Do you feel you're being punished by God?"

"No." Yes.

"Something prompted you to come here. What was it?"

I closed my eyes, a swell of sorrow, fear, and revulsion that I'd been trying to keep at bay for days suddenly threatened to swamp me. "I nearly died a couple of days ago. The thought haunts me—scaring the—" I'd been about to say shit. "Heck out of me."

"I see," the priest said in understanding. How often had he heard a tale like mine? "Something must weigh heavy on your soul."

"I was mugged eighteen months ago. I almost died then, too. I don't know who hurt me—I never will—but I can't forgive, and I certainly will never forget what happened."

"But forgiveness will lift the burden from your heart. Turn the other cheek, my son."

"I can't," I said as the uncomfortable mix of emotions seemed to swell within my chest, "and I guess that's the sin that weighs heavy on my soul."

Suddenly there wasn't enough air. The wooden panels seemed to be closing in on me.

"Thanks, Father," I said, and opened the door of the confessional. I had to get the hell out of there.

"But we haven't finished—" he called after me.

Head bowed in shame, I stalked out of the church without taking in my surroundings, hurried down the concrete steps and down the walk before I turned the corner for the side street and got back in my car. I stuffed the key into the ignition, but didn't start it. Instead, I stared at the dash.

It had been stupid to think a few Hail Marys could lift the burden from my soul.

Stupid, stupid, stupid.

My cell phone rang. I yanked it out of my pocket and looked at the number on the small screen. Sam.

"Yeah?"

"Sorry to hear about Richard's boat. I don't have anything on the registration number yet, but I have set up an interview an hour from now. Are you available?"

I cleared my throat. "Yeah." I'd already told Richard I'd be meeting Sam; now that statement was no longer a lie.

"Good."

"Are you okay? You sound funny."

"I'm fine."

"Great. I'll give you the address and you can meet me there. Bring your camera along. That way it'll look like you're a valued member of the team."

"Are we a team?"

"We are for this."

"Where are we going?"

"To Jack Morrow's former residence. It's on the fore-closure block, but I managed to sweet talk a lady at the bank into arranging a visit for me, and believe me, it wasn't easy."

"Will there be anything left for me to touch?"

"We'll find out when we get there."

He gave me the address. I knew the area, so I didn't bother to write it down. "See you there in an hour," I said and ended the call. I was glad Sam had contacted me. About then, I needed a major distraction. I didn't want to dwell on how I'd made a fool of myself in the church. And I was still no closer to figuring out what it was I needed to get past the feeling of impending doom.

I sat, hands on the steering wheel, staring at nothing, thinking. What I should have done the night before was done a Google search on Jack Morrow, but by the time I'd gotten home from the bar, I'd been too wiped to do much more than check the fridge, find nothing of interest, and fall into bed.

I glanced at my watch. I still didn't want to go home to my computer, but the library nearby did have computers for use by the public. It would only take me twenty minutes to get to Morrow's house, which meant I had nearly forty minutes to do my research.

I plunked down at one of the computer carrels and logged into Google. Sure enough, most of the articles from the *Buffalo News* were retrievable at the click of a mouse. Even if Sam wasn't interested in the murder, I was.

John Francis Morrow had been found shot to death in a leased late-model Lexus. The reporter, Alison Kiefer, had made of point of saying that his Jaguar had been re-possessed and he was forced to drive a low-end luxury car to court. I was more surprised that his team of attorneys had let him loose without a leash.

The motive for the murder was up for grabs. Revenge, retaliation, perhaps he'd also stolen candy from a baby—

but I wondered if the person responsible had had the same idea as Sam—finding those millions in hidden assets.

Morrow's car had been found parked in Delaware Park at two in the morning. The jury had been scheduled to receive their instructions for deliberation some eight hours later. And, of course, they never did.

The autopsy conclusively established murder. After all, it would've been rather difficult for Morrow to shoot himself in the back of the head—especially as there was no gunshot residue on either of his hands. The police figured the shooter had been sitting in car's backseat.

Several other articles looked interesting, and I copied the URLs into an email and sent them to myself for later reading.

I was headed for my car when I remembered that Sam had asked me to bring my camera. Damn. I'd have to stop at home anyway.

As I pulled out of the library's lot I thought about what I'd seen when I'd handled Sam's mystery envelope the evening before. I hadn't flashed onto Morrow's face, but Da-Marr's.

I needed to analyze that memory a bit further. The kid I'd met was full of swagger, but his expression during that flash of insight had been one of fear and indecision. Unfortunately, it was only his face I'd seen. Nothing in the background, not even the clothes he was wearing.

Part of me didn't give a shit. I didn't like the kid and I never would. And yet, from what I'd seen, I couldn't imagine him ever being scared.

And here I was—deathly afraid of him.

SEVEN

I stopped at the house to grab my camera and managed not to run into Richard or anyone else. Brenda's car was gone. Maybe she'd taken her guests and gone shopping. That suited me fine.

Despite my unexpected stop, I still made it to the address Sam gave me before he did. But then, I didn't have a day job to attend to.

The gates were open—not surprising, as someone was expecting us—and I drove through, but parked near the end of the drive to wait for Sam. I gave the big house a thorough once over. What a palace. No wonder this guy had been about to go to stir for stealing mega millions. I guessed the house was worth a couple of million. In another part of the country, it would be worth five or ten times that, and not surprisingly it wasn't far from Millionaire's Row, where robber barons from the previous century had gathered along Delaware Avenue.

Maggie would've killed to get a look inside the two-and-a-half story Tudor revival made of limestone. Its bay windows, parapets, dormers, arched balustrades, and carved rosettes made Richard's house look like positively cheap in comparison.

Sam's SUV pulled up next to my rattletrap and he got out. His work clothes didn't look all that different from what he'd worn at the bar the night before, except for his tie. It didn't depict dancing girls, but it wasn't exactly mainstream, either. Pineapples?

We walked up the drive.

"Have you had any new flashes of insight?" Sam asked, hopefully.

"No. But I did do a little research on Morrow."

Sam stopped dead and glared at me. "Don't do that. I want your perceptions to be free of bias."

"Can't I just be curious?"

"You can be curious after all this is over."

"All what?" I asked suspiciously.

"Our investigation."

So, he *did* think of me as a team player. Funny, I didn't hold that distinction at my last day-job.

We stopped before a massive oak door tucked under a carved archway. Sam grasped hold of the heavy iron knocker and gave it a good bang, then we waited in self-conscious silence. He knocked again.

Eventually the door opened and an old, gray-haired woman dressed in a long brown skirt, ratty maroon sweater, with sensible shoes and heavy support hose, stood before us.

"Mrs. Walburg? I'm Sam Nielsen. We spoke on the phone this morning." Sam brandished his *Buffalo News* ID.

She scrutinized it before opening the door wider to take a good look at me.

"This is my colleague, Ernie Pyle," Sam said with a smirk.

She scowled. "You're joking, right?"

"It's a nickname," I offered. Mrs. Walburg was obviously better informed than the last person Sam had used that line on. And had he just put the old lady off? "I'm Jeff. Nice to meet you." I didn't offer her my hand. She nodded.

"Did you work for the Morrow family for long?" Sam asked.

"I worked for *Mr.* Morrow for over thirty-five years.

Longer than he was married to either of his wives."

Did she consider herself to be a walking font of information on the dead man, or was she just angry that she had only been an employee and not something more?

"So this is where Jack Morrow used to hang his hat," Sam said, looking past her.

"When he was in Buffalo. He had a house on Grand Cayman, and apartments in San Francisco, Chicago, and New York."

"Did you ever see them?" Sam asked.

She shook her head. "I was their employee—not one of their pampered Pomeranians," she added bitterly.

Okay. There was major animosity going on there. Had she wished to be more than just an employee, or had the whole bankruptcy thing ruined some kind of financial arrangement she thought she might get as a long-time employee? We weren't likely to ever know.

"And now you're a caretaker?" I guessed.

She nodded. "Until it's sold."

"And what's taking so long?" Sam asked, huddling further into his jacket. Wasn't she ever going to invite us in?

"The price. Do you know anyone with five million bucks?"

Sam shook his head.

I'd guessed wrong on the home's worth; either that, or the bank wanted to squeeze every penny they could from Jack Morrow's assets.

"Come in if you're coming," she said at last, and ushered us inside where the ambient temperature wasn't much higher than outside. It was probably set low to keep down maintenance costs.

The place was rather ostentatious with its high-beamed ceilings and stonework, reminiscent of pictures I'd seen of the formal entry at Biltmore in Asheville, only on a much smaller scale. Nothing decorated the space, nor the formal living room to the right. The whole place had probably been stripped of everything that could be sold to pay off Morrow's creditors and victims. I was beginning to think this little foray would be a gigantic waste of time, as there didn't seem to be anything other than light switches for me to touch.

Mrs. Walburg motioned for us to follow her. "Come on. I'll show you the game room."

"Did Mr. Morrow spend a lot of time in there?" I asked as we followed in her wake.

"He liked to play billiards," she said, and opened an antique cherry door to what was obviously Morrow's personal domain. A beautiful old and impeccably maintained pool table stood near the far wall, away from what might have once been a seating area. Above the fireplace was a place to plug in a very big flat-screen TV, but of course there wasn't one there now.

Mrs. Walburg walked over to the table. "It's a Brunswick and Balke Exposition Novelty table circa 1880. It's made of rosewood, with ivory inlays."

"It's a beauty," I said, admiring the intricate patterns along its sides and legs.

"It was completely restored before Mr. Morrow purchased it some fifteen years ago. The baize was replaced to match the curtains five years ago when Mrs. Morrow redecorated," she recited, as though we were tourists.

The cue sticks were lined up in perfect order up on the wall. A rack filled with balls sat at the far end of the table. "Do you mind if I give it a try?" I asked.

"Yes, I mind. It's been sold. The new owners will take possession as soon as they hire someone qualified to move it. That in itself is going to cost thousands of dollars."

"How about you let him just hold one of the cue sticks?" Sam suggested.

Mrs. Walburg looked appalled. "You came here to

look—not touch," she admonished.

How wrong she was.

I snapped eight or nine shots of the table and the room, although I wasn't sure Sam actually intended to use the pictures to accompany his article. If nothing else, it allowed me to look the part of sidekick.

"Can we continue the tour?" Sam asked.

Mrs. Walburg scowled but led us to the grand staircase. "There are five bedrooms upstairs, all with en suites. The formal dining room and kitchen are this way." She held out her hand to indicate where.

"Would it be all right if we just wandered around the place and took a few more pictures?" Sam asked. He flashed his most winning smile.

She sighed. "I suppose so. But I'd appreciate it if you could do so as quickly as possible. I do have my regular duties to perform."

And what would that entail? A stint with a broom—before she rode it?

"We'll try to take up as little of your time as we can," Sam said sincerely, gave her another smile, and started up the stairs. I followed. Neither of us spoke until we'd reached the landing. "Getting any vibes?" Sam asked.

"Only that I'm not a fan of Mrs. Walburg."

He held out a hand, indicating the door to my right. As Mrs. Walburg had said, we found the first of the five bedrooms. The walls were painted a warm apricot with an accent wall covered in what looked like a hand-stenciled fleur de lis pattern in gold leaf. I bent low and scratched one of the emblems and, sure enough, a fleck of gold came off on my thumbnail.

"Expensive," Sam noted.

"I guess wallpaper was just too gauche."

No furniture or art graced the room. It wasn't a large space, but big enough to hold a queen-sized bed and a small sitting area. At least the dents in the carpet seemed to indicate that. I flipped the light switch and a small chandelier glowed overhead, the prisms sparkling like diamonds. Had this been a guest room?

"You said Morrow had kids," I reminded him.

"A son and a daughter, but I don't believe either of them lived at home when he was led away in handcuffs."

I wandered into the bathroom, which was small, but adequate with a shower-tub combo, toilet, and pedestal sink. I turned on the light. The medicine cabinet over the sink was empty. I ran my hand along the doorframe, but got no psychic signals. Touching the faucet handles brought me no information, either.

"Nothing?" Sam asked.

I shook my head.

We turned and went back out into the hall. The next room was a lot bigger, just as empty, and just as clean as the first. Clean in terms of tidiness and of psychic imprints. Though painted and wallpapered in other colors, the next two rooms were just the same. We were wasting our time.

The master suite took up the south end of the second floor. Dual skylights lit the room, with built-in shades, as evidenced by the remote I found sitting on a windowsill. The room was huge, with enough space for a king-sized bed and a formal sitting area with a fireplace and floor-to-ceiling bookshelves. I wandered around, standing in a number of places to try to soak up vibes … and picked up anger. It took me a few long moments to figure it out. Not so much anger, but frustration. Female frustration. Mr. Morrow, for all his supposed power and position, hadn't been satisfying his wife for quite some time. Was it because he knew his whole Ponzi scheme was doomed to collapse or was it just the ravages of age? I had no clue.

I wandered around. The room sported two walk-in closets, each bigger than my bedroom over Richard's garage. I found myself gravitating to the closet on the left, and switched on the light. A ripple of something seemed to crawl up my spine and I suffered an involuntary shudder.

"Now we're getting somewhere," Sam commented. "I take it this was Morrow's closet."

I nodded, not that there was any physical evidence to prove it. But it had contained his clothing, his shoes, and they'd left an imprint on the walls and floor. Something flashed in my mind—like a light. Was it that damned near-death vision again? Unfortunately, whatever else I'd picked up wasn't concrete.

"You're frowning," Sam said.

"I don't know what it is I'm supposed to be picking up. If the guy was a prick, it's not blasting through me."

"I haven't given you too much information because I want you to tell me about him."

"I need something more substantial than walking into rooms where he'd been. Let's face it; he hasn't been in this house in what, a year or more?"

Sam frowned. "I hadn't thought of that."

"Just what is it you want me to learn about the guy—besides where he hid the millions they haven't yet found?"

"Anything that will help."

"Help what?" I practically pleaded.

"I don't know. And that's why I wanted you on-board."

I thought about it for a moment. "The fact that he had a house on Grand Cayman—doesn't that say it all?"

He shook his head. "There are rumors that he converted money to jewelry, stamps, and coins, and that it's spread out all over the Buffalo area."

"Sounds more like wishful thinking on someone's part," I commented, switched off the light, and sidled past him to check out the bathroom which was nearly as big as the home's smallest bedroom.

"Whoa," Sam said with awe. "Check out that

shower."

The steam shower was not only big enough for half a football team, but had enough controls to outfit a rocket to the International Space Station. Multiple sets of water jets were positioned along the walls. A Jacuzzi soaker tub sat under a window with no curtains or blinds.

"Why is it rich people never have window coverings in their bathrooms?" I mused.

"Maybe they're all a bunch of exhibitionists," Sam suggested, looking through the window to the backyard beyond. A large in-ground pool had been covered for the winter, which reminded me that we only had days left to play with Richard's boat before it, too, would again be unavailable for months on end. That is, if we could play with it at all. I wondered what his insurance agent had said. Maybe I'd call him later to find out. Much later.

Dual sinks sunk in granite lined the east wall, with separate medicine cabinets overhead—both empty. The cabinets below held nothing but cleaning products, extra boxes of tissues, and a couple of rolls of toilet paper.

"Unless the kitchen has anything the guy actually touched, we're done," I told Sam.

"Do you think you might get something off of one of those cue sticks?"

"They're likely the only things left in the house that he touched. How are you going to distract Mrs. Walburg?"

"With my charm and good looks," Sam said wryly.

Charm he had. Good looks? They had disappeared with his thinning hair. "I'll corner the old lady and then you make a beeline to that game room. You might only have a minute or two."

"Got it."

We left the upstairs behind and went back downstairs, where we found Mrs. Walburg in the kitchen, polishing the already shiny taps. I kept to the far end, feigning interest in the wet bar, while Sam cornered Mrs. Walburg. "I have a few more questions for you, if you don't mind," he said smoothly, while I snapped a few more pictures.

"I suppose," she said, her attention still riveted on the task before her.

I snapped a couple more photos and wandered out of the room. Once out of earshot, I hurried back to the game room. In the minutes since we'd checked out the back yard, it had begun to rain. Already the windows overlooking the yard were beaded with drops.

I set my camera on the pool table and grabbed the first cue from the rack. It had been polished with what seemed like beeswax. She had not only obliterated any fingerprints that might have been on the stick, but any auras left behind as well. They were all like that. No one could say that Mrs. Walburg was shirking her duties. I put the last one back in the rack and heard voices approaching. I went to grab my camera and noticed a well-worn piece of blue billiards chalk in one of the table's pockets. I grabbed it and stashed it in my jacket pocket before hurrying over to the window so that I would appear to be evaluating the yard.

"I hope you haven't been messing with that table," Mrs. Walburg scolded as she entered the room.

I turned and held my hands up in surrender. "I wouldn't think of it. Could you tell me who does the landscaping?" I asked, and looked back toward the yard.

"Why would you care?"

I pivoted to meet her gaze. "I'm looking for someone to take care of my place."

She looked me over and frowned. Okay, so I wasn't wearing a suit and tie—just jeans, a black turtleneck, track shoes, and a denim jacket. Steve Jobs had mega millions and always seemed to wear the same outfit and nobody claimed he couldn't afford a gardener.

"It's time for you to leave," Mrs. Walburg sharply.

I didn't argue, and without a word headed for the entrance.

"Thank you for all your help," Sam said sincerely.

Mrs. Walburg walked us to the door, opened it, and let us out. The door slammed behind us. She hadn't said good-bye.

Sam pulled up his collar as we started walking back down the drive toward our cars. "Well, that was a complete waste of time."

"Maybe not," I said. "Let's go sit in your car for a minute."

The rain pelted us and we picked up speed. Once inside the car, I reached into my pocket for the chalk. The second my hand clasped it, I got a jolt of something.

"What've you got?" I showed Sam the paper-wrapped piece of blue billiards chalk. "Hey, where'd you find that?"

"In one of the table pockets."

"Are you getting anything from it?"

I closed my eyes, folded my fingers around the chalk, and was assaulted with a myriad of sensations.

"Well—well?" Sam badgered me.

"Shut up and let me concentrate."

Whoever had last held the chalk had been upset—about money. A hazy image of a pool cue slamming into the cue ball, and all the other balls scattering across the table flashed through my mind. There was no way to tell if it was Morrow, his son, or anyone else who might have been in the house, but whoever it was had taken out his—and it was definitely a male—frustrations via the pool table and accoutrements.

I opened my eyes and shook my head. "Money."

"Yeah?" Sam asked eagerly.

"But I don't know who it was, or what they were thinking."

"Is there a chance you might get more? You know,

think about it a while. Maybe things could get clearer."

"There is that chance," I admitted.

He nodded. "Okay."

I pocketed the chalk once more. "What's up next?"

"I'm going to do some more research. I don't want you doing the same. That might taint whatever it is you get from other more tangible sources."

I shrugged. "Suits me."

"Then again, if you get more vibes, you might want to take some notes—no matter how odd or demented they seem. At this point, we don't know what could be relevant."

It seemed a reasonable request.

"I need to get going. Like Mrs. Walburg, I've got duties to perform."

"All the cleaning in the world isn't going to get rid of that woman's anger. And by the way, did you get anything off of her?"

"Just that she's afraid she's going to lose her home. You can't blame her for being pissed about that."

Again, he shook his head. "She's living in the basement of a goddamn mansion. That's not so bad."

"It is if you have nowhere else to go." I thought about it for a moment longer. "She loved the bastard. She never gave up hope that he would one day turn to her, but it was never going to happen."

"He saw her as an employee, nothing else?" Sam guessed.

"Exactly. "

"Poor lady." He shook his head as though in commiseration. "I'll call you tomorrow—or maybe Thursday."

"I'll be around," I said, and got out of his car. I hadn't been lying when I said I had duties to perform. The laundry basket in the bottom of my closet was overflowing. As I climbed into my own car and started the engine, I wondered if it would be better to toss everything into a garbage bag and head for the nearest Laundromat, rather than head over to Richard's to wash my stuff. If the pantry door to the kitchen was closed, I might not have to run into anyone. I could toss in a load and get out of there in a minute or so, then come back to throw them in the dryer half an hour later.

With my plans made, I backed out of the drive and headed for home. The pocket that held the chalk seemed warm, and I hoped that later it would give up more of its secrets.

EIGHT

Brenda's car hadn't returned by the time I got home. I grabbed my dirty clothes and went directly to the dungeon that housed their laundry room. I kept my own supplies in a cabinet by the side of the washer, dumped in my clothes and the liquid detergent, and hit the power button. The cycle ran a full twenty-three minutes, so I headed back to my apartment over the garage, dodging the raindrops.

Once back home, I set the timer on my microwave and then settled on my couch. I retrieved the chalk cube I'd set on the coffee table and rubbed it between my fingers. Before I had time to absorb anything, my cat Herschel jumped on my lap, head-butting my chin—a ritual I endured, yet enjoyed, at least a dozen times a day.

While Herschel purred his brains out, I pressed the chalk to my forehead and again the hazy images of Morrow's pool table surfaced—game in progress. I ground my teeth, willing the image to solidify, but instead an odd image of dull gray pebbles being tossed on a beige carpeted floor came to mind.

That hadn't made a damn bit of sense.

The microwave timer pinged and I set Herschel down on the floor and headed for the door, stuffing the chalk into my pocket.

Brenda's car was still AWOL, so I hurried down to the basement and stashed my wet light-colored clothes in the dryer and hit the start button. I put my darks in the washer and got that load going, too. Settling my weight against the washer, I withdrew the chalk from my pocket, once again pressing it against my forehead.

Again, the image of greasy dark pebbles were imprinted upon my mind. What the heck? I shook my head and tried again.

Sam had said Morrow's money could have been converted to other things, such as stamps, and sure enough I saw rows and rows of carefully preserved vintage stamps. Stamps with old airplanes. Stamps with silhouettes of heads of state. Stamps with flowers, faces, and everything in between. But where were they?

I kind of got lost in the crazy array of images, for the next thing I knew the dryer buzzed, bringing me back to the here and now. I shook myself and opened the dryer door. I folded my clothes on autopilot, still thinking about stamps and wondering how much I could learn about their value online when the washer finished its cycle, and I transferred those clothes to the dryer.

Again, I leaned against the washer and contemplated the images that worn out piece of chalk had already conveyed. Of course, all this psychic mental exercise started my head pounding. It was just too bad that physical pain seemed to be part of the process.

I was staring at the chalk, turning it over and over, inspecting its every imperfection when I suddenly realized Brenda stood before me, waving her hand before my eyes.

"Hey, pay attention to me," she ordered none too kindly.

I shook myself. "Sorry. I was lost in thought."

"You seem to be lost in more ways than one these past few days," she said tartly, her expression fierce. "You haven't made an appearance in almost two days."

I shrugged and shoved the chalk back into my pocket. "I've had a lot on my mind—and a lot on my plate."

Her penetrating glare seemed to cut right through me.

The buzzer went off on the dryer, and I opened the door, pulling out the chocolate brown towels and washcloths, piling them onto the top of the washing machine.

"I understand you have a problem with my houseguests."

"I don't have a problem."

"You haven't been at all friendly to Da-Marr."

I wasn't sure how to respond to that statement, and continued to fold my laundry.

"You never told me about the people who mugged you," Brenda said.

My gaze remained on the bath towel I folded. I didn't want to be having this conversation.

"Were they black?"

I didn't say anything. My silence was answer enough for her.

I could feel her anger building.

"I'm sorry, Jeffy, this black face just doesn't rub off. And I can't take responsibility for what other people of my race do, just the way you can't for those white boys who steal their parents' guns and blow people away in schools, movie theaters, and coffee joints."

"I didn't ask you to take responsibility."

"And you can't blame Da-Marr for what happened to you."

I folded the last washcloth, gathered up everything, turned, and walked away.

"Don't ignore me—and don't stalk off in a huff."

But I did leave without another word. I didn't understand exactly what it was I felt, but I knew I couldn't discuss it with her.

I trudged up the stairs, emotion swelling within me once again. It was fear—and even worse—the growing fear of having to face that fear.

I hadn't yet arrived at a place where I was ready to

deal with it. And after my experience with Dr. Krista Marsh, I wasn't sure I'd ever be able to explore what I felt with any kind of so-called qualified health professional. And I'd never get past the guilt I felt for the pain I'd caused Grace Vanderstein at Krista's manipulation.

The rain was just a drizzle as I crossed the driveway for my apartment. Brenda's car was still among the missing, and Richard's was gone, too. Had Brenda loaned her car to Evelyn? Aw, who cared?

I trudged up the stairs to my apartment and let myself in. Herschel was waiting for me behind the door and gave a yowl. "No treats right now, buddy." Instead, I dumped the laundry basket on the breakfast bar and headed to the bathroom. I grabbed a dose of my migraine meds and downed it with some water, and then stood for a long time before the medicine cabinet's mirror studying the haunted expression on my face, wondering what I should do next. I didn't have to work that night, but I didn't want to be alone, either. And I certainly wasn't prepared to spend another evening with Evelyn and Da-Marr, even to placate Brenda.

The truth was, I loved Brenda. In fact, I felt more for her than a brother-in-law should. Why couldn't she understand what that beating at the hands of a couple of young thugs had cost me? Okay, typical macho things like maybe my manhood. Eighteen months later, I still had these stinking, often crippling headaches, and probably always would. That limited my ability to work, to support myself. I was dependent on Richard and his generosity, and I hated it.

No, she couldn't understand all that those punks had taken from me. And I could never begin to tell her, either.

I wandered into the living room and stood there for a few minutes, soaking in the silence. When I had one of my skull-pounding headaches, silence was a welcome respite, but right then I felt antsy. I knew better than to seek out my psychic mentor, Sophie Levin, until the wee hours; she simply was not available until then. That left me only one person I knew I could trust, and even that was tenuous.

I sat down on the couch and once again, Herschel was there, but it wasn't his comfort I needed. I reached for the telephone that sat on the end table.

I dialed the number and waited to see if voice mail would pick it up.

"Hello?"

"Hey, Maggs."

"Oh. It's you." She didn't sound angry. She didn't sound happy, either. She sounded … indifferent?

Okay, so we hadn't been on the best of terms since the spring. Not that we'd fought, either. What we hadn't done was talk much about her infidelity. I hadn't wanted to confront her about it—just in case she decided to dump me for good, but not discussing it kept us from going back to the way things had been before her sister had instigated our breakup.

Wasn't it ironic? She and Brenda both had a bossy older sister, and both of them seemed content to let them rip their lives to pieces. Irene had done that last spring; Evelyn was doing it now. Were Maggie and Brenda in contact with one another, comparing notes?

"Are you busy tonight?"

"What did you have in mind?" Maggie asked, sounding resigned. Well, at least she hadn't told me to fuck off.

"I dunno. How about a pizza? I could really use some company, and I can't think of anyone I'd rather be with."

"Really?" Was that hope in her voice.

"Yeah, really."

"I'd like that. Why don't you come over around seven?"

"I'll be there."

Neither of us said good-bye. I hung up the phone and sank deeper into the back of the couch. Herschel settled onto the couch beside me in perfect contentment; I wished I could tune into that emotion with such ease.

I hadn't been lying to Brenda. I did have more on my mind than Da-Marr and Evelyn, and even Sam and his quest to find Morrow's hidden millions. I hadn't called an allergist. I suppose I'd have to get a referral. It might take weeks—months—before I could even get an appointment. And then there was that whole near-death thing that kept hovering at the back of my mind.

I could have died.

The way things were going, maybe that wasn't such a bad thing.

Stop it.

I'd had that thought far too often back in May—not my doing— and abruptly got up from the couch, startling Herschel. I stepped over to the window overlooking the driveway. The rain had started once again, pelting the glass.

Brenda's car rolled up the driveway and pulled up behind my car, effectively blocking me in. Da-Marr got out, his expression smug. I took a step back, not wanting him to see me, but it was already too late. He glared at me for a long moment before he turned and sauntered for the house.

That kid gave me a very bad feeling, and it had nothing to do with psychic insight.

The better part of Richard's day had been spent on the telephone dealing with insurance agents who shunted him from one department to the next. But when he'd set the receiver down for the last time, it had been after a conversation with the claims adjustor who'd just finished assessing the damage to the still-unchristened Betsy-Ruth.

He liked the name. He was really going to enjoy that boat, or at least if Brenda finally came to like the boat he'd be better able to enjoy it.

He'd planned to pour a celebratory Scotch in the solitude of his study—that is until Brenda dragged him into the kitchen while Evelyn prepared dinner. While Brenda hadn't said so, he could tell Evelyn's presence had completely unnerved her. But there was something else going on with her, and he knew they weren't likely to discuss it in front of their houseguests.

Richard poured himself a drink and settled at the table next to Brenda while Evelyn yammered on about the difficulties in raising the funds for a new roof for her church. Richard had a feeling Brenda would be writing a generous check to that institution before the end of the visit. Why couldn't the woman just ask for a donation? Why did she feel she had to guilt them into contributing? Feeling stubborn, Richard ignored the not-so-subtle hints.

He reached for his glass and drained it before he got up from the table to retrieve more ice from the freezer. He tried to ignore Evelyn's disapproving glare.

"Do you *really* feel you need that?" she asked.

Richard managed a smile. "Yes. Today I do."

"I wouldn't mind a glass of wine. A big one," Brenda muttered from her seat at the table where she'd been sitting on her hands, no doubt to keep from clenching them. "It's been eight long months since I tasted the grape."

"We'll have champagne when the baby's born," Richard said.

"You will not," Evelyn said, her fierce glare now pinned on Brenda. "Not if you're going to breast feed that child."

Richard poured himself another Scotch, slopping it onto the counter. He waited for the rebuke.

"Perhaps you've already had enough," Evelyn said, and swooped in with a piece of paper towel.

"I can get it," Richard said, fighting to keep his tone neutral, but Evelyn ignored him. He retreated back to the safety of the table.

Outside, Brenda's car pulled up and he watched as Da-Marr got out, turning to look up at Jeff's apartment. It occurred to him that the kid had been gone an awful long time just to get a spark plug, but he wasn't about to interrogate him.

The outside door banged shut and Da-Marr trudged into the kitchen.

"Hang up that coat, young man," Evelyn ordered, and Da-Marr dutifully turned around and shucked his jacket before he returned to the kitchen. Evelyn checked on the pot roast simmering on the stove. "Wash up for dinner. It'll be ready in five minutes.

Without saying a word, Da-Marr headed for the bathroom.

Richard threw a glance at the clock on the wall. It wasn't even six. They normally didn't eat dinner until at least seven, but since Evelyn's arrival they'd been on an eight, twelve and six o'clock meal rotation. Didn't the woman understand the concept of spontaneity?

Da-Marr returned and, without a word from Evelyn, went to the cupboards to collect dishes, and then set the table. She had him well trained.

"You were gone an awfully long time, Da-Marr," Evelyn said with an edge to her voice.

Da-Marr gave her a wide grin. "I went exploring, Aunt Evelyn. I got the new spark plug for the lawnmower, but then I drove around just to see what I could find. Sorry, Cousin Brenda, but the gas tank needs to be filled."

"Don't worry about it," Brenda said, sounding weary.

"If it don't rain tomorrow—"

"Doesn't rain," Evelyn automatically corrected him.

"—I'll cut the grass," Da-Marr finished. He turned to his aunt. "Can I help you with anything, Aunt Evelyn?"

"No, dear. You sit right now. Brenda, do you have an electric knife?"

"It's in the cupboard to the right of the sink."

Da-Marr took what was usually Jeff's seat. "Hey, Richard, when can we go out on that boat again?" he asked, sounding keen for a new adventure.

"Depending on the weather, tomorrow or the day after."

"Does the weather really matter when you're driving it from inside the cabin?" Da-Marr asked.

Richard shrugged. "I guess not."

"Don't be ridiculous. Of course it does. The river could be terribly choppy," Brenda said, annoyed.

"Why do you want to drive that boat anyway?" Evelyn asked, plugging in the electric knife.

Da-Marr shrugged. "I sure as hell ain't gonna get the chance to do it once we're back home."

Richard had to bite his tongue not to ask just when that happy day would be.

"Da-Marr!" Evelyn called sharply. "Please do not swear in my presence."

Thoroughly chastised, Da-Marr hung his head. "Sorry, Aunt Evelyn."

Evelyn transferred the roast to a waiting serving platter and began to cut the meat into thin slices. "Will someone please strain the vegetables?"

Brenda made to get up, but Richard motioned her to sit and got up to help. "That pot roast sure smells good," he said, trying to sound jovial.

"Brenda told me how much you enjoy home cooking and I made it especially for you."

"That's very sweet of you. Thank you."

"You're welcome. I'm so glad Brenda invited me to come and look after the two of you and the baby, for surely you need it."

Richard opened his mouth to refute her assessment, but a warning look from Brenda made him back down. Somehow they'd managed to survive together for almost nine years without outside interference; why did Evelyn intimate that Brenda wasn't capable of managing a home, let alone a dinner? She was a nurse, a respected researcher, and was the kindest, most generous woman Richard had ever met. Sharing these past few days with Brenda's oldest sister had given Richard a whole new insight into how a teenaged Jeff must have felt when their mother had thrown Richard's success at the young boy who'd grown up without the same advantages and security. Being made to feel inadequate was something Richard had experienced far too many times. To endure it from a guest was even harder to swallow. But for the sake of family harmony—Brenda's family harmony—he was willing to do so.

Richard strained the water from the pot of lima beans and dumped them into the waiting serving bowl before setting them on the table.

Seconds later, Evelyn set the gravy boat and an enormous bowl of mashed potatoes on the table. Next came the platter of meat. She set it down, too, before taking her seat. She bowed her head and closed her eyes. "Dear Lord," she began. Da-Marr bowed his head, but stared at the potatoes, looking ready to pounce as soon as the prayer ended.

Richard tuned her out and reached for his glass, but a stern look from Brenda kept him from that last mouthful of Scotch.

Thoreau said, *"The mass of men lead lives of quiet desperation."*

At that moment, Richard understood exactly what he'd meant.

NINE

It was already dark when I got out of my car with a cold six-pack of beer and walked around to the front entrance of Maggie's house, noting that the lower portion of her duplex was dark. I was later than I'd planned, thanks to having to move Brenda's car to unblock my own.

Though I had a key, I rang the bell and waited. I could hear the sound of barking. A minute later, the door opened and there Maggie stood, looking tired after a long day at work. Looking beaten. Looking better than anything I'd seen in a long time.

"No pizza?" she asked flatly as her dog Holly nosed past her. I could see her tail already wagging.

"It'll arrive in about half an hour. Can I come in?"

She shrugged. "I guess." She stepped away from the door and started back up the steps to her second-floor apartment. Holly waited until I was inside and had locked the door before she threw her golden retriever body against me in greeting, looking up at me with adoring eyes, before following Maggie back up the stairs. I liked the dog's greeting better.

I recognized Maggie's favorite new-age CD playing softly in the background. We ended up standing in the center of her living room. "I come bearing gifts," I said and offered her the beer.

She took it from me. "Thanks. Want one?"

"I wouldn't say no."

She nodded and went into the kitchen to fetch a couple of glasses. I took off my coat and sat on her couch. A plate with the remnants of a pound of Watson's chocolate-covered sponge candy sat on the end table. So, she was having one of *those* kind of days.

Maggie returned to the living room carrying two glasses of beer, each with a tall foamy head. She set them on the coffee table and sat beside me, but not too close. Holly, however, pressed herself again my left leg, resting her head on my thigh.

"Don't be a pest, Holly," Maggie chided.

"She's fine," I assured her.

"So, how have you been?" she asked, not really sounding all that interested.

"Not so good. It turns out I'm allergic to bees. I got stung and almost died the other day."

"Yeah, I heard."

So, she'd talked to Brenda. Apparently, my almost leaving this earth hadn't made much of an impression on her.

We sipped our beer. Maggie's gaze seemed focused on the carpet. The silence felt awkward. I thought we'd gotten past that. It was time to clear the air.

"You know, Maggs, if it was just up to me, we'd both forget that May ever happened and could go back to the way it used to be between us."

"Well, it isn't up to you, and it really did happen, and I'm the world's biggest shit to have treated you that way," she said and still wouldn't look at me.

"If I can forgive you, why can't you forgive yourself?"

Her eyes widened and she turned to face me. "Looks who's talking about forgiveness?"

"What's that supposed to mean?"

She took another sip of her beer but didn't answer.

And then I understood. She'd spoken to Brenda *after* Brenda had spoken to me that very afternoon.

"I can't talk to Brenda about what happened to me back in the city."

"I guess I can see why."

"I kind of hoped I'd be able to talk to you, but I can see now that nothing I have to say would make any difference." I nudged Holly aside and stood, grabbed my coat from where I'd left it on the other chair and donned one of the sleeves.

"Wait." She sighed, looking distinctly unhappy. "This isn't the way I meant for things to go."

"Would you like me to come back in through the door and we can start over again?"

She said nothing.

I shrugged into the other sleeve, walked to the door, and out onto the first step, closing the door behind me. Then I opened the door and walked back into the living room. She'd moved to stand where she'd been when I'd first arrived.

"Hello, Maggie," I said and walked right up to her and planted a tender kiss on her lips. I was surprised when she wrapped her arms around me and returned it. I pulled back. "I've missed you, lady. Where've you been?"

I felt her slump in my embrace. "It's been a terrible couple of weeks."

"Let's sit down and you can tell me all about it."

I shucked my coat and took my former seat; she settled beside me, this time leaning her head on my shoulder like she'd done hundreds of times before. "Lily had a stroke," she said, her voice breaking.

Lily. Her ex-mother-in-law. Her beloved mother-in-law who lived in the bottom apartment of her duplex. I sometimes wondered if she loved that old lady more than her own mouse of a mother. I can't say I had a very good opinion of most of Maggie's family. Her sister Sandy and her husband and kids were all right, but her older sister, Irene, rode roughshod over the rest of the clan and apparently had her entire life and they continued to let her do so.

"When did this happen?" I asked.

"A week ago, Thursday."

"Why didn't you call me?" I asked, meaning it.

She shrugged. "I didn't want to bother you."

"How is she?"

Maggie sighed. "They moved her to rehab on Sunday."

"That's good, right?"

She nodded, but looked like she wanted to cry. "They *think* she'll be able to come home in a couple of months. Her speech is getting better every day, and she can walk with a cane if someone holds onto her, but she has to relearn so much. Getting dressed, washing—stuff she took for granted—now seems insurmountable. I've been to visit her every day. Gary," her ex-husband, "and I are both on her health care proxy, but so far I've had to make all the decisions so far."

"Didn't he come up to see her?" I asked, more than a little surprised.

She shook her head. "He says he can't leave work."

"I don't believe it."

"I don't, either. Lily asks for him every day. I think he's decided that she might die and he wants to remember her as she was."

"What does Brian say?"

She shrugged. Brian was now her ex-husband's husband. "That Gary's a shit if he doesn't get his ass up here. He told me he'd get him on a plane this weekend or kill the sonuvabitch."

"Will he?"

She managed a laugh. "Damn right." She reached for her beer and took a healthy sip. I did likewise.

She set the glass back down and nestled against me once again.

"What about Holly?" I asked. I hadn't even noticed that she had once again attached herself to my leg. She looked up at me with sad dark eyes.

"I've got her in doggy daycare when I'm at work. She misses Lily something terrible." The dog usually spent the day with the old lady, keeping her company, and Lily let her out into the yard for comfort calls. "But the home allows pet visits. I'm taking her back on the weekend. It'll help cheer Lily—make her work harder on her rehab so she can come home faster."

I reached over to stroke the soft hair on Holly's head. She let out a doggy sigh of contentment.

"I'm sorry I didn't call after your accident," Maggie said softly. "I wanted to. I should have, but I was just so overwhelmed by Lily's situation that I didn't think I could take on one more thing. And Brenda did say you were okay, anyway."

"Yeah. I am."

Maggie chewed on her lip for several long moments. "She's really upset with you."

"I know. As I said before, I really can't talk to her about what's bugging me, because … I'm really not sure I understand it myself. It hurts to know Brenda thinks I'm a racist."

"Are you racist?" Maggie asked, with one eyebrow raised inquisitively.

"I never thought so. But it was a couple of black guys who jumped me."

"And Da-Marr is black."

"Yeah, and just about the right size and age, too. But it's more than that."

"What do you mean?"

"That's the trouble; I haven't been able to pin it down. He's trouble—and he's headed for even bigger trouble."

"But you don't have a clue what."

"Yeah, and that scares me even more."

The CD stopped and we sat there in deadly silence.

I wondered if I should tell her about my adventure with Sam earlier in the day. I glanced at the clock. We still had ten minutes before the pizza was going to be delivered. But instead of talking about Jack Morrow, I chose another subject.

"I went to church today."

She pulled back and looked at me with surprise. "You? Church?"

I gave an ironic laugh. "I needed someone to talk to."

"And you went to *church?* I need a drink to digest that news," she said and grabbed her beer, taking a gulp. She turned back to look at me. "Who did you talk with?"

"A priest. I went to confession."

"They don't do confession anymore. But as you haven't been to church for decades, you probably didn't even know that."

"I didn't, and it hasn't been decades since I went to church. I went eighteen months ago." The day Richard was shot. I hadn't been in a hurry to return during the intervening time, either. Until that morning.

"Did you find what you were looking for?"

I shook my head. "I guess I didn't think I would. I'd just figured it wouldn't hurt to try. When I took that tumble off the ladder, I kind of had a near-death experience."

"With the white light and everything?" she asked incredulously.

I nodded.

Maggie sobered—if that was possible for someone who sounded as depressed as she did. "I know you won't want to talk to a counselor—"

"You got that right."

"But Father Mike at my parish is a pretty good guy."

"I don't want to talk to yet another old fart in a dark suit."

"He's not old. In fact, he's younger than me."

"I didn't think anyone was called to the priesthood these days."

"You thought wrong. I could call and ask him to talk to you. I'm not saying he'll have any insight, but he won't bullshit you, either."

I shrugged. "If you want." I took another hefty sip of my beer.

The doorbell rang—saved by the bell. The pizza was early, and Holly jumped to attention, barking a warning. I really didn't want to discuss the subject any longer.

I got up and went down to retrieve the pizza, giving the guy a nice tip. By the time I got back upstairs Maggie had retreated to the kitchen and had plates and napkins set out on the table. I plunked the box in the middle, grabbed a couple more beers from the fridge, and sat in my usual chair. Sharp knife and spatula in hand, Maggie opened the box and separated the pieces, doling out a fat slice for herself and giving me the smallest. She knew I wasn't likely to eat more than that anyway.

Holly settled between us, looking hopeful. Maggie took her seat and looked down at the dog. "You've already had your dinner and you didn't share it with me." Holly looked away, duly chastised. Maggie took a bite of her pizza and set it down on the plate again. She chewed and swallowed before speaking. "Are you in a hurry to go home tonight?"

"Not especially, why?" Was I going to get lucky?

"Just wondering," she said and cracked open her new beer, pouring it into the glass before her. "I kind of don't want to be alone."

"Just kind of?" I inquired.

"Yeah."

I shrugged. "I could stay and keep you company for a while."

"That would be nice." She smiled at me—like she hadn't done in way too long, then she reached across the table and clasped my hand. "About what you said before...."

My mind raced. "What?"

"About us ... and moving on from the past. Do you think we could really do it?"

"I'd like to try."

She squeezed my hand harder. "Me, too."

TEN

Richard stared blankly at his computer screen, trying to concentrate on a recent JAMA article on the cost effectiveness of bariatric surgery but found he'd read the same paragraph four or five times and still hadn't absorbed the content. He looked over the top of his reading glasses. Brenda hadn't said a word in hours, patiently working on her latest needlepoint project while Evelyn sat on the other end of the couch, knitting and talking at her. He frowned. It seemed almost impossible to have a decent conversation with the woman, who only appeared to enjoy the sound of her own voice.

Richard stared at the screen once again wishing Evelyn would find something else to do in the evenings. He missed his quiet time with Brenda. But, like them, Evelyn wasn't a big fan of cop shows or reality programs and had joined them in his study—intruding on *his* sanctuary.

Was he being too hard on Evelyn? The woman had had a brilliant career helping at-risk kids to not only improve their academic test scores, but actually graduate high school and go on to college, lifting them from the stranglehold of poverty and putting them on the road to success. She was good at that, but she wasn't much good at being a big sister.

Ha—that from the guy who'd neglected his own younger brother twenty odd years before. Well, he was making up for lost time—they both were, even if things were a bit strained at the moment.

It was no use trying to finish the article. He removed his glasses, closed the document, and powered down the computer before getting up to join the ladies, taking the wing chair adjacent to his wife. He watched as his sister-in-law pulled at the skein of fine, pale-blue yarn. "What are you working on, Evelyn?"

"A baby cap. The women from my church knit them for the preemie babies at Children's Hospital. I've got a bigger one made for Betsy Ruth to wear home from the hospital. I meant to give it to you before now, Brenda, but goodness knows somehow it slipped my mind."

Brenda looked up from her work and smiled. "Thank you, Evie."

"Looks like you'll be done with that piece before the baby comes," Richard said, indicating the needlework canvas where bunnies hopped against a green and yellow background.

"Maybe," Brenda said, noncommittally.

"That was a very nice pillow you sent me for Christmas," Evelyn said, and yanked on the yarn once again. "It sits in a place of honor in my guest bedroom."

Did she ever have houseguests? Would anyone but her ever see it?

"I'm glad you liked it," Brenda said. "This one will go in the baby's room, on the glider."

"Just where is that child going to sleep? There's no crib in the nursery," Evelyn said.

"We've got a cradle in our room. She'll be with us for the first few weeks. The crib was supposed to be delivered last week, but there was a mix up. It should arrive either tomorrow or the next day."

"You've left it rather late to do all the things that need to be done."

"After what happened last year, I didn't want to jinx things just in case...." Her voice broke, and she left the sentence hanging. They'd lost their first baby just eleven months before.

"Well, you'll soon have a full house—perhaps too full," Evelyn said, and looked over her glasses at Richard.

"What do you mean?" he asked.

"If there's one thing I learned in all my years in education, it's that a child must be prepared for self-sufficiency when he or she goes off into the world. It seems to me your brother could use a push for independence. A thirty-seven-year-old man should not be sponging off his relatives."

"Jeff is not sponging off us. He more than carries his weight around here," Richard said.

Evelyn shook her head sadly. "You're an enabler, Richard. Just as affirmative action crippled weak individuals in the past, you've taken away your brother's incentive to find meaningful work, to take responsibility for himself."

"Evelyn, Jeff suffered a devastating head injury only eighteen months ago. And while his recovery has been remarkable, it's by no means complete."

"He doesn't appear to be suffering any ill effects."

"Appearances can be deceiving."

"Yes, they can. I submit that your brother has been deceiving you for quite some time. You've given him a comfortable home—"

"The apartment has been there since this house was built. It was used by caretakers who worked for my grandparents."

"I understand you paid for serious upgrades before your brother moved in. A new furnace, central air conditioning, new appliances—"

Richard shot Brenda an angry glare, and she had the decency to look guilty for supplying her sister with so much information. "I know you mean well, Evelyn, but this is my family business."

Evelyn schooled her face before she got up from the couch, suddenly towering over him. She was a couple of inches taller than her youngest sister. "I've said my piece on the subject. I won't bring it up again. Good night."

"Good night," Brenda called.

Richard didn't say a word until he heard Evelyn climb the stairs to her room. "I know you're angry at Jeff, but did you have to drag Evelyn into our personal business?"

Brenda set down her needlepoint. "Jeffy living under our roof is my business, too."

"What do you want me to do—kick him out? Where would he go? How would he support himself?"

"I never said he had to leave."

"But you'd like it better if he did?"

"Of course not. I'm just angry that he hasn't shown my guests the kind of respect they deserve."

"Has he been rude to Evelyn?"

"No, but he hasn't been at all friendly to Da-Marr."

"And we've been over why."

Brenda stuffed her needlepoint project into a canvas tote. "It's time for him to get over the mugging. It happened, he's better. He should move on."

"Would you be that callous about a woman who'd been raped?"

"Don't even compare the two," she warned.

"Why not? They're both traumatic, life-altering situations."

"Now you're trying to make me the bad guy."

"And you're doing the same to Jeff."

Brenda pursed her lips, and he could see she was close to tears. "Look, no one says Jeff has to like Da-Marr or that Da-Marr has to like him. Why don't we just ask both of them to stay out of each other's way?"

"If that's what you want, then you do it. I don't need the aggravation right now."

"I know, and I'm sorry we've had to deal with this. I'll

talk to both of them tomorrow."

"Be my guest."

Silence descended, hanging heavy between them.

Richard spoke first. "Just how long are Evelyn and Da-Marr going to stay?"

"I'm not sure. Evie bought a one-way ticket for both of them. She said she'd go home when she was sure I could handle the baby."

"It seems I have a lot more confidence in your abilities than your sister does. You are a nurse, for chrissakes."

"Yes, but not a pediatric nurse."

"And how many first-time mothers are?" he muttered. "It's getting late. We should probably get ready for bed."

"You'll get no argument from me," Brenda said, and struggled to get up from the couch. Richard helped her to her feet. "I'll be glad when my old center of gravity returns."

Richard followed Brenda out and switched off the lights before they started for the stairs. "Where's Da-Marr?" he asked.

"I think he went to his room to watch TV."

"Are you sure?"

"No, but what else is there for a young man to do around here?"

They climbed the stairs. The lights were on behind the two guest rooms, and Richard could hear at least one TV blaring. Somehow, knowing Da-Marr was tucked in for the night made him feel better, but he was smart enough not to mention it and rile Brenda once again.

It was almost midnight when I arrived home from Maggie's. I swear, I drove the entire way there with an idiot grin on my face. We'd had sex a few times since her fling with her ex-fiancé, but it wasn't satisfying and we hadn't really reconnected until now. We were back in sync and I reveled in it.

I hadn't stayed the night because she had to get up and go to work at what I now considered an ungodly hour, so it made more sense for me to just go home. She assured me she didn't mind. Besides, I needed to feed Herschel.

Richard's house was dark as I pulled my car into the garage and hit the button to close the overhead door. Lost in thought, I got out of my car and opened the door to the stairwell. Shuffling up the stairs, I paused and listened. A faint pounding seemed to shake the walls like a ghetto wagon going by, only this wasn't out on Main Street. This was closer—inside my apartment. Every muscle in my body tensed as I grasped the door handle and gingerly tried it. Locked. I fumbled with my keys and opened the door. The room was dark, just the way I'd left it, but rap music thumped on my stereo. The sweet, acrid odor of marijuana wafted at me. It took every bit of courage I had to turn on the light.

With his feet propped up on my coffee table, Da-Marr lay sprawled across my couch, his glazed eyes staring at the ceiling.

"How the hell did you get in here?" I demanded.

Da-Marr looked up at me, a stupid grin plastered across his wide face. "The door was open, man."

"The hell it was." Either he was good at picking locks or, more likely, he'd never returned Brenda's key ring to the kitchen rack where she kept it.

He struggled to sit. "I can't listen to my music over there. They listen to classical shit. Not even R&B."

"I don't care what your excuse is. You're *their* guest, not mine. Now get the hell out."

"Aw, man." Da-Marr staggered to his imposing six-foot height.

I backed up a step, flashing onto the night I was

mugged. The baseball bat slamming into my skull.

Adrenalin pumped through me as I stumbled into the doorframe and caught hold of the jamb before I fell down the stairs.

"Fucking pussy." Da-Marr pushed past me, saying nothing more as he trotted down the steps.

The door to the driveway banged shut. I slammed the apartment door shut and flipped the deadbolt. What good was that against a key? I strode across the room, grabbed one of the dining chairs and hauled it across the floor, shoving it under the door handle.

Hands shaking, I somehow managed to hang my jacket in the closet before I crossed the room and backed the music down to a more tolerable level. Then I hit the first of the stereo's programed buttons. More rap. Hit the second button. Same station. The fucking little—correction, huge—bastard had reprogrammed every button to the same station. I smacked the power button, plunging the apartment into silence.

I looked around the room as a different kind of panic filled my gut.

Where the hell was my cat?

"Herschel? Where are you, boy?"

The darkroom door was open. Holy Christ, what if he'd gotten into any of those hazardous photo chemicals?

Everything was sealed—at least I'd left it that way, having dumped the last batch of chemicals the day before. But the cat wasn't inside. I turned off the light, my hand still shaking as I closed the door.

There weren't many other places for a cat to hide.

The ceiling light blazed when I threw the bedroom switch, I looked around. The closet door was still shut, the bedspread was unwrinkled. I crouched down, lifted the dust ruffle Maggie insisted I needed under the mattress, and found two frightened amber eyes staring back at me.

"It's okay, pal, he's gone. You can come out now."

Herschel glared at me as if to say, "No way."

I struggled to my feet and headed for the kitchen, finding the counter behind the breakfast bar littered with empty chip bags, an empty bread bag and a jar of open peanut butter, with smears of it on the sink where the dirty knife had been tossed. I looked across the way to see a couple of what I'd bet were empty beer cans sitting on my coffee table.

Trying to throttle back my sense of rage, I retrieved a can of cat food from the kitchen cabinet, pulled the flip tab and dumped it into a bowl. Returning to the bedroom, I again crouched down and offered the cat a treat, but even his favorite flavor couldn't entice Herschel to venture out from his safe hiding place.

"I don't blame you, pal." I slipped it under the bed and replaced the dust ruffle.

Returning to the living room, I opened the windows to air out the place, then returned to the kitchen to pour a glass of Maker's Mark on the rocks. I settled on one of my living room wing chairs, kicked off my shoes, and tried to decide just what it was I felt. Anger, for one, but also a sense of violation. If I was honest, I'd felt that way since the minute Da-Marr had walked into Richard's study three days before.

All the good feelings I'd experienced with Maggie had been obliterated.

I raised the glass to my lips to take a sip and then thought better of it. I held the glass up to the light. Something wasn't right. I sniffed it, wrinkling my nose. Something had been added to the dark amber liquid, and I didn't want to speculate what that might be. I tossed it in the sink and put the glass in the dishwasher before disposing of the rest of it. The bottle of Jack Daniels hadn't been opened. I grabbed more ice and poured it into a fresh glass.

The chilly night air wafted through the opened windows and I figured the place had been aired out enough. Where the hell had Da-Marr gotten the pot? While he'd been out on his little joy ride during the afternoon? How had he found a dealer so fast?

I was on my second drink when Herschel finally crept into the living room. He warily studied his surroundings and, crouched low, made a circuit around the room before he jumped onto my lap. He nudged my chin, and I scratched his head. It took him a minute or two to settle down. A minute after that, he began to purr. He didn't sit on my lap often. Usually he'd perch on the back of my chair or beside me, but he must have felt terribly insecure to need so much reassurance.

"I'm gonna fix this, buddy," I said as I scratched his chin. "I'm not sure what I'll do, but I'm going to fix this so that you won't have to be frightened by that asshole ever again."

Herschel head-butted my hand and purred even harder.

I'd had maybe three hours of sleep before I got up, dressed, and took off in my car. The mega hardware store opened at eight. I arrived at the parking lot about seven-fifty and waited, as rain spattered my windshield.

The drizzle had stopped when Richard showed up at my place about nine. I was turning the last screw on the sturdy new bolt I'd attached to the inside of my door as he came up the stairs.

"What are you doing?"

"Ensuring my privacy."

"Don't be stupid. What if there was a fire?"

I turned the screwdriver one last time. "Then I'd fry." I got up and headed into my once-again tidy apartment.

I topped up my tepid coffee. I didn't offer Richard a cup.

"Is that a new lock as well?"

"It sure is."

He held out his hand. "I want a copy of that key."

"Not until your guest leaves."

He stood on the other side of the breakfast bar, his body coiled with tension. "Da-Marr told us what happened. What's your version?"

"Version?" I echoed, ready to bite his head off. "He was in *my* house, smoking pot at midnight. I didn't invite him here."

Richard looked back at the shiny new lock and bolt. "Jeff, don't do this. It looks like we don't trust Da-Marr. It looks like—"

"I don't care how it looks," I grated in a tone I'd never used with Richard.

"Take it off, now," he said, the timbre of his voice matching mine.

I straightened and met his deadly gaze. "Is that an order?"

We stared at one another for a very long time.

The new hardware wasn't the real issue, and he knew it. Was he going to choose some punk kid he'd known for less than a week over me?

Finally, he looked away. "I'm sorry Da-Marr invaded your privacy. He won't do it again."

"Says who?"

"Says me."

"Are you going to babysit him every hour of the day and night?"

"Look, he'll only be here a few more days—"

"Have you got that in writing, because from what Maggie tells me, Evelyn hasn't given you guys a departure date."

"You've talked to Maggie?"

I nodded. "We're back together again. *Really* back together."

"I'm glad to hear that." He let out a breath. "How can we get through the next week or so until they leave?"

"Keep that kid out of my way. And if you're smart, you'll keep him on a short leash. I don't know where he got that pot, but he sure as hell didn't find it here."

Richard sniffed and frowned. The odor still hung in the air. At least he knew that part of my so-called story was true. "I'm sorry," he said at last. "I don't doubt a word you've said. But I have to live with Da-Marr, with Evelyn, and with Brenda. She's the most important person in the world to me and I'm willing to do anything to make her happy."

"Is she happy having company right now?"

He didn't reply. We both knew the answer to that question.

"What do we do about the boat?"

Richard looked uncomfortable. "Da-Marr wants another shot at driving it."

"Hey, I'm still waiting for my first shot."

"I'm sorry about that. The adjustor came yesterday afternoon. I thought I'd try to get someone to give me an estimate on fixing the upholstery. Otherwise, I was going to head over to the marina just to clean out everything that's busted. I could use some help."

"I'd be glad to give you a hand. But not if the kid comes."

He nodded. "Fair enough."

A banging noise came through the floor from the garage below. "What's that?" I asked, pretty sure I already knew the answer.

"Evelyn thinks Da-Marr needs to stay occupied. She wants him to cut the grass."

"It's wet. And we don't have a working mower."

The sound of an engine roaring to life made mock of that statement.

"Apparently he fixed it."

"Then he's good for something, at least. Maybe we should take advantage of the situation and head to the marina."

Again he nodded. "I'll tell Brenda and meet you back here in a few minutes."

"Right."

I watched in him leave, pulling the door closed behind him, then I wandered over to the window that overlooked not only Richard's driveway but gave me a view of a chunk of the backyard. Sure enough, Da-Marr had already started cutting a swath through the lawn.

I gave up on my coffee, tossing it down the sink and putting the mug in the dishwasher before I grabbed my jacket. Herschel was nowhere in sight, probably sacked out on my bed. I locked the door and hoped he wouldn't be terrorized again during my absence. Hell, I hoped that when I returned I wouldn't be terrorized again, either.

ELEVEN

We made one stop on the way to the way marina, hitting the closest Wegmans to buy a box of trash bags. From what I'd seen the day before, we were going to need all thirty of them.

A slice of blue sky had somehow managed to cut through the bank of clouds overhead as Richard drove through the marina's opened gates. Though in one respect it seemed like ages had passed since we'd been there the day before, I was surprised to see that the number of boats now missing from their slips had substantially increased. The thought of impending winter depressed me, and yet there was no place on earth I'd rather be. For better or for worse, Buffalo was home, and I now regretted those eighteen years I'd stayed away.

Richard unlocked the trunk and I grabbed Baby Suck—my mini shop vac. We didn't speak as we made our way to the boat. Richard already had the okay from Frank, the marina manager, to dump the trash in their Dumpster. Sure, it was worth letting us do that to try to avoid a lawsuit, not that he blamed them. The truth was, I was pretty sure there was no negligence on their part. We still had no clue who had owned the boat before that auction, and someone had obviously been looking for something. Drugs probably, but if there'd been any, I was pretty sure some pot- or coke-sniffing dog would have found it long before the boat had been released for auction.

We stopped in front of the outside deck and stared at the lock the vandal had smashed to gain entrance to the boat. Someone at the marina had used duct tape to secure the door, but in the damp environment, the filament tape had failed miserably. Richard looked heartsick, so I took the lead and rolled back the sliding glass door to gain us entrance.

"Brenda hasn't even seen the boat and already she hates it," he muttered.

"She'll feel different come summer," I said, trying to sound hopeful, but I had a suspicion Brenda's lack of enthusiasm was going to be difficult, if not impossible, to overcome.

When we'd first scoped it out at auction, I'd been as elated as Richard to board Easy Breezin'. I'd been caught up in the excitement of the prospect of lovely summer evenings spent with him and Brenda, and seeing Maggie sunning herself on the bow, while little Betsy Ruth toddled around chewing on her toys while giggling uproariously. That little girl was going to be a perpetual bucket of giggles. The thought brought a smile to my lips.

Richard wasn't smiling—and why should he? He'd probably already heard way too many utterances of "I told you so," if not from Brenda, then from Evelyn. "We'd better get to work. Then, if there's enough fuel in the tank, we can take her out for a spin."

"I do owe you your turn at the helm."

I laughed. "You make it sound like a starship."

"Mr. Sulu you ain't," Richard said with a laugh.

I wish we could have kept that level of levity, but once we entered the salon and started cleaning up the aftermath of vandalism we were both somber. Hell, I thought for a moment Richard might cry. The salon had been so sleek and comfortable, but now it lay in virtual ruins, with every flat surfaced covered in black fingerprint dust. The damage was far more extensive than we'd seen standing on the dock the day before. Not only had the ivory leather upholstery been slashed, and the couch and chairs eviscerated, but the cupboards had been emptied and anything that could have been smashed—was.

"I'm sorry, Rich," I said as we scooped handful after handful of cushion stuffing and ruined upholstery into the plastic bags.

"Yeah, well … it is what it is," he said, sounding defeated.

"There are many happy summer days ahead of us," I said.

"On this boat?" he asked, sounding just a little skeptical.

I wasn't sure about that, but I answered in the positive anyway.

It took twenty-eight of the thirty garbage bags, and five trips to the Dumpster, before the boat looked tidy, if spartan, once again. Richard stood before the controls about to fire up the engines when a voice called out that chilled me to the bone.

"Hey, I thought you were gonna let me drive this sucka."

I cringed and turned around to glare at Da-Marr.

"IIow did you get here?" Richard asked, trying, but not succeeding, to hide his displeasure.

"Brenda's car's got GPS," the kid said smugly.

I turned around to glare at Richard. "You promised me," I grated.

To be fair, what could he do but shrug?

Da-Marr bypassed the steps and jumped onto the back end of the boat. His knees were seventeen years younger than mine. He brushed past me. "Sorry about last night," he said without sincerity and went directly to the bridge deck and the boat's controls. "Are you gonna cast off?" he asked Richard.

The fact that Rich didn't protest and went to the dock

to untie the lines and pull in the bumpers hit me like a slap in the face. I stood there, immobile, too stunned to move—or protest—and the next thing I knew we were drifting away from the dock as Da-Marr started the boat's powerful engines.

Richard climbed back to the bridge deck and stood beside him, giving him the instructions he'd learned by studying the online articles he'd read and the few actual instructions he'd been given two days before. And once again I couldn't help but feel I'd been fucked. By Da-Mar—and worse—by Richard. And now as we traveled farther and farther away from the dock, I felt trapped.

The memory of the mugging came back to slam my psyche. I was helpless once again. I steadied myself and tried to swallow the bile that rose to try and choke me.

Da-Marr gunned the engines, and the momentum nearly sent me onto the deck. He let out a whoop of pure joy as the boat cleared the marina and headed north out on the river.

I staggered across the open deck and into the salon where I collapsed onto one of the wooden benches that had been a comfortable upholstered couch just two days before. And then it occurred to me that none of us was wearing life jackets, either. Richard and I had disposed of the three that had been destroyed.

Did I really care?

"Jeff, come on up," Richard called, but I ignored him.

I was behaving like a spoiled child, and I didn't give a shit.

The drive home was silent. What could I say that wouldn't make me look like the petulant jerk I was? I stared out the passenger window while Richard held the steering wheel in a death grip. We were almost home when he finally spoke.

"Sorry about all that."

"Yeah."

"Listen, I could use your help on something."

He had the gall to ask for another favor?

"The baby's crib could arrive today."

It was supposed to have arrived weeks ago.

"There's just one problem. It's coming unassembled."

Richard was fine with the tools of his trade—a stethoscope, thermometer, etc.—but put a real tool in his hands and he was all thumbs. I knew where this was going.

"You want me to build it?"

"Well, give me a hand at least."

"Sure." I was quiet for a moment. "Brenda doesn't know it's coming unassembled?"

"No. It was the only way I could get it here before the baby came, and—"

I held up a hand to stave off the rest of the explanation. "Sure. But I have to go to work tonight."

"Tomorrow morning then?"

I nodded. "Sure."

He pulled up the driveway, opened the garage door, and pulled in. He opened the trunk and I retrieved my shop vac, putting it away. I was about to head upstairs when I noticed Richard standing in the driveway, staring at something. I joined him and my rage ignited once again.

The garden that had ringed the backyard had been filled with annuals when we'd left, but now all that was left were the chewed-up remains. All my hard work—gone. They wouldn't have lasted much longer, but they wouldn't have been so thoroughly destroyed by a mulching lawnmower, either.

"I don't know what to say, Jeff. I'm sorry."

I didn't trust myself to speak and turned and stomped off for my apartment. I needed to change clothes and feed Herschel before I headed for The Whole Nine Yards.

I needed to cool off.

I wanted to commit murder.

I don't think I was ever so happy to get to my minimum-wage job. Still, the tedium of washing glasses and drawing beers wasn't mind-numbing enough for me to work off my anger and a few of my customers took their drinks and went to sit closer to the TV. The tips were going to suck.

It was a good two hours into my shift before I began to feel like a regular human being again. About that time a guy about my age, dressed in jeans and a Red Sox sweatshirt, entered the bar and sat down on one of the stools. I finished pouring a Molson on tap for one of the regulars before I wandered over to wait on him. "What can I get you?"

"Got any Guinness?"

I shook my head. "Sorry, no. But we've got Sam Adams black lager in a bottle."

"That'll do," he said, and shifted his gaze to the TV mounted on the wall to his right where a playoffs game was just about to start.

I set a clean glass and the beer before him and gave him the total. He gave me a five and while he poured, I made change, handing it to him.

"My name's Mike Ryan."

"Jeff Resnick," I said, and indicated the pin on my shirt that gave my first name.

"I was told I could find you here," he said, taking the first sip of his beer. He nodded in approval.

"Oh, yeah?" I asked, suddenly wary.

"Maggie Brennan said I'd find you here."

For a moment, I was confused. Then it hit me. "Father Mike from Maggie's parish?"

He nodded and smiled. "That would be me."

I offered him my hand, wanting to make a good impression for Maggie's sake. "Good to meet you."

"And you," he said. His grip was firm and I got no blast of insight from him that I often got when meeting someone new. That could be seen as good or bad depending on how the ensuing conversation went.

"Maggie said you'd recently had a crisis of faith."

I laughed at the absurdity of that statement. "I'm not even sure I have faith, so I don't know why'd she come up with that description."

Mike's expression was absolutely serious. "She said you had a near-death experience and that it had frightened you."

I didn't remember mentioning the word fear to Maggie, but he was right on that count. "Let's just say I was extremely disconcerted."

"And who wouldn't be? Do you have time to talk now?"

I glanced around the bar. The few patrons who'd shown up were either steeped in conversation or had their eyes glued to the game on the tube. "I guess so," I said, and reached under the bar to come up with a small bowl of potato chips that I sat before him.

"I'm fascinated by the whole concept of near-death experiences. I did my dissertation on the subject."

"You've got a degree in death?" I asked with an ironic laugh.

"As a matter of fact, I do. Not only am I a Catholic priest, but I'm also a hospice chaplain. I've ministered to people of just about every faith."

"What are you doing in Clarence?"

"It's a temporary assignment."

I nodded. I thought about what he'd said. How I wished the concept of hospice had been more common when my mother had been dying of cancer. She died friendless, but not entirely alone. Richard—who she'd barely known—had been there with her. Not me, who had taken care of her through all the years of her drunken depression. The boy who had taken on the responsibility of filling in the checks to pay our bills. The boy who had her sign her name before mailing them so our utilities and phone wouldn't be cut off. Or handing them to the landlord—opening the door to our apartment on a chain so he wouldn't see my mother lying drunk on the couch. How stupid I'd been to think that he—or anyone else—wouldn't notice the handwriting in the TO and AMOUNT portions of each check was different than that of the signature. But my efforts had kept us afloat for years. I'd had to grow up awfully fast.

Still, it was Richard—not me—who'd been allowed to be there during her last moments. He'd held her hand as she'd left this earth. Worst of all was knowing she probably preferred it that way.

Father Mike squinted up at me. "What are you remembering right now? It doesn't look like it's particularly happy."

I shifted my gaze. "No, it isn't."

He took another sip of his beer, savored it, and set the glass back down on the bar. "Maggie thought you could use a new sounding board. Someone neutral."

"Did she?" I asked, not sure how I felt about that.

Mike lowered his voice. "She told me what happened back in May and how unhappy she's been about the strained relations between you two."

I wasn't sure how to reply to that statement, so I said nothing.

"For what it's worth, I believe she's genuinely sorry."

Sorry didn't erase the past, but it made it more tolerable to accept. We'd made our peace the night before—I'd somehow have to do a better job of convincing her of it.

Mike took another sip of his beer and shifted his gaze to the TV where a base hit had just occurred. He turned back to his glass and took another sip. "I don't expect you to open up to me here at the bar. Hell, I didn't know if you'd be interested in talking about it in depth at all. But I wanted you to know that when and if you are, I'd be happy to listen." He reached into his pants pocket, came up with a slightly wrinkled business card, and handed it to me.

I scrutinized it. "I didn't know priests carried business cards."

"Hey, when it comes to phone numbers—even my own—I've got a mind like a sieve. This way I can hand it out without looking like a complete jerk."

After talking to Mike Ryan for only a few minutes there was one thing I was sure of—he was no jerk.

"Thanks. I'm not sure I'm ready to expose my soul to you or anyone else, but I appreciate the offer. And that Maggie respects you is a pretty damned good endorsement."

Mike upended his glass and drained it. "Gotta go," he said, and set the glass back down on the bar. "One of my parishioners is going to cross over tonight. He's been in a coma for the past two days."

"Then why do you have to be there?" I asked.

"Oh, it's not for him, but his children are in real distress. One daughter in particular. She was her dad's favorite. She's just a teen and is absolutely heartbroken. She hasn't accepted that his death is imminent and her mother asked if I would mind being present."

I met his gaze and somehow understood that even if I wasn't sure of the great beyond, that I could understand that the man before me was capable of comforting someone facing mortality—even if it wasn't her own.

"Thanks for coming here tonight," I said and offered Mike my hand once again. "I don't know if I'll call you, but I do appreciate that you came here for Maggie's sake. She means the world to me."

He smiled. "I know things have been rough for you two these past few months, but I honestly believe she feels the same way about you."

A spark inside me ignited into a full-blown flame, not that I would share it with this virtual stranger. It was the hope that after a long lonely summer apart, we'd somehow be able to recapture what we once had. Hope made the impossible suddenly seem within reach. We had a long way to go, but my gut told that the effort it would take—and it was not going to be easy—would be well worth it.

Mike slipped a buck under his glass, stood, and nodded a good-bye.

I had a feeling I'd be talking with Mike Ryan again.

For the first time since her arrival, Evelyn had very little to say at dinner that night. The fact that one of the seats at the table stood empty was the cause. Brenda chattered on and on about the novel she was reading, about the diaper service she had hired, and even on the kind of baby food she intended to make for Betsy Ruth once she was able to tolerate solids, but all Evelyn did was stare at the driveway and dare Da-Marr to return from wherever he'd gone after his joy ride on Richard's boat.

The long silences were nerve-wracking, which made Richard more antsy and aching to pour himself yet another Scotch, which he didn't dare do.

After the dinner plates were put in the dishwasher, the ladies joined Richard in his study where the strained silence continued. No one wanted to acknowledge the elephant in the room—or the lack of his actual presence. Richard turned on the stereo, playing Vivaldi, which always sounded so light and cheerful, but he could tell Evelyn thought it frivolous and annoying. She hadn't voiced her musical preferences, and he was afraid to ask.

He hadn't told Brenda about Da-Marr smoking pot in Jeff's apartment. He hadn't told her that Jeff had changed the lock. Life on LeBrun Road had become too tense these last few days to mention anything that could be taken in a negative connotation.

It was almost nine when they heard the thump of heavy footsteps pounding on the hallway leading to the study.

"Anybody home?" Da-Marr called cheerfully.

Slowly, Evelyn's head swiveled toward the door, her face tight with anger.

Da-Marr paused in the doorway, his expression bland.

"Where have you been, young man?" Evelyn demanded.

Da-Marr laughed. "I've got a friend here in Buffalo, Auntie. I told you about him the other day. We met at the marina. After we put the boat away, I saw him and we sat in his boat and talked until it was dark. Then we got something to eat. You brought me here to see a different kind of life and do different stuff. Isn't this what you wanted?"

Evelyn opened her mouth to speak, but then closed it, looking disconcerted.

"Did you have a good time?" Brenda asked, her voice sounding subdued. She probably wasn't eager to suffer her sister's wrath.

"Yeah. We went for pizza at some joint near the marina."

"And what's the name of your new friend?" Evelyn asked, her voice brittle with suppressed anger.

"Bobby. Isn't that the whitest name in the world—next to Richard?" he said and laughed.

Nobody seemed to find that comment funny—least of all Richard.

"You could have called," Evelyn said.

"I don't have a cell phone," Da-Marr said flatly.

"But I'll bet your friend did," Evelyn said, her voice even sharper.

"I don't know anyone's number," he said and laughed again.

"I'm sure Richard will give you a list," Evelyn said and looked pointedly at him.

"Sure," Richard said, trying to keep his voice even.

Evelyn held out her hand. "I think you'd better give me the keys to Brenda's car."

"Oh, come on, Auntie. I was just having some fun with a friend."

"I'd like to meet this friend. Are you willing to bring him home to meet us?"

It was Da-Marr's turn to look disconcerted. "I guess," he muttered.

Evelyn's hand still beckoned.

Da-Marr's mouth tightened, but he dug into the pocket of his jacket and handed over the keys, which he clearly found difficult to do.

Evelyn grabbed them and stuffed them into the pocket of her sweater. "You need to apologize to Brenda for missing dinner. It was rude. Your hosts have a pile of leftovers."

"Sorry, Brenda. But I'll bet I could eat them for lunch tomorrow," Da-Marr said and laughed again.

Brenda shot Richard a worried look, but then turned back to Da-Marr with a forced smile. "All is forgiven," she said, but her voice sounded strained.

Evelyn wasn't quite as generous. "Let's see that it doesn't happen again."

Instead of being contrite, Da-Marr's expression hardened. "Auntie, you want me to make more of myself. Didn't you tell me you want me to stop hanging with low lifes and find a higher class of people?"

"Yes, but—"

"Then you've got to trust me. You *do* trust me, don't you?"

Evelyn swallowed. "Of course I do," she said, but the

set of her mouth said anything but.

Da-Marr gave his most charming smile. "I love you, Auntie," he said, and sauntered over to give Evelyn a kiss on the cheek. Her anger seemed to melt and she gave him a loving smile.

"I'm going to bed now. See you all tomorrow," Da-Marr said.

"Good night," Brenda said, and Evelyn and Richard echoed that.

Their collective gazes remained on the hall as they listened to Da-Marr travel down it and then up the stairs. Finally Evelyn turned back to Brenda, digging into her pocket, she handed back the keys. "Don't let him drive your car anymore."

"Are you worried about him?" Brenda asked, her voice sounding carefully neutral.

"You better believe I am," Evelyn said, but whatever it was that preyed on her mind, she didn't share it. Still, as she resumed her knitting, the lines on her forehead seemed even deeper.

"Why are you so worried about him?" Brenda asked.

Evelyn turned on her sister. "He's a young black man. He's a good boy. But if you're a black man in a white man's world, you are a target. He could end up dead because he's wearing a hoodie. A rich white boy can be just as dangerous as a black gang member to someone who's vulnerable."

"You don't think Da-Marr will show good judgment?" Brenda asked. Richard would have asked the same question, but was wary of Evelyn judging him.

Evelyn seemed to think long and hard before she answered. "No." She looked back down at her knitting, saying nothing while The Four Seasons continued in the background, but her knitting needles seemed to click with aggression, or maybe it was redirected anger, then suddenly she stopped, picked up her yarn and stuffed it and the baby's cap into her work bag. "I'm going to bed," she said, got up, and hurried from the room.

"Good night," Brenda called after her, looking worried.

The CD ended, and the room went deadly silent.

Brenda was the first to speak. "Evie's got it, too."

"Got what?" Richard asked.

"The second sight. Just like Jeff. Just like our grandma. Just like me sometimes. She knows."

"Knows what?" he asked, feeling totally confused.

"That something bad is going to happen with Da-Marr. She's been trying to save him from whatever it is, and she thought bringing him here would do that, but it was the worst thing she could have done."

"And what is going to happen?" Richard asked, fearing the worst.

"I don't know. But I suspect she does, and she's never going to tell me or anyone else."

"And what part do we have to play in this? Is there anything we can do to stop it?"

Brenda shook her head, her expression grave. "No."

"Will this hurt our daughter?" he asked, suddenly alarmed.

Brenda's head tilted to one side and she seemed to concentrate for a moment. "No."

Richard breathed a silent sigh of relief. But then he wasn't brave enough to ask his next question aloud: would whatever happened to Da-Marr affect Jeff?

Brenda turned to look at him with an odd expression, as though she'd heard the unspoken question, and the hairs on the back of his neck bristled. "Yes."

She didn't say anymore and neither did he.

And he felt like a goddamned coward for it.

TWELVE

It was almost one by the time I parked my car in Richard's garage. The night had dragged, which was unusual for a Wednesday evening, with my conversation with Father Mike being its only highlight.

I got out of the car. The light on the garage door opener would stay on for three minutes, but I wasn't about to wait that long. When I flipped the switch to the stairwell, nothing happened. Had my previous night's visitor made a return call, found he couldn't get in, and removed the bulb from the fixture?

I mounted the stairs, stepping carefully as I headed for my apartment. At least with a new lock on the door, I knew no one could have invaded my home since I was the only one with the key.

I was wrong.

Something was very wrong.

I hesitated before touching the door handle, but knew whose aura would still be attached to the metal: DaMarr's. But he couldn't have gotten in. Still, he'd touched the door and found it locked, and he'd been frustrated and angry.

I fumbled with the key, knowing that behind the door was danger, I could feel it. He'd gotten through my new set of defenses; he had been inside my apartment and ... could he have booby-trapped the place?

There was only one way to find out.

Slowly, I opened the door. The place was pitch-black. I flipped the light switch, but nothing happened. Had he taken the bulbs out of all my light fixtures?

I fumbled around in the dark, making my way to the kitchen, threw that switch and still no light came on. I opened the microwave door and it lit a small portion of my galley kitchen. So, there was still power in the place. I opened the fridge, letting its light spill into the kitchen as well. I kept a big flashlight in the cabinet under the kitchen sink, and I retrieved it and hit the switch. Nothing. Were the batteries dead, or had Da-Marr dismantled it, too? Back under the sink it went.

The outside light was on. In my haste to cross the room, I nearly fell over my coffee table and cursed the asshole who had put me in this position. I drew the drapes and the room was flooded with shadows and enough light for me to finally see where I was going.

I made my way to the bathroom, but the light bulb was missing from that room as well, and a breeze chilled the air from the open—no, broken—window. I moved closer and stepped on shattered glass. If I looked out, would I find a ladder standing at the back of the house?

"Herschel?" I called. He was probably under the bed again.

It seemed as though I could hear an odd hum coming from the vicinity of the dining area. I doubled back and the hum got louder.

"I don't like the sound of this," I muttered to myself, and something whizzed past my head.

Something crackled under my foot, and I leaned against the counter to take a look. A shudder passed through me as I recognized exactly what I'd stepped on: a wasp. By the sound of it, there had to be a hell of a lot more of them buzzing around, too. And if one of them stung me....

I had to get out of there. I was sensitive to bee venom; would I have the same nearly fatal reaction to a wasp sting? Logic said yes.

And what about Herschel? What if the angry insects had attacked him? Would he be safe under the bed?

Next stop, the bedroom, but the light had been tampered with there, too. I'd kill that slimy little bastard. I heard more buzzing, and fumbled my way back to the darkroom which doubled as my supply closet, but more glass cracked under my feet and I knew every spare bulb—including the curly and expensive fluorescents—had been thrown on the floor and smashed in anger. Why was that bastard so pissed at me? What had I ever done to him?

I groped in the darkness until I found Herschel's cat carrier. My presence must have angered the wasps, for more of them seemed to be buzzing around the living room. I paused to pull my jacket over my head before I charged forward for the bedroom. Keeping my voice low, I called for the cat, but as this was the second night he'd been traumatized, I knew I'd probably have to frighten him more just to capture him. I closed the door behind me, but I could still hear buzzing.

Suddenly I remembered the small flashlight I kept in my nightstand drawer, and edged my way alongside the bed until I bumped into it. The bastard hadn't found that light; its sharp narrow beam pierced the darkness. A wasp whizzed by my head once more and I knew I'd have to get out of there fast.

I crouched down, again lifting the dust ruffle and shining the light. Two frightened red eyes peered back at me. "Come on, Herschel, I'm getting you out of here." But instead of moving toward me, the cat made a break for the head of the bed, moving just out of my reach. He was no fool. He'd heard the door of his carrier swing open when I'd entered the room and knew that meant a trip to the vet. "Not this time, buddy," I said and shoved the bed over a foot until I could grab him by the scruff of his neck and hauled him out from under the bed, stuffing him into the carrier.

I struggled to my feet and made my way through the darkened apartment, kicking something light that bounded into the air. A paper wasps nest? Suddenly the air was filled with the sound of angry buzzing and I pulled the jacket lower over my brow as I charged for the door.

Somehow, I managed to hold onto the carrier as I slammed the door shut without locking it. A couple of the wasps had gotten out with me—I could hear them—and I nearly fell down the steps in my haste to get the hell out of the stairwell.

The cold air hit me like a slap as I ran into the center of the drive, unsure of what my next step should be. I had a decision to make and I wasn't sure what I should do.

I set Herschel's carrier on the ground. He gave a plaintive cry as I pulled the cell phone from my jeans pocket, staring at it from the glow of the light above the garage door.

My first inclination was to call the police and report a break-in, but what additional hot water would I be in with Brenda if I did? Their house was dark. Calling Richard's landline meant waking up the whole house. Why should I care? Da-Marr's little stunt could be viewed as attempted murder. Being stung by one of those wasps could have killed me, especially since I wasn't carrying the epi pen as Richard had instructed me to do. Who the hell thinks they need to be protected from angry wasps in their own apartment?

But I thought better of calling that number. It would upset Brenda. If Richard ever got calls in the middle of the night from the hospital about one of his patients, they always called his cell phone. Not that he was doing direct patient care anymore, but maybe out of habit he still kept the phone by his bedside. I took the risk and hit speed dial.

It rang four times—about to go to voice mail when a sleepy voice said, "Hello?"

"My cat and I are standing in your driveway."

"My what?" he asked, sleepily.

"Your driveway. Someone broke into my apartment and left a nest of angry wasps. I'm asking your permission to call the police." I waited, letting my last two sentences sink in.

"Is this some kind of a sick joke?"

"It's me, Jeff. Someone broke into my apartment," I repeated. "Can I call the cops and report it?"

"Why wouldn't you—?" He stopped, no longer sounding half-asleep. "I'll be right there."

I pocketed my phone and watched as a trail of lights came on over at the big house. A minute later, Richard opened the back door and shuffled through it in his bathrobe and slippers. I didn't cross the distance to meet him.

"What the hell is going on?" he asked, more than a little annoyed.

"You tell me. Or rather, have Da-Marr tell me. And then he can tell it to the cops."

"Are you sure the place is full of wasps?"

"I bent down and took off my shoe and shoved it at him. Half a wasp body still protruded from the edge of my sole.

Richard swallowed. "How do you know Da-Marr did it?"

"How many people know I'm allergic to bees—and possibly wasps? Let me guess," I said and calmly counted them off on my hand, amazed that I hadn't already exploded in anger. "You, Brenda, Maggie—and I'm assuming Brenda told Evelyn, and who would have been sitting right next to her? Da-Marr."

Richard looked back down at my shoe still in his hand. "Shit."

"What are you going to do about it?" I demanded.

He looked up at me. "Me?"

I grabbed my shoe, slipping it back on my foot. "It's your property."

He sighed, looking panicked. "I can't call the cops. Brenda would—"

"Do you think she'd condone this?"

"Of course not, but—"

"What's going on?"

We both turned to see Brenda standing at the door, backlit by the pantry lights.

"Go back to bed," Richard called.

"How can I?" she answered, sounding worried.

I reached for the cat carrier and turned for the garage.

"Where are you going?" Richard demanded.

"Where else? Maggie's. If she'll have me. Christ knows I've got nowhere else I can go," I said, and opened the side door to the garage, slamming it.

I stowed the carrier on the backseat of my car, got in, and pressed the garage door button. The door went up and I started the engine, pulling out.

Richard was standing on the steps by the time I hit the button and the garage door started on its way back down. I turned on my headlights and hit the gas, my tires spinning.

I didn't look back. I wasn't sure I wanted to see either of them ever again.

Don't you dare call the police," Brenda grated. She held the cup of steaming cocoa up to her lips but didn't take a sip.

"This is more than a prank, Brenda. Being stung could

literally kill Jeff," Richard said. Screw cocoa, he took a sip of Scotch, neat.

Brenda set her cup back on the kitchen table, her eyes welling with tears. "I can't believe it. I won't."

"But you said yourself—"

She looked up, glaring at him. "We are *not* going to accuse a guest of such a heinous thing."

"Okay, if you don't want to believe in attempted murder, how about malicious mischief? Every light bulb in the place is missing—it looks like they were all smashed. And the place is full of wasps." He held out his hand to show the swelling welt where he'd been stung. "It was just dumb luck that Jeff isn't dead from anaphylactic shock."

Brenda kept shaking her head. "No. Da-Marr may be troubled, but he's not malicious. Evie says—"

"That he can be rehabilitated? You saw what he did to Jeff's garden. You saw how upset Evelyn was this evening. Admit it, both she and you are afraid of what this kid might be capable of doing."

That she didn't protest said a lot.

"Evelyn is—*we're*—a positive influence on Da-Marr. I refuse to believe that he could do something this terrible. I refuse to believe that he is responsible."

Richard chose his words carefully. "I understand that you want to give Da-Marr the benefit of the doubt, but admit it; is this someone you want around our baby?"

Brenda turned away. "I trust Evie's judgment."

And suddenly you don't trust mine or Jeff's? he dearly wanted to ask.

"Richard, this boy has had a hard life. His family has more or less given up on him. All of them—except for Evie. She's worked miracles with kids. She's sure she's turned him around. She's sure—"

"Why does she care so much? Why this boy?" Richard shook his head. "And that's the thing; he's not a boy. He's a man. He's twenty years old."

"But he deserves a second chance. Evie doesn't champion losers. In all the years she's been a teacher and a school administrator, she's never had a failure. She's that good."

Or was she willing to dismiss whatever failures she'd had?

Richard drained his glass, already wanting to pour another. But he wouldn't because he could see the hurt in her eyes. More than once he'd had too much to drink. His mother had been a drunk. Brenda worried that he might succumb to that obsession. He couldn't bear to see that look of disappointment in her eyes.

"So what do we do next?" he asked.

"Give Da-Marr the benefit of the doubt," she said vehemently

"And the wasps up in Jeff's apartment?"

"Call an exterminator. And we'll get our cleaning service to see if they can send someone by in the morning."

"And after that?" he asked.

She let out a shuddering breath. "Pray."

Pray? They might as well make a wish on a falling star.

"And how do we keep this from happening again?"

"It won't."

"How do you know it won't?"

"I will make sure it doesn't," she said, and then winced.

"What's wrong?" Richard asked.

Brenda shook her head. "The baby kicked." She reached for his hand and placed it on her abdomen. The tiny foot once again jutted against its fleshy prison.

"It won't be long now," Richard said. Judging by the position of the foot, the baby was starting to turn. He looked up at her, but neither of them could muster a smile. They'd so looked forward to this birth and now discord and enmity supplanted their joy.

They weren't going to talk about it anymore that night. Brenda got up and poured her nearly full cup of cocoa down the sink, and Richard followed, placing his glass there, too, then they headed down the hall to the stairs.

No lights shone under the guest room doors. The house was as quiet as a tomb.

They climbed into bed and Richard molded his body against Brenda's, but he could feel the tension emanating from her.

It was a long, long time before either of them fell back to sleep.

THIRTEEN

*S*ince his arrival, Da-Marr seemed to have grown in stature. *He was not only taller, but beefier, and an angry sneer per-petually covered his brooding, thug-like countenance.*

The three of us stood at the stern of Richard's boat, which seemed to have grown as well. The open deck was nearly the size of a tennis court.

"You still haven't recognized me," I accused. It had taken every ounce of courage I possessed to challenge him.

Da-Marr's gaze shifted from my face to the deck, his shoulders hunching like a prize bull getting ready to charge.

I forced myself to continue. "I used to have a brown leather bomber jacket. Man, I loved that coat. I had it almost twenty years. They cut it off me in the Emergency Room."

Da-Marr's eyes remained locked on the deck.

"Did Lester's balls ever recover?" I asked.

No reaction. I'd kicked his cohort hard where it counted, but that had only increased Da-Marr's killing rage.

"Are you still friends with Reggie?"

That got Da-Marr's attention, and he looked up sharply. He'd wielded that vintage baseball bat, using it to smash my skull. The bat had come down, over and over again.

"What the hell are you talking about?" Richard asked, sounding both confused and concerned.

"Da-Marr's got himself a collector's item. A Reggie Jackson special—one quality baseball bat. It had to be at least thirty years old, too. I saw the signature burned into it just before it

plowed into my skull."

Richard's mouth dropped open in horror.

Da-Marr still said nothing.

"I figure you owe me a computer, a camera, binoculars, a stereo, TV, microwave, and a gun. Want me to continue with the list of what you cleaned out of my apartment?"

Da-Marr still said nothing.

"But most of all, you took my fucking life!"

"What are you saying, Jeff?" Richard demanded.

"Big Brother, meet the man who caved in my skull."

Richard shook his head in denial. "You don't remember what happened. How could you—?"

"You're right. At first, I didn't remember. It started coming back to me in dreams. Little snippets at a time. How many nights did I wake up in a cold sweat seeing one face. One black face, starkly lit by a sodium vapor light. Oh yeah, brother, I remember the face. I remember the hands that wielded the bat that hit me. I remember every fucking detail."

Richard looked from me to Da-Marr, his face a study in growing terror.

"Say something," he told Da-Marr. The kid kept looking at the deck.

"A man's gotta survive," Da-Marr said at last. "You don't know what it's like out on the streets."

"Are you the one who mugged Jeff and left him for dead?" Richard demanded.

"There were a lot of guys in bomber jackets. A lot of apartments I emptied."

"What happened to Lester?" I asked again.

"Knifed in an alley—tried to rip off his crack supplier."

"At least one of you got what you deserved."

"And now you're going to get what you deserve." He reached into the pocket of his long black duster and pulled out a semi-automatic. I recognized the gun. It had once belonged to me.

"Da-Marr! You can't!" Richard pleaded, but his words held

no sway.

Da-Marr aimed the gun at my chest, and pulled the trigger.

A loud bang on the glass next to my left ear woke me with a start. It was still dark out, but the porch lamp lit the upper half of the driveway. I turned, feeling half-frozen and terminally stiff.

Maggie's face peered at me, her expression a mix of annoyance and worry. I rolled down the window.

"What in God's name are you doing here at six-twelve in the morning?"

"Waiting for you to get up."

It looked like she was barely awake. Her hair was tangled. She wore her blue quilted robe and a pair of moccasin slippers, and held the newspaper in her hand. She looked through the back passenger window. "Is Herschel in there?"

"Yeah. I need a favor."

"You know he doesn't get along with Holly."

"Yeah, but I thought since your mother-in-law is in rehab he might be able to stay in her apartment for a few days."

"Lily doesn't have a litter box."

"I bought one on the way over. The poor cat's been stuffed in that carrier for five hours. By now he might need to use it."

"Five hours?" she cried in disbelief. "Let's get him out of there." She went inside ahead of me. I hauled Herschel and his supplies out of the car and we waited for Maggie to get the key to the apartment. She unlocked the door, then grabbed the bulky bag filled with a ten pound sack of litter, food, and cat treats in one hand, hauling in the new litter box with the other.

Maggie flipped the light switch and crossed the threshold ahead me. Her apartment above was decorated in what she liked to call eclectic contemporary—with refurbished yard sale finds mixed with contemporary furniture and a smattering of antiques. In contrast, entering Lily's home was like to stepping back into the 1970s. The shabby green furniture was badly faded, and the air hung stale, no doubt from the place having been unoccupied for nearly two weeks.

"You'd better put the litter box in the bathroom," Maggie advised.

I shucked my jacket, tossed it on the couch, and grabbed the bag of supplies and the box. Two minutes later, I let Herschel out of the carrier. He made a beeline for the box and we turned away to give him his privacy.

Maggie flipped on the kitchen light switch, found a couple of bowls, and filled one with water, setting it down on the floor. "When was the last time he ate?"

"Before I went to work last night."

She took one of the cans of cat food and dumped half into the other bowl, setting it down next to the water.

"So, do you want to come upstairs for a cup of coffee and tell me what the hell is going on?"

"It's a long story, and you're going to have to get ready for work."

"Give me the abridged edition," she said, and started back for the front door. I left the lights on for the cat and followed.

Holly met us at the door to Maggie's apartment. She seemed to know something was wrong about the timing of my visit, and whined quietly as she followed us into the kitchen. The coffee was indeed ready, and Maggie poured me a cup, dumping just the right amount of milk into it and handing me a spoon before we sat down at the table.

"Okay, I'm listening," she said, and took a big gulp of coffee, as though to fortify herself.

I did give her the short version.

She listened, without interruption. "What are you

going to do now?" she asked, and I could tell from her tone that although I was welcomed back into her life, she didn't expect me to move in with her. Fair enough. I didn't want that either. Crummy as it often was, I wanted my old life back. The life before Evelyn and Da-Marr entered it, that is.

"I'm not letting that punk drive me from my home, but I can't risk Herschel getting hurt and being terrorized. Can he stay at Lily's—just until Da-Marr is out of our lives?"

"And when do you think that will be?"

"It had better be damn soon, but even Brenda doesn't have a clue when Evelyn intends to leave."

"So she said."

"I'm sure Richard will be on the phone calling an exterminator and his cleaning service the minute either of them opens this morning. He'll make it right, at least in that respect."

"He really doesn't have proof Da-Marr did it, and what's he supposed to do, kick out Brenda's houseguests a day or so before the baby arrives? You know that isn't going to happen."

I looked away.

"Oh, come on, Jeff. You've been married. You know how it is."

"Yeah," I grudgingly admitted, "I do."

She reached over and touched my hand, gave me a wan smile, and then got up to scrounge for something to eat. With her harried life these past couple of weeks, I knew her cupboards had even less in them than mine. In desperation, she zapped a couple of slices of the pizza from two nights before.

I sipped coffee and attempted to read the paper while Maggie got ready for work. What I really wanted to do was try to catch another hour or two of sleep.

Maggie donned her coat and grabbed the canvas bag

she hauled around with her current novel and work shoes. "You're welcome to stay as long as you like." She handed me a key on a ring. "It's the extra one for Lily's apartment. I'm going to stop and visit her on the way home from work. She likes me to stick around and watch TV with her for a while every night, so I probably won't be home until at least seven."

"I don't know if I'll be here or not. I don't have to work, but I'm expecting a call from Sam."

"Whatever you guys are up to, I don't want to know about it—at least not now. Tell me all about it when it's over."

"You got it."

She bent down to give me a kiss. It was perfunctory, nothing more, and yet as she pulled back we shared what I would call a loving smile. Then, she was all business again. "Come on, Holly. Time for doggy day care." She grabbed the leash and hooked it to the dog's collar.

The apartment seemed unnaturally quiet after she'd gone.

For once, I was glad Maggie drank decaf coffee, and I decided to sack out on her couch. I must have conked out right away, because when I came to and looked at her living room clock it was nine-thirty. I checked my cell phone and was surprised to find that Sam hadn't called. That was okay. I had another call to make.

I reached for my wallet and pulled out the card I'd been given the evening before. I studied it long and hard before I worked up the courage to punch in the number and expected voice mail to kick in. "Hello."

"Father Mike? It's Jeff Resnick. We spoke at The Whole Nine Yards bar last night."

"Of course. So, you decided to talk about your experience after all."

"Yeah—if only to get it behind me."

"Great."

"Are you free today?"

"Yeah. Would you like to come over to the rectory?"

"Uh," I hesitated. It was less than a mile down the road, but ....

He laughed. "I don't blame you. Are you doing anything for lunch today?"

"Not a thing."

"I'm loving those beef on weck sandwiches here in Buffalo. I'll sure miss them when I'm reassigned. I have to be up at Sisters Hospital this afternoon. There's a tavern near there that's got some wicked-fresh horseradish. It's call Ivy's."

"I know the place."

"See you at noon?"

"I'll be there."

I hung up, wondering if I'd made a mistake. Why was I willing to talk to a stranger about what was bothering me and not to Maggie or Sam? Okay, Maggie wasn't available to me for that kind of shit just yet, and I wasn't sure I wanted to bare my soul to Sam. We were fine talking about his investigations, but we didn't talk about personal stuff—ever. And Richard was on my shit list. No doubt, I was on his list, too.

I wouldn't need to talk to Mike Ryan if Brenda didn't have houseguests. Before Evelyn and Da-Marr arrived, I could talk to her about anything. I'd really disappointed her by not warming to her houseguests. Disappointed? The word wasn't strong enough to describe what she felt about that. Words weren't necessary, either—I could experience it firsthand, and it wasn't pleasant. She had no clue how much that hurt—that she'd chosen Da-Marr— someone she'd never met before—over me. I thought after what the three of us had been through during the previous eighteen months that we'd forged a bond that nothing could shatter. That I could be so wrong shook me.

I replaced my phone and got up from the couch. I'd

check on Herschel, and then it would be time to go home.

I still wasn't sure I wanted to face Richard.

"I don't care what it costs, I need this done today," Richard said for the third time in less than an hour. He closed his eyes and let out an exasperated breath.

"Our mobile unit can be there by three this afternoon."

"I'd be willing to pay more if it was by noon."

"I'll have to look at the schedule and see what I can do," said the manager at Erie County Glass.

"I'd appreciate that."

"I'll call you back within ten minutes."

"Thank you." Richard hung up the phone and looked up to see Da-Marr standing in the doorway of his study. "What's up?" he asked, and it took all his self-control not to sound angry.

"Aunt Evelyn says I can't drive Brenda's car anymore. Tell her I can."

No hello, no please. No nothing.

"I can't do that."

"Why?" Da-Marr asked, the anger in his voice was positively menacing.

Richard shrugged. "She feels a certain responsibility toward you. As your guardian, I have to bow to her judgment."

"She ain't my guardian. I'm over eighteen. And she's wrong."

"About what?"

Da-Marr stepped up to the desk. "I should be able to do what I want when I want." He sounded ten instead of twenty years old.

Richard leaned back in his chair, taking another tack. "We had some trouble overnight."

"Oh, yeah?" Da-Marr's tone had softened; he sounded wary.

"Last night my brother's apartment was broken into."

Da-Marr said nothing.

"Some vandal broke the bathroom window and got in. All the light bulbs were unscrewed and smashed. Not only that, but whoever did it also left three wasp nests in the living room."

"That's weird," Da-Marr said with little inflection.

"Yes, it is," Richard said, staring into the young man's deep brown eyes.

"Why didn't you call the po-lice? Isn't that what white people do?"

"I've been asking myself the same question. You see, my brother is deathly allergic to bee and wasp venom. If he'd been stung, it could have been murder."

Again Da-Marr said nothing.

"It's going to take a lot of money to remedy the situation."

Da-Marr shrugged. "Hey, you got it."

"That's not the point. My brother could have *died,*" Richard reiterated. "Whoever attacks him—attacks me."

Da-Marr's expression remained impassive.

"I'm sure you can understand my concern," Richard pressed. "Evelyn tells me you come from a close-knit family. We have that in common. There isn't anything I wouldn't do for my family."

Da-Marr shrugged.

"I understand your parents and sisters have been worried about you getting mixed up with the wrong element, and that's why your aunt has taken such an interest in your future."

"She treats me like a kid."

"I think she loves you very much and wants you to be successful."

"She don't ask me what I want to *do* or *be*. Are you

gonna let me drive Brenda's car or not?"

Richard shook his head. "Sorry. You know your aunt better than I do. She's made a decision and I have no intention of crossing her."

Da-Marr turned away in disgust. "Pussy-whipped asshole," he grated and left the room.

Ungrateful idiot who can't see a golden opportunity when it's handed to him.

The phone rang. Richard leaned forward to pick up the receiver.

"Mr. Alpert, this is Bill at Erie County Glass. Our mobile unit can be at your house within the hour."

"Thank you. I really appreciate this."

"No problem, sir."

Richard hung up and leaned back in his chair once again. Da-Marr's question haunted him. Why hadn't he called the police? He knew he'd better come up with an explanation before the next time he spoke with Jeff.

FOURTEEN

Ivy's On Main was a dump. It seemed to have changed hands at least twice since I'd come back to Buffalo some eighteen months before. Its proximity not far from UB's south campus meant that the student foot traffic was high, and so was the rent, even if the décor sucked. At least the walls had recently seen a coat of paint, and the ancient tile floor looked like it had been pressure-washed since the first—and only time—I had darkened its door.

As predicted, the place was full of students and others grabbing a beer with lunch. A table in the back was empty, so I snagged it. There were no individual menus. The bill of fare had been written on a blackboard in different colored chalk, featuring burgers, fries, and sandwiches. I had a feeling Mike and I would be ordering the same thing.

It was already a little past noon, with no sight of Mike Ryan. Good thing, too. My phone rang. I looked at the number.

"Hi, Sam. What's up?

"Did you get anything else off that piece of chalk?"

Crap. With everything that had gone on in the previous sixteen hours, I'd forgotten all about it. I couldn't even recall where I'd left it. Somewhere in my apartment. After my visitor the previous evening, I wasn't even confident it would still be there.

I answered simply. "No."

"Too bad. Are you doing anything important this afternoon? Care to take another field trip?"

"Where to this time?

"An auction of Jack Morrow's personal possessions."

"Why haven't I heard about this before now?"

"Well, if you read my paper you might have," he said sounding annoyed. "There's a piece in this morning's business section."

"Sorry. I only got as far as the comics."

"You need to expand your horizons."

"I've heard that before. Where and when?" He gave me the address and we agreed to meet at two that afternoon.

"Can you bring your camera?"

"Don't I always?"

"Good. See you then."

I ended the call just as Father Ryan approached the table.

"Sorry I'm late," Mike said, looking like he'd just stepped out of a men's clothing store ad. His dark suit didn't look like it had come off the rack, and the scarf around his neck looked like cashmere. He obviously hadn't taken a vow of poverty.

"They were gifts," he said as though reading my mind and took the seat opposite me. "I have a rich aunt who dotes on me—I'm the son she never had."

The word aunt caused me to wince, painfully reminding me of Richard's houseguests. Hadn't Brenda told me that Evelyn had three daughters—no sons? Is that why she doted on Da-Marr? And what did her daughters think of that?

"Have you ordered?" he asked.

"Not yet."

Mike turned and raised a hand to get the waitress's attention, dazzling her with a smile. Did Catholic priests with loving aunts also have their teeth whitened?

"Are you ready to order?" asked the slim, blue-haired coed in black pants and shirt. Gold studs marred her nose and lip.

"Beef on weck and a Molson for me."

I nodded. "I'll have the same."

"Coming right up."

Mike leaned forward. "I wear the scarf to hide the collar. It's just easier that way."

"I know you don't have a lot of time," I guessed, "so where should I start?"

"Why don't you tell me what happened. Maggie said you were stung by a bee."

I nodded. "The next thing I knew, I was on the ground looking up at the sky."

He shook his head. "If that was true, we wouldn't be talking now."

I sobered. "Yeah. Well, as you're an expert on this kind of stuff, I was kind of hoping you'd tell me what it all means."

"I don't know that it means anything. You need to discover what your experience means to you. And you still haven't explained it to me. Is there a reason?"

I shook my head. "I saw the classic white light and it scared the shit out of me."

"Were you frightened before the experience, during, or after?"

I hadn't thought about it before now. "During and after."

He nodded. "Most people feel a sense of peace as they approach the light. But before we go into that, can you tell me more about what you remember and felt just prior to your experience?"

I shrugged. "I remember looking at my hand and watching the bite turn into a welt before falling from the ladder. And then things get murky. I was being sucked into this glaring white light."

"Have you ever had an out of body experience before this? Did you see yourself, your surroundings, from above as your soul left your body?"

I frowned. "My soul never left my body. I was aware that I was still me, but ... not. I know that doesn't make much sense."

His expression darkened. "Did you feel weightless?"

I shook my head. "I could feel the pull of gravity." I closed my eyes to blot out the sight of the bustling bar, to better concentrate, and felt my fists clench. "I was being sucked up, into the air, but it wasn't...." I had spent far too much time trying not to think about what had happened, and now I wasn't sure what it was I'd gone through. I opened my eyes, finding Mike looking at me intently.

"Okay, if you can't tell me what it was, can you tell me what it wasn't?"

I let out a breath, unsure of how to answer. "I've gone online. I've read near-death accounts. Many people find it to be an enlightening thing. It wasn't for me. Or is it that I'm just a coward and am afraid to face death?"

"From what I've heard, you've faced death more than your fair share of times, so I don't think that's your problem."

I wasn't sure I liked hearing that. How much had Maggie told him about me? But as I thought about it, it became apparent that *I'd* made this experience a problem. It nagged at me. I found myself thinking about it at odd moments. I'd let it bother me in waking hours, and it had reawakened the nightmares from the mugging, giving them a new and more terrifying ending.

"What do you think is my problem?" I challenged.

Mike laughed. "I have no idea. But I suspect you do."

"Now you sound like a shrink."

He shrugged, just as the waitress brought our beers. "Your sandwiches will be ready in a couple of minutes," she said, and went to the next table to check on their progress.

Mike turned back to me. "You don't strike me a person of faith."

"Sorry."

"No apologies necessary. I may be a priest, but I don't go around criticizing what people believe or don't believe."

"That's not exactly church doctrine."

"I prefer to think—or at least hope—that as time goes on there'll be more forward-thinking leadership. Hey, Pope Francis took the first steps. I'm encouraged that more progress will happen in the coming years no matter who's wearing the white cassock."

"You're a heretic," I accused.

He laughed. "It's not the worst thing I've been accused of."

"And the worst would be?"

"Just don't get into a poker game with me."

I couldn't help but smile, but it was short-lived. A beer and a good conversation over lunch weren't going to change the fact that I couldn't seem to let this whole near-death thing drop. It was going to come back the minute I shut my eyes for sleep, and the flashback to the mugging was going to come back to slam me the next time I saw Da-Marr.

Maybe I did need a shrink, but there was no way I was going to voluntarily go that route.

True to her word, the waitress arrived and plunked down our sandwiches and fries, along with a bottle of ketchup and a pot of horseradish to share between us. "If you need anything else, give a holler."

"Thanks," Mike said, and turned to his lunch. "This is what I've been waiting days for." He removed the top of the roll and slathered on a generous helping of horseradish. I did the same before taking a bite. Ivy's might be a dump, but they made a damn fine beef on weck. The horseradish was so pungent it brought tears to my eyes. Perfection!

Mike swallowed his first bite, coughed, and wiped his mouth with a napkin. "When your mind replays the sequence, how long would you say it lasts?"

"Forever."

"Do you get stuck at a certain point in the nightmare?"

I took a sip of my beer and thought about it. "As I spiral up into the blinding light, it gets bigger and bigger until it's about to—" I tossed my hands in the air and made a noise like an explosion.

Mike took another bite and looked thoughtful. "Do you hear any sounds?"

"Come to think of it, no."

"Some people describe celestial noises, although what they sound like changes from person to person."

I'd once thought I heard celestial noises after whacking my head after being pushed down a flight of stairs. Only for me, the sound was reminiscent of wind chimes.

"Have you thought about writing down your experience? You might find clarity if you could put it down on paper."

"I don't know if I'm looking so much for clarity or understanding." Once I'd said it, I knew it was the latter, not the former. "Why did this happen to me? Lots of people go into anaphylactic shock and don't see a bright light. When I got mugged, I saw the bat come at me, but it wasn't a bright light I saw, it was—" I stopped myself. "What else did Maggie tell you about me?"

"Not much, really. In fact, she mostly talked about herself. She's terribly afraid she's going to lose her mother-in-law."

Then she hadn't told him about my gift—not that I thought of knowing things about people, glomming onto their emotions, and sometimes experiencing clairvoyance as a gift. I sure as hell wasn't going to mention it.

"You were saying?" Mike prompted.

I shook my head. "Nothing." I took another bite of my sandwich.

"Not to be a braggart, but if you'd like to read my dissertation, I'd be happy to loan you a copy."

"Not to be rude, but I don't think so. I almost wish I hadn't checked the Internet to read up on the experience. I think it may have colored my memory of the experience."

"That's a valid observation."

"The more I think about it, the better I like your idea of writing down what I remember. Maybe I will get clarity and understanding."

He shrugged. "It can't hurt." Mike changed the subject. "So, what do you think of the Bills this season?" It turned out he was a Patriots fan, and we discussed past games and predicted the outcome of the upcoming game.

When the check came, I grabbed it.

"Thanks," Mike said. "I've enjoyed our conversation. If you'd like to talk some other time, I'd be happy to meet again.

"Thanks," I said, leaving the invitation open.

When we left the tavern, he went left while I turned right. I still had more than an hour to kill before I had to meet Sam. Up the street was a college bookstore where I knew I could buy a notebook.

I did just that, and then sat in my car for the next twenty minutes writing down my thoughts and memories of the mugging and the near-death experience. My pen had practically danced across the pages as I wrote. When I finished, I looked at my watch and realized I had twenty minutes to make it across town to meet Sam.

Mike had been right. I may not have found clarity or understanding, but writing down my experiences had been cathartic. Not that the memories wouldn't surface again, but somehow I felt better for having acknowledged them in a concrete form.

I closed the notebook and set it on the passenger seat before starting the car. I'd acknowledged one set of angst. Would examining Morrow's personal possessions bring on another?

FIFTEEN

I was glad I'd left my camera in my car's trunk after our last investigative foray, since that meant I didn't have to go back to my place to get it.

When Sam and I arrived at Adam's Mark's East Ballroom, a long line snaked out into the lobby and out the front door. I felt sorry for the poor schmucks who didn't have umbrellas, and even those who did have one looked pretty damp around the edges.

Sam flashed his newspaper ID and waited to be let in to have a preview of the auction preview. The guard made a call and we waited for our escort to arrive.

We turned away, trying to get a glance inside the ballroom.

"If I'm supposed to be your photographer, how am I going to touch the stuff? Won't they expect you to hold onto whatever you want me to scope out while I take the shot?"

"Hmm. I hadn't thought about that," Sam admitted. "We'll just have to fake it."

"This doesn't bode well," I said under my breath as a handsome woman of perhaps fifty approached. Her hair was not a natural strawberry blonde, but it suited her and complimented the coffee-colored suit she wore.

"Hello, I'm Diane Kelly. I'm the PR liaison for Meier's Auction House, which is coordinating the sale for Bison Bank. I'm happy to accompany you while you look through the items going up for auction tonight."

"Thanks," Sam said and introduced us; she shook both our hands. I got no bright flash of insight from her, which was fine with me since I didn't have a clue what I might encounter when touching Morrow's stuff.

"If you'll follow me," Diane said, and Sam dutifully fell into step, with me a half-pace behind them.

"I've read through the program," Sam said, "but what's your take on the assembled goods?"

Diane paused and sighed. "The sole reason for the sale is to try to recover as much revenue as possible to repay those who lost their life savings through poor financial decisions."

"That's a nice way of saying the people who trusted Morrow were swindled," Sam said.

Diane did not dignify his statement by agreeing.

I wasn't sure what I'd experience upon entering a room that housed so many of Jack Morrow's possessions. The word that best describes it is overwhelming, but the sensation bore no resemblance to the aura still attached to the chalk cube. It wasn't so much Morrow I sensed in that ballroom, but an overwhelming sense of greed, which was uncomfortable to say the least.

I viewed the large ballroom through the lens of my Nikon and snapped a picture. It seemed to have been divided into sections, with one corner set up to look like a clothing store with racks of suits, boxes and boxes of new and barely worn shoes and monogrammed slippers, and tables of other clothing.

I paused to take another photo as we walked along the aisles of merchandise on offer, and Sam turned to me. "The catalog lists clothes, shoes, household accessories, and sports memorabilia. What do you think will give off the strongest vibes?"

"I have no idea," I said as we started off again, passing a table piled with expensive, custom French-made shirts.

"Is it likely Diane is going to let me handle anything?" I asked, keeping my voice low.

"All we have to do is ask."

But we didn't—at least not just then. Instead, we walked along the rows and rows of largess: shelves filled with Jack Morrow's books; his artwork collection; his stereo equipment and collection of CDs, which favored classical composers. Richard could have enhanced his own collection from the pickings. Also among the loot were knick-knacks, souvenirs of Morrow's travels to other countries, and several sets of antique French and Russian dinnerware. I snapped pictures of gold-plated cutlery, as well as baroque mirrors, along with gold- and silver-leafed picture frames with images of Morrow's family still gracing them. It was like an estate sale: one person's lifetime collection of flotsam and jetsam up for sale to the highest bidder.

Sam paused and turned to Diane. "Is it okay if we take a closer look at some of this stuff?"

"Are you registered to bid?" she asked.

"No, but I figured it might be a more powerful experience to hold something that Jack Morrow might have actually touched," Sam said, laying it on thick.

"Mr. Nielsen, don't tell me a hardened newsman like yourself actually admired a man like Jack Morrow."

"Not admire, but perhaps I'm in awe. How did the man sleep?"

Diane shrugged. "Go ahead," she said, amused.

Sam picked up one of the silver frames with a picture of good-looking man—an ivy leaguer, for sure. "What do you think about this, Jeff? Wouldn't a picture of your girl-friend look great in this?"

He handed me the frame, which I held in both hands, staring at the photo.

Wrong, wrong, wrong!

I let out a breath. "Maggie looks great in every picture," I said.

"And who's the guy in the photo?" Sam asked Diane.

She shrugged. "A family member, I would guess. I've seen photos of Morrow's wife, but I can't say I've seen pictures of any of his other family members."

I knew Sam would be on it like a tick the minute he could get a moment to check Google images.

A big, locked display case held an assortment of rings, watches, cufflinks, and tie tacks. I didn't even know people still wore tie tacks. Sam eyed a watch in its original case. "Is that really a Rolex?"

"It's been authenticated," Diane said with a nod.

Sam looked almost coy. "Any chance we could...?"

"Try it on?" Diane finished.

"I may never get another opportunity to see the real thing."

"You can get a knockoff on just about any corner in Manhattan," I commented and could tell by Sam's glare that my opinion was not welcome.

Diane withdrew a set of keys from the pocket of her skirt and unlocked the case. She reached for the Rolex and handed it to Sam. He slid the stretch band over his wrist and smiled, then he looked at me and seemed to realize his mistake. He might have just tainted the piece so that I'd get his vibes—and not those of its former owner. "It sure is nice," he said, flexing his wrist to try and make it catch the light. I took a picture of it, figuring Sam might like it for himself.

He took it off and handed it to me. "Try it on for size. Who knows, if it looks good, you may even get one in your Christmas stocking."

"Is that an offer?" I asked, slung my camera strap over my left shoulder and took it from him, sliding it onto my right wrist, which felt awkward and unnatural. I stared at the face of the watch, and it wasn't Sam's aura that came through, but must have been Morrow's. A man who'd once felt powerful and unstoppable, but during the last days he'd worn the watch, he'd felt panicked and emasculated. A looming jail sentence would certainly have had me sweating in the same manner. If I'd had more time to wear the watch, would I have picked up more? Like where he'd supposedly hidden a chunk of his ill-gotten gains? Maybe, maybe not.

I took the watch off and handed it back to Diane, who put it away and locked the case once more. "Shall we continue the tour?" she suggested.

Finally, we came to the land of sports memorabilia, which included baseball cards, signed footballs and several framed jerseys from Buffalo Bills players that spanned the years from O.J. Simpson to Jim Kelly. How much would Morrow have been willing to pay for a ring if the Bills had ever won a Super Bowl? The prospect of the team going to the playoffs seemed possible early in the season.

I studied all the items on offer. To think all this stuff had once graced the walls of the home we'd seen the day before, or had some of it come from Morrow's office, or maybe his sky box at Ralph Wilson Stadium?

"Damn, look at that," Sam said and pointed to a baseball encased in a cube of Lucite. "A signed Ty Cobb baseball. What do you think something like that would go for?" he asked Diane.

"Anywhere from two to eight thousand, but we're hoping to get at least five."

Sam winced. "Out of my league, I'm afraid." He eyed the rest of the collection, his envious gaze coming to rest on a bat signed by Joe DiMaggio.

Uneasy, I took a step back.

"What's the estimate on the Yankee Clipper's bat?" he asked.

"Anywhere from two to four thousand. If we get three, we'll be quite happy," Diane said.

"Any chance I could hold it?"

Diane forced a smile; she was getting tired of show and tell. "Of course." With great care, she picked up the bat and handed it to him.

Sam studied the signature on the barrel end and whistled. "It's dated, too. During the time he was married to Marilyn Monroe." He shook his head in admiration. "What I wouldn't do to have this baby hanging on my living room wall."

And then time seemed to slow to a crawl. I watched in horrified fascination as Sam gripped the handle with both hands and assumed a batter's stance.

The image of a Reggie Jackson special flashed before my eyes, the bat arching down at me from above.

Sam drew the bat back toward his shoulder.

I took two steps back but something was in my way.

The bat swung toward me, but it wasn't Sam who held it.

The teenage thug's fury-filled face loomed before me once again.

Panicked, I pushed at whatever was in my way, stumbled, and fell to the floor with the sound of shattering glass ringing in my ear.

"What on earth?" Diane practically screamed in my ear. "Get off of me."

Suddenly Sam loomed over me, pushing me away as he tried to pull Diane to her feet.

Shame burned within me and I struggled to my feet, making a grab for my camera, which had hit the floor. I heard the rattle of the broken mirror within it and my heart sank. "I'm so sorry, I—I—" but I didn't have a decent explanation for my abhorrent behavior.

Diane pulled her suit jacket down and tried to brush the wrinkles from her skirt. She raised her angry gaze to take in my face and her annoyance immediately dissipated. "Are you all right?"

I suddenly realized how hard it seemed to breathe. "Yeah."

"You don't look it," Sam said.

I didn't feel it, either. My heart pounded, and the back of my collar was damp with sweat. I coughed and cleared my throat. "I think I need a drink. Water fountain?" I asked hopefully.

"Hang on a minute. I'll see if I can get you a glass," Diane said kindly.

She hurried away, almost as freaked out as I was.

"What the hell was that all about?' Sam asked once she was out of earshot.

I turned away. "I'm sorry. I—" But there was no way I could explain it to him what I'd just experienced.

"Wait a minute. When you got mugged—didn't they come after you with—?"

He didn't finish the sentence.

I suddenly felt frozen and realized I was shaking.

And I felt stupid, and panicked, and emasculated—just like Morrow had felt when he'd last worn his Rolex.

Or was the already-fading sense of terror a remnant of Morrow's anxiety?

Not a chance in hell.

"I've gotta get out of here," I told Sam.

"I'm sorry, Jeff. I forgot. You know I wouldn't have—"

"Forget it. I've had a bad couple of days. Too many reminders of what happened...." I didn't—couldn't—explain farther. "Make my excuses, willya?" I asked, but didn't wait for his reply and dashed for the exit.

I barreled through the doors and into the corridor, which was seething with even more people. Gaze leveled on the floor, I charged down the corridor and headed for the lobby.

Once outside, I practically ran for my car, though I couldn't have said why. No one was chasing me, and yet

I couldn't seem to let go of the feeling that I had to escape. And escape to where? Maggie had too much on her plate to indulge me and my insecurities. I didn't have to work. There was only one other place I could go—back to Richard's. Back to what, until just a few days before, had been the first real home I'd had in way-too-many years. I knew I wasn't ready for that. Not yet.

I unlocked my trunk, but took a moment to try out the camera. I looked through the viewfinder, but everything was a blur. My beautiful Nikon was ruined. I placed the camera inside and shut it, then got in my car and headed for the only friendly place of comfort I knew.

Richard looked at the platter overloaded with four, inch-thick Angus steaks Evelyn had picked out at the grocery store. He and Brenda could have shared one between them, and it was more than apparent that Evelyn hadn't expected—or wanted—Jeff to join them for dinner. Not that he could have convinced his brother to do so.

"Here's a clean platter to put the steaks on when they're cooked, and the fork to turn them. And remember, I like my steak cooked through," Evelyn said, practically pushing him toward the door. Thank goodness it wasn't raining, although he wasn't sure that would have deterred Evelyn from her dinner choice.

"I like mine rare," Da-Marr said as he entered the kitchen from the hall.

"Then you go out and supervise. You stayed in your room all day, you could use some fresh air," Evelyn said, and pushed him toward the back door as well.

Richard threw a look over his shoulder as he passed into the pantry for the outside door and saw his wife give him a pained smile. *Only a few more days,* he reassured himself, *only a few more days.*

Richard headed out to the backyard and the barbecue,

wishing the house had a more direct route. Built in the 1920s before people added decks and patios, the house was lovely but not always user friendly.

He set the steaks down on one of the low tables and lit the grill. A thoroughly bored Da-Marr dragged himself up the deck steps and settled on the rail. He'd spent the day sulking.

Richard put the first of the steaks on the grill and glanced over at Da-Marr, who stared vacantly at the large expanse of lawn, its fringes no longer decorated with the last remnants of summer.

"So, you're going to school in January," Richard said.

"I guess," Da-Marr muttered.

"Are you really going to take criminal justice?"

Da-Marr shook his head.

"Then what will you take, or do you really care about going to college?"

Da-Marr shrugged. "I'm going because my family has decided it would be the best thing for me."

"And what do you think would be best for you?"

A sly smile crept across Da-Marr's lips and he sat up just a bit straighter. "Being a hip-hop producer. Yeah. People would be begging me to get their shit out in front of the masses. Everyone would kiss my ass. I'd have respect. *Real* respect."

"And how likely is that to ever happen?" Richard asked, trying not to sound entirely negative.

Da-Marr's posture took a hit. "Shit, man—it ain't never gonna happen. Truth is, I don't wanna go to college. I got more street smarts than school smarts."

"Everyone needs to do something with their life," Richard said.

"Like you?" Da-Marr said with contempt.

"Hey, I'm a doctor. That's not an insignificant achievement."

Da-Marr snorted. "From what I hear, you're too soft to

be any good."

Richard's back stiffened. Just what had Brenda told Evelyn, and how much had she shared with Da-Marr?

"You're kinda old to be havin' a kid, too."

"I wasn't aware fatherhood was dependent on a time-line."

"I had a kid," Da-Marr bragged.

Richard hadn't expected that revelation. "Oh?"

"Sure. I got a picture." He reached into his back pocket and withdrew a wallet. He fumbled inside and pulled out a creased and rather fuzzy photo of an infant. "Da-Marr Junior," he said with pride.

"How old is he now?"

Da-Marr shook his head. "He died. He was born too soon. That's why Aunt Evelyn knits baby hats for pre-emies."

"Are you and your son's mother still together?"

Da-Marr shook his head. "She's a real bitch. Wanted to get married. Hey, I got things to do before I get tied down. And since our kid was dead, why bother?"

Richard couldn't help himself. "Why indeed?"

"I'm gonna make something of myself and she woulda weighed me down."

"I don't know. Brenda's the best thing that ever happened to me."

Again, the young man shrugged. "You're lucky. You got born to rich people."

Maybe, but he hadn't been happy—really happy—until Brenda had entered his life.

"What do you see yourself doing for the next couple of months before you start school?"

Da-Marr moved his head to look at Richard. "What do you mean?"

"Maybe you should get a job."

"I ain't got no skills."

"As far as I know, McDonald's is always hiring."

"I ain't working no shit minimum-wage job."

"Have you ever had a job?" Richard asked.

"Yeah, a shit minimum-wage job. I ain't doin' that again."

"You've got no major in mind, and no job skills. What do you see yourself doing in five years?"

Da-Marr's expression was blank. Had he—or Evelyn—thought that far ahead?

"Is there a chance you'd prefer to go to a vocational school?"

Da-Marr shrugged. "For what?"

"Construction."

"That's hard work," Da-Marr said angrily.

"Plumbers made good money."

"And are up to their elbows in everybody's shit. No way."

Richard added another steak to the grill and poked at the first. "You did a good job fixing that lawn mower. Have you thought about being an auto mechanic?"

Da-Marr shrugged once again. "Maybe."

"Or how about an aviation mechanic," Richard suggested.

The kid turned his head toward Richard, his eyes widening. "Working on planes?"

"Sure, why not? Because you're right; not everyone wants or needs to go to college, but there are lots of great-paying jobs out there that need skilled workers."

Da-Marr's expression soured. "You don't think I'm smart enough for college."

"Not at all. But if you don't want to be there, you aren't going to succeed. You'd disappoint your parents, your aunt, but most of all yourself."

"My aunt has really pushed to get me into college. If I changed plans now, I'd never hear the end of it."

Richard kept his gaze on the spitting steaks. "Part of growing up is figuring out how you're going to live the rest of your life." He was quiet for a long moment, and then decided to be honest. "You were right about me."

Da-Marr looked up, confused.

"I am too soft to deal with direct patient care."

"Scared of blood or something?" Da-Marr guessed.

Richard shook his head. "Nothing like that. I don't like people dying on me. I don't like when they come to me asking how to get well, and then don't do what they need to do to get better."

"So what do you do now?"

"I volunteer my time with the hospital foundation. But before that, I had to figure out what I could do as a doctor that didn't involve patient care."

"Which was?"

"For a lot of years, I worked for a think tank out in California. We evaluated medical equipment and did a lot of other cool stuff. That's where I met Brenda. We worked together for almost eight years." He smiled at the memory.

"So what're you sayin'?" Da-Marr asked.

Richard shrugged. "If you like working with your hands—figure out what you could do that would bring you a living wage and what you could do for the rest of your life that wouldn't bore you to tears."

Da-Marr looked away, his expression unreadable. "Aunt Evelyn wouldn't be happy knowing you're trying to talk me outta going to college."

"I'm not trying to talk you into or out of anything. You're the one who seems iffy about college." Richard added the last two steaks and turned the others. "Would you go in and tell Brenda these steaks will be ready in a couple of minutes?"

Da-Marr got up without a word and headed for the kitchen. Richard watched him disappear around the corner of the house. Was it his imagination or had the kid stood just a bit taller than he had before their conversation? Richard smiled but then soon sobered. If Da-Marr decided he wasn't going to go to college, Richard knew he'd catch hell from Evelyn.

His phone rang and Richard extricated it from his pocket and glanced at the caller ID. He didn't know who the caller was, but the number looked vaguely familiar. He picked up the call. "Hello."

"Hi, Richard. It's Sam Nielsen. Jeff's friend."

"Hi, Sam. I'm sorry, but Jeff's not around. I don't know where he is or when he'll be back. But I'll tell him you called."

"I'm not looking for him this time," the reporter said and the timber of his voice was different from the other times Richard had spoken to him, which immediately raised his hackles.

"What's up?" Richard asked guardedly.

"That's it. I'm not sure, but I'm worried about him."

The hackles rose even higher "Oh?"

"As a reporter, I protect my sources. But as a friend…."

"Sam, what's wrong?" Richard asked.

A long interval of silence followed before Sam answered. "I asked Jeff to help me on a story for the paper. I wanted him to touch stuff. To tell me what kind of vibes he got. This afternoon we went to an auction preview and one of the items on offer is a vintage baseball bat."

"Oh, God," Richard breathed, his heart sinking.

"I swear; I completely forgot that he was hurt by a mugger wielding a baseball bat. The thing is, I picked it up and went to swing, and—" He let out a tormented breath. "The guy absolutely freaked out."

"Jesus," Richard swore.

"He bolted, ended up on the floor, smashed his camera—the works. I tried to call him on his cell, but he hasn't picked up.

"When did this happen?"

"A few hours ago. I figured he'd head for home, but I

called his cell and landline. Nothing." His tone changed. "As his brother—his only family—I think you should take this incident seriously. I'm no shrink, but I've been around enough vets to know a case of Post-Traumatic Stress Disorder when I see it. He obviously hasn't gotten over the mugging. I think he needs help."

The steaks, now forgotten, continued to sputter.

Sam's opinion was not unanticipated, but unsettling nonetheless. "I appreciate you calling me, Sam. The truth is, our lives have been turned upside this past week." He wasn't about to go into how.

"Then you know what's going on with him?"

"I've got a pretty good idea."

Sam let out what sounded like an exasperated breath. "Jeff and I aren't exactly friends, but even I can see he's hurting and confused. I thought you should know."

"Thanks."

"When you see him, ask him to give me a call, willya?"

"I will, thank you."

"Good night."

Richard ended the call, staring at his phone for a long moment, then he hit autodial. Jeff's cell phone rang and rang before an automated message said, "The wireless customer you are calling is not available. Please try again later." Next, he tried Maggie's cell number. She picked up on the third ring.

"Hello, Richard, what's up?" Maggie asked without enthusiasm.

"Have you seen Jeff?"

"Not since his morning. He dropped Herschel off and was going to crash on my couch for a few hours."

"This morning?" Richard asked. He'd last seen his brother around one in the morning.

"Yeah, they slept in his car out in my driveway. He didn't want to wake me," she said wearily. She sounded awful—depressed. "Is everything okay? Brenda hasn't gone into labor or anything?"

"Everything's okay," he lied, "I was just wondering where Jeff was. He hasn't checked in since last night.

"He might be at my place. I gave him a key to Lily's apartment—that's where Herschel is. Herschel and Holly don't exactly hit it off."

"How is your mother-in-law?"

Maggie sighed. "She had a setback today," she said, her voice breaking. "She fell."

"Did she break anything?"

"No, but her face is a mess. It's terribly bruised. I feel so guilty that she's stuck in the rehab facility and not at home where I could take care of her—*if* I could take care of her."

"You have to work," he said reasonably.

"That's for damn sure." She changed the subject. "If you find Jeff at my place, tell him I'll be late tonight. I don't want to leave Lily until they put her to bed, and that won't be until at least nine."

"I'll do that."

"Tell Brenda I'll try and call her tomorrow."

"Will do. Bye."

"Bye." He punched the call end. Sure as shit Jeff wasn't going to find comfort in someone who could use a mega dose of it herself. There was only one other place he could think of to call. He punched in the number.

"Whole Nine Yards, this is Tom. What can I do for you?"

"Tom, it's Richard—Jeff's brother."

"You found him," Tom said, without Richard even asking. "Been sitting in the corner nursing a double shot of Mr. Jack. Dave and me, we left him alone. He doesn't seem to want to talk. I figured if he didn't move in another hour I'd give you a call."

"I appreciate that. Listen, I can't get over there for at

least half an hour—maybe forty-five minutes."

"Don't worry. He ain't going nowhere. I'll make sure of that," Tom said.

"Thanks. See you."

Richard pocketed his phone, turned off the gas, then switched off the burners before stabbing the steaks with the big fork and dropping them onto the clean, waiting platter. He hoped Evelyn liked hers as well-done as she'd indicated, because he doubted any of them had any juice left.

As he rounded the corner for the house, he saw a strange car in the driveway. Da-Marr stood near the driver's door talking with its occupant. As he got closer, Richard recognized the make: a steel gray Infinity no more than a couple of years old.

"Who's your friend?" Richard called.

Da-Marr stepped away from the car and Richard saw a white male who looked to be almost a decade older than Da-Marr sitting behind the wheel.

"This is Bobby. His father has a boat at the marina."

Richard switched the platter to his left hand and held out his right to shake hands. "Richard Alpert. Nice to meet you."

Bobby focused on the steaks. "I guess you like them well done."

"Yeah," Richard said. "I don't mean to rush you along, Da-Marr, but you know how your aunts gets if you're late."

"I'll be right in," he said.

Richard nodded. "Nice to have met you."

Bobby nodded and smiled, and Richard started back for the house.

Was Da-Marr's friend going to delay dinner? As it was, Richard wondered how he was going eat and then run to The Whole Nine Yards without giving a detailed explanation as to why. And no way did he want to give Evelyn the excuse of making it her business.

SIXTEEN

I'd been staring at nothing for so long, trying not to think, that it took three taps on my shoulder before it registered that someone was trying to get my attention. I looked up.

"Mind if I sit down?" Richard asked.

I turned back to face the wall. "It's a free country. Or, at least it used to be."

Richard took the seat opposite me, setting a glass and a bottle of Molson Blue on the table. "I'd offer to get you something, but I see you're already taken care of."

I glared at him. "I'm not drunk."

"I didn't say you were."

I watched as he poured his drink. "You missed supper. Good thing, too. The steaks were charred—just the way Evelyn likes them."

I couldn't look him in the eye and felt myself squirm. "I suppose Sam called you."

"Yup. He said you broke your camera."

"I dropped it. It's toast."

"Cameras can be fixed—or replaced. People can't."

"You're not telling me anything new," I said and wet my lips with my drink. I didn't have the stomach to actually sip it.

"I talked to Maggie." He let out a breath. "She's really bummed. Lily took a tumble today."

I looked up. "Is she okay?"

"She will be, but man—doesn't it seem like the world has been shitting on everything and everybody we know?"

"I'll drink to that," I said, and actually took a minute sip of my bourbon.

Richard raised his glass and took a sip. "Is Herschel okay?"

"He was last time I saw him." Damn, he was going to need to be fed—and soon.

"Speaking from personal experience, I don't think Maggie's in a position to have a guest right now." I looked up, met his gaze, and found it full of concern. "She sounds pretty damned depressed."

"Are you trying to lay a guilt trip on me?"

"No," he said, adamant. "It's just an observation. Do you want to stay in a hotel for a few days?"

"I've thought about it. The idea really doesn't appeal to me. I like sleeping in my own bed—or Maggie's, but as you inferred, that ain't gonna happen for a while."

"Your bathroom window's fixed. The place has been cleaned, exterminated, and all the light bulbs replaced."

"Thank you."

"It's the least I could do." He drank more of his beer while I stared into the depths of my glass.

"I had a locksmith come over, too. I've got an extra key to your place. The only extra key. Brenda—and Maggie—can have one after our guests leave."

"And do you have a departure date?" I asked, already knowing the answer.

"No. My point is, nobody but me is going to get in without your say so."

"Unless they break a window."

"That isn't going to happen."

"And you know this because?"

"I had a talk with Da-Marr."

I let out a breath and polished off the rest of my drink,

letting the glass smack the table with a thunk. Richard drained his glass, too.

"I'm damned sorry the kid has badgered you—and I'm not trying to trivialize what he's done. I don't blame you for being pissed off, and I'm in awe of your restraint. I let him know that I won't tolerate him stepping out of line again. If he does, that's it—I don't care what Brenda says—he's out of my house. But I also feel sorry for him. Evelyn has good intentions, but she hasn't figured out that she can't make Da-Marr do what he doesn't want to do. I want to trust what she says, that he's basically a good kid, but I'm just not sure."

I had no comment. At least not one that I was willing to voice.

"In a way, he kind of reminds me of you."

I looked up sharply. "Me?"

"In your misspent youth, you did climb a ladder with a pumpkin on your head, rap on my grandmother's bedroom window, and nearly scare her to death."

Shame washed through me. Yeah, I had done that.

"Are you ready to go home now?"

I shrugged. "I guess."

He pushed back his chair and stood. "Come on."

I got up. We carried our glasses to the bar, where Richard left a ten-dollar tip. "Thanks, Tom. See ya, Dave," he called as we headed for the door.

"See you on Friday," Tom called after me, and I waved a hand in acknowledgment.

But it struck me as I headed for my car, that I didn't know if come Friday, I'd be in any condition to go to work.

And I didn't know what that meant, either.

Oh, for the days of boring routine. They were never likely to come again once Betsy Ruth arrived. They'd have to get used to a new normal. But Richard still longed for one more day of his old life. A day spent with Brenda. A day when they ate when they wanted, a day when they went where they wanted without company. An evening when they watched the eleven o'clock news before going to bed.

Evelyn wasn't noisy. She went to bed early, she got up early, and she didn't expect her hosts to follow the same schedule. Unfortunately, Da-Marr didn't exist on the same timetable. Late to bed, with the TV blaring, and not-so-early to rise. Even with the guest room door shut, as well as their own bedroom door, the sounds of sirens and explosions could still be heard. Evelyn had to wear earplugs, but it didn't seem to bother her.

As Richard undressed for bed, he made a decision.

"We have to talk," he said as he watched Brenda pull back the bedspread.

"Isn't that my usual line?" she asked, warily.

"You've taught me well," he said as he climbed into bed.

Brenda sat on the edge of the bed, painfully drawing her legs up one at a time, but she didn't lie down. She sat there, her belly straining against her nightgown, looking terribly uncomfortable. "Am I a rotten person to just want this over?" she cried in frustration.

"Of course not," he said, and reached for her hand.

"I wasn't just talking about the pregnancy." She sighed, tears brimming her dark brown eyes. "I'm sorry. It's the hormones. And don't you damn well dispute it."

He couldn't help but smile, but it soon soured. "Jeff is helping his reporter friend, Sam, with a story. He had a bad experience today, and—"

Brenda plastered a hand over her eyes, and he saw her mouth tremble. "You're right. I don't want to hear this. Not now. I'm at my rope's end and I just can't take any-more."

"Then it can wait," Richard said and squeezed her hand.

"You must think I'm a terrible bitch—" she began.

He laughed. "To the contrary. But man, the four of us are living in hell right now."

"Which four?"

"You, me, Jeff, and Maggie."

"Maggie?" she asked, her interest piqued.

"I spoke to her earlier this evening. She said she would call you, but I don't think she will. I suspect she isn't willing to dump her garbage on you when you aren't in a good place."

"Is it Lily?"

He nodded.

"Oh, dear. If I wasn't like—" she looked down at her belly, "—this, I could go and be with her. But right now—"

"You have to take care of yourself. I think she realizes that."

"And what about Jeffy?"

Richard shook his head. "I don't think we need to talk about him now."

"Why?"

"Because you need to concentrate on you. On us. On our baby. Things have a way of working themselves out. Soon Evelyn and Da-Marr will go home, and then it'll just be the five of us."

Brenda looked at him askance. "The five of us? You make it sound like we're a real family.

"Maybe because that's the way I think of us."

"Even though Maggie hurt Jeffy so bad back in May?"

"Yeah. I don't want to judge her. I don't even want to judge Evelyn and Da-Marr. I just want to get through this and go on to what will become our new life. And, I'm sorry, Brenda, but Evelyn and Da-Marr are not ever going to be part of our everyday lives. I think you know that, too."

Brenda's head drooped. "Of course I do."

"Then … we just have to get through the next week or so. Right?"

She turned to look at him, her lips quirking into a smile. "You're right. Damn, but you're almost always right."

"Only almost?"

"Nobody's perfect," she said.

"Come on. Turn out the light and let's go to sleep."

She smiled, but it was short lived. "Sorry, but, damn—I have to pee. I can't wait until this is over and I don't have to pee every five minutes," she said, swung her legs over the side of the bed, eased herself off, and headed for the bathroom.

More explosions rattled the windows. Guest or not, it was simply rude to disturb the rest of the home's residents with a blaring TV. Richard got up.

He crossed the dark hall. He could see the flickering shadows under the door from the TV. He knocked. "Da-Marr, can you turn that thing down?" he said, not shouting, but he hoped loud enough to be heard over the din. No answer. He knocked again and waited. Still no answer. He tried the door handle and it opened. He stepped inside.

The TV was on, but the room was unoccupied. There wasn't even a wrinkle in the bedspread.

Da-Marr had said an early good night some three hours before, which was when the TV went on.

Richard switched off the set and closed the door, then hightailed it down the stairs. He could call Jeff to ask if Brenda's car was still in the garage, but he didn't want to disturb him, not after the day—and night before—he'd had.

He'd neglected to put on slippers when he'd left his bedroom, and all his shoes were in the walk-in closet, but he did have a pair of winter boots in the butler's pantry. He slipped them on, unlocked the back door, and ventured onto the drive. Crossing the expanse of asphalt, he stopped at the door that led to the stairway to Jeff's apartment. He didn't have his keys, but he could look through the window and see into the garage. All three cars were snug in their berths for the night. Da-Marr hadn't lifted Brenda's keys for another joy ride.

So where the hell had he gone—and how?

SEVENTEEN

Home, sweet, home. I can't say I felt a hundred percent safe to be back in my own digs, but I had to trust that Richard was right and that my problems with Da-Marr were over.

Despite making it an early night, I got up late, feeling more settled, but still on edge. I made a pot of coffee and automatically opened a can of cat food before I remembered that Herschel wasn't just asleep under the bed or birdwatching on one of the windowsills. I missed the little guy, but there was no way in hell I was going to bring him home as long as Da-Marr was around.

I snagged my coffee, flopped down on the couch, and grabbed the TV remote, intending to find out what had happened in the world during the past forty-eight hours, when I spied the chalk cube on my coffee table. Whoever had cleaned the place hadn't tossed it.

I picked it up. Now that I had a better sense of who Jack Morrow had been, maybe I'd get more from the cube. For a long moment, I just looked at it, turning it over and over, noting each imperfection. It had been well used, but the aura still attached to it hadn't been Morrow's.

Sam had said the guy had a son. He'd also asked me not to go looking for information on the kid—young man...whatever—in case it tainted my perceptions.

I held onto the chalk, closed my eyes, and concentrated.

I got no image of the man who'd used the chalk, rubbing it on the tip of a cue. He'd been good at the game. Cunning. I got the feeling he was also cunning when it came to business.

I thought long and hard, trying to come up with other descriptors.

Cold. Calculating.

A murderer.

Jack Morrow had known his killer, had played pool with him in his own home on many occasions. Morrow had lost to him, not only in a game of skill, but also the game of life.

I should have been creeped out by that insight. Funny, looking at Da-Marr scared me shitless, but touching the soul of a murderer had become rather commonplace for me. But then the stakes were different this time. We weren't looking for a murderer, and he had no idea we were looking for the same treasure. Still, there was the possibility that our paths could cross, which was an unsettling thought.

The phone rang. It could only be one of two people: Sam or Richard. "Hello."

"Hey, Jeff. It's Sam."

A flush of embarrassment coursed through me. "Sorry I ran out on you like that yesterday. I–"

"No apologies necessary."

There seemed to be a *but* hanging between us.

"Go on," I urged.

"Are you still up to digging around with me? After yesterday—"

"Yesterday had nothing to do with Jack Morrow or his killer."

"Whoa—who said anything about his killer?"

"Me. I've been inspecting the chalk cube. I'm pretty sure whoever used it last killed Morrow, and with the same mission as you—to find Morrow's hidden assets."

"Then we're on the right trail."

"I thought you said you weren't interested in the killer."

"Well, I didn't mean that literally, but that finding the assets could be as big a story as finding the killer."

I put the chalk down and picked up my coffee cup, took a sip and winced. Cold. How long had I sat there entranced by a lump of blue chalk? "What do you have in mind?"

"I've got an opportunity to inspect the car Morrow was killed in. I wouldn't ask you to sit in the driver's seat—I don't want you to freak out on me again, and I'm not saying that for my own sake. I'm honestly worried about you."

"I appreciate that," I said, but didn't want to dwell on it, either. "So you want me to sit where the killer sat and see if I can glom onto whatever vibes he left behind?"

"Something like that. But only if you feel up to it."

I considered the offer. Except for visiting Herschel, I had nothing better to do that day. "I guess. But are we likely to get anything of use? The guy was looking for the same thing we are."

"Yeah, and why would he have killed Morrow without that information?"

"Out of spite or frustration?"

"You have your funny feelings, I have mine, and I think you're going to come up with something spectacular from sitting in the back of that Lexus."

"Yeah, most likely a skull-pounding headache."

"I'll take you to lunch afterward," he offered, which wasn't much of an inducement.

"Then you want to do it this morning?"

"I'm supposed to be at the impound yard at eleven. Can you make it?"

I looked at the lump of chalk sitting on my coffee

table, remembering that it aroused more curiosity than fear from me. "I guess."

"Great. Do you know where the impound yard is?"

I didn't. He gave me the address.

"I'll see you there in about an hour."

"I'll be there. See you." I hung up the phone, got up from the couch and poured my cold coffee down the sink, then fixed myself a fresh cup. I needed caffeine—and one of my little blue pills—if I was to keep at bay the headache that was beginning to form behind my eyes. I needed to be thinking clearly when I got into the back of that Lexus and once again try to soak up the soul of a killer.

The police impound yard was located in a seedy, ramshackle neighborhood. The police presence hadn't seemed like much of a crime deterrent as evidenced by the graffiti and abundant litter. I parked near the entrance's chain-link fence and hoped it wouldn't be stolen or vandalized.

With his collar turned up against the wind, an impatient Sam waited for me outside the yard. "Sorry I'm late," I said as I slammed the driver's door. "It's a damn maze of one-way streets around here."

"We've got a very short window of opportunity here," Sam said and beckoned me to follow.

"You mean the boss is on a coffee break and some flatfoot who owes you a favor is letting us play detective?" I asked as I fell into step with him.

"Something like that," he admitted.

We marched past the open gate as a uniformed officer approached. "Hey, Rodriguez, good to see you," Sam called.

Rodriguez didn't seem to share that sentiment. "You said you'd be here fifteen minutes ago," he grated.

"We're here now. And we'll be out of your hair in just a couple of minutes," he promised good-naturedly.

Oh, yeah? I shot Sam an annoyed glance. Time often played tricks on me when I tried to soak up vibes—if I was even able to pull off that little parlor trick. It was never a given.

"Let's get this over with," Rodriguez said, "You've got ten—fifteen minutes at most, and then my obligation to you is over."

I gave Sam a sideways glance. What had he done for Rodriguez that gave him this kind of access to police evidence? I might never know.

The place seemed oddly absent of other police personnel as Rodriguez led us through a garage with many bays to a cream-colored Lexus that sat at the end of the row.

"Did they get any fingerprint evidence?" Sam asked.

Rodriguez shook his head. "Nothing. The entire car was wiped clean. Morrow's own prints weren't even on the steering wheel. They figured out the killer used antiseptic wipes bought at any supermarket to clean up the evidence, but the blood splatter was everywhere else, as you can see.

Oh, yeah. The splatter pattern on the windows was absolutely spectacular. It had ruined the cream-colored upholstery, marred the floor mats, and covered the electronics panel. And there was other matter that had dried on every surface, as well. Probably bits and pieces of Morrow's skull and brains. I'd seen similar crime scenes in my work for a major insurance company back in Manhattan—and of course when I'd first come back to Buffalo and entered Matt Sumner's love nest. Crime scenes had been my specialty—for a time. Then downsizing ended that career, and the rest, as they say, is history.

"My friend here," Sam said, without introducing me, "has an uncanny ability to observe things not readily apparent to folks like you and me."

Rodriguez gave me a sullen glare.

"We're wasting time," I said and waved my hand toward the car. "Shall we?"

Rodriguez pulled a few latex gloves from his pocket, donning one, and handing me two. He opened the driver's side door. A shudder ran through me. Sam had indicated I wasn't going to have to relive Morrow's death, but he didn't protest, either.

Coward that I am, I didn't want to appear weak in front of this beefy looking stranger and swallowed down my revulsion as I scooted onto the driver's seat.

Almost immediately, Morrow's residual terror enveloped me. He'd stared straight ahead at the darkened expanse of lawn, the headlights cutting a swath through the night, with the barrel of a gun pressed against the back of his skull, pleading for his life. He'd invoked the names of his wife and children, he'd begged, he'd appealed, but the one thing he wasn't prepared to do was divulge the whereabouts of the millions and millions of dollars he'd stashed in some safe place, somewhere where no one—least of all his killer—was ever likely to find them.

That same flash of light—remnant of the near-death vision?—caused a shudder to run through me and I practically jumped out of the driver's seat, feeling unnerved.

Rodriguez turned his hard stare from me to Sam as if silently asking, what the hell?

It took a couple of deep breaths for me to regain some tiny semblance of normalcy. Sam said nothing, but gestured toward the car's back seat.

My head was already beginning to thump. Why had I ever agreed to put myself into such an unpleasant situation? For a free lunch? Crap, I could eat a box of store-brand mac and cheese for far less than a buck. I didn't need to be bribed with filet mignon.

And still, there Sam stood, expecting me to lay aside all my fears and just thrust myself into what was literally the hot seat of a killer.

Stupid me. I did it—but not without reluctance, which I was pretty sure Sam could tell by my expression. He looked worried, but his concern wasn't enough to put a stop to this little endeavor.

My ass hit the seat and I was enveloped by an aura with which I was already familiar. It was the same one that had been attached to the chalk cube.

He'd held a Glock with a full clip. His voice had been reasonable, chillingly reasonable, as he'd outlined the consequences of not giving the answers he required, but after sitting in the driver's seat, I knew that Morrow had believed—known—that no matter what this monster promised, he was as good as dead—and he'd been right. But things that hadn't been clear to me when sitting up front came into sharper focus when compared with the sensations the killer had experienced in those final minutes—seconds—before the world, and Morrow's head, had exploded in a shower of blood, brains, and bone.

Again, I practically jumped out of the back passenger seat, my breathing harsh, as though I was suffering from an asthma attack.

"Are you okay?" Sam asked.

I had to hold it in. Rodriguez was staring at me like I was some kind of imbecile, while Sam looked cautiously optimistic.

"Yeah," I said, my voice tight, and felt anything but.

Rodriguez slammed the car doors shut and held his hand out to collect the gloves. It was a struggle to peel them off my sweaty hands. The cop stuffed them into his uniform slacks and then held a hand out to usher us out of the garage. I had no choice to but meekly follow in his and Sam's wake.

Once we arrived at the place where we'd first entered

the garage, Rodriguez turned to Sam, his expression hard. "We're done. Don't ever call me again," he said in a tone that held no semblance of friendship.

"It's been a pleasure," Sam said with a smile, but I could tell by the timbre of his voice that he wasn't happy about the situation. Had my expression revealed that much?

Sam turned and confidently strode toward his car. I followed a step or two behind, feeling pretty damned fragile. There had better be a double—maybe two of them—glass full of bourbon to accompany the lunch Sam had promised me, not that I was sure I would be able to eat more than a mouthful or two.

"Are you up to driving, or should we leave your car here and come back after lunch?" he asked, as though nothing had happened back at the garage. Any why not? For him nothing had happened.

"I can't drive right now," I said, trying to keep a quaver out of my voice.

He nodded and pressed the unlock button on his key fob. I got in the passenger side of his SUV, he backed up, and we took off.

While he drove, I stared at the vast sea of gray plastic dash in front of me, trying to figure out the mishmash of sensations and information that had pummeled me when sitting in both the Lexus's seats. I'd known that it wasn't going to be pleasant, and yet I'd once again let Sam talk me into soaking up the sensations of power and the deliverance of death. I wanted to be angry at him, but if I was honest, I could have refused to help him. There was nothing in any of this for me. Unlike Rodriguez, I didn't owe Sam a damn thing.

Of course, that wasn't true. I'd never be able to repay him for loaning me that gun four months before—for giving me the tool to save Richard's, Maggie's, and my own life.

Eventually, we arrived at our destination, a low brick building with a sign that proclaimed ANDREA'S RISTORANTE. The landscaping was low-key, but impeccable. As it was only eleven-fifty, just a few cars were parked near the entrance. We got out of Sam's car and entered.

The lights must have been set on a dimmer switch, because it took a few moments for my eyes to adjust to the dark interior. The walls were exposed brick—real or faux, it was hard to tell—with linen napkins and oil lamps on every table.

"Sam, you devil, you," said the attractive hostess, who strode right up to my old high-school buddy and planted one hell of a kiss on his smiling lips. A slim brunette with blonde highlights, she looked like she could have walked the catwalk in a high-class fashion show in a city much larger than Buffalo.

"Hey, Margot, we need a quiet table," Sam said.

"Only the best in the house for you," she said, then grabbed a couple of menus and beckoned us to follow her.

She led us to the back of the restaurant and set the menus on the table before a banquette that could easily have sat six. Sam slid in on the left while I moved to the right.

"Can I get you something from the bar?" Margot asked.

"I'll have a Flying Bison," Sam said, "and a double bourbon for my friend, here."

Margot flashed her pearly white teeth, nodded, and quickly disappeared.

I focused my attention on the table. I did not want to be there. I wasn't hungry and the last thing I needed was a drink.

"I'm sorry," Sam apologized. "I should have realized after yesterday that you weren't in any shape for any of this crap."

I looked up. "What do you mean?"

"You look like shit. Like you're about to keel over. I don't think I understood until just yesterday how much this psychic stuff drains you, and then I asked you to do it again today. I'm sorry."

I studied his earnest expression. The rather snooty high-school newspaper editor I'd barely known so many years before had certainly changed. He saw himself as a crusading reporter from another age and though he tried hard to hide it, he was a lot more softhearted than he let on.

Before I could answer, a waitress arrived with our drinks, placing cocktail napkins on the table before setting them down. "Ready to order?"

Sam looked to me, but I shook my head. "I don't want anything."

"You have to eat something," he chided, reminding me of Richard.

I let out a resigned breath and looked up at the waitress. "Could I get a hard-boiled egg and some dry white toast?"

"You're kidding," Sam said, giving me an odd look.

"That's what I want."

"Not a problem," the waitress assured me, and turned to Sam.

"I'll have a slab of lasagna, and a side salad with bleu cheese dressing."

She nodded and departed.

Sam turned his attention back to me. "Are you ready to talk about what you experienced in that car?" he asked, not unkindly, and then took a sip of his beer.

So much for sympathy.

I lowered my gaze to stare at the table. A crisp white linen tablecloth was protected from spills and crumbs by a slab of beveled plate glass. "Morrow died with his secrets."

"He didn't try to save his neck by telling his killer

where to find his money? He didn't even bluff?" Sam asked, surprised.

"He knew the minute the gun was shoved against the back of his skull that he was a dead man." I closed my eyes and placed my right index finger against the middle of my forehead where a headache was beginning to blossom. With my other hand, I reached into my jacket pocket and withdrew my prescription bottle, glad I'd thought to bring it. I doled out a pill and washed it down with a sip of bourbon—not exactly as per the pharmaceutical company's instructions.

"Did you learn anything else?"

"Morrow's killer must have been a friend, or at least a regular visitor to his home."

"How do you know that?" Sam asked.

"That billiards chalk I found at Morrow's house. It held the same vibes as the back of the leased Lexus."

"Damn. That's something the cops should know—but would totally blow off if we told them."

"It wouldn't hold up in a court of law, that's for sure."

"What else did you learn?"

"I'm not sure. Sometimes it takes a while for all the stuff I absorb to make sense."

"Is there any way to speed up the process?" Sam asked, taking another sip of his beer.

"Not so far."

From the corner of my eye, I saw the waitress approach with a tray. "Luncheon is served," she said, and set Sam's salad and lasagna before him. Next, she set my plate down. The egg had been split in half and sat in the middle of two slices of dry toast cut into triangles. "I had the chef zap the egg in the microwave so it would be warm. I hope that's okay."

I gave her a wan smile. "Just the way I like it. Thanks."

She gave me a much warmer smile and briefly touched my shoulder. "Enjoy."

Sam grabbed a shaker filled with parmesan cheese and doused both his entrée and salad before taking a bite. He chewed thoughtfully before swallowing and speaking. "You must know something more about the killer than he plays pool and shoots people."

I bit the end off of one of my toast triangles and thought about it. "Morrow had always underestimated his killer. He'd dismissed him as a non-threat, and wrongly so."

"Was he a business colleague? An underling perhaps?"

I thought about it. "I don't think so."

"A disgruntled client?"

I shook my head. "Not that, either."

"That leaves a friend—or at least an acquaintance," Sam suggested.

I nodded. "That seems about right."

Sam cut another piece of his lasagna and frowned. "And how many friends and acquaintances did the guy have over the years?" He stabbed at a chunk of sauce-covered pasta and stuffed it into his mouth.

I grabbed the pepper shaker and shook it vigorously over my egg halves, thinking about the killer. "Morrow knew this guy for years, but I sensed that they weren't close."

"And yet they regularly played pool at Morrow's home?"

I frowned. "That does seem odd."

"Could he have been one of Morrow's personal employees?" Sam suggested.

"You mean like a gardener or something?"

Sam nodded.

I popped half of the egg into my mouth and chewed. It was barely warm; I should have eaten it first. "I don't think so."

"A regular visitor to the house, then?" he asked.

I picked up another toast triangle. "Maybe."

Sam chased a grape tomato around his salad plate, captured it, and dipped it in dressing. "Looks like I should try to have another conversation with Mrs. Walburg."

I chewed my toast thoughtfully. "I wonder if she's had her suspicions about the killer all along."

"I doubt it. Who besides you would have associated the man's killer with a piece of billiards chalk? But I'll bet she knows the name of every regular visitor who came to that house."

"Wouldn't she have already shared that with the police?"

"If so, they may or may not have acted on it."

I shook my head. "You'd better be careful. Ask too many questions and you could put the old lady in danger."

"Hey, I'm a pro. I'd ask enough bogus questions that she'd have no clue as to my real interest."

I sipped my bourbon and considered dipping a piece of toast into the glass … but decided against it. "So you say." I ate the other half of my egg. "Our original intent was to find the assets. Now it seems like you're more interested in the killer. But he didn't get Morrow to tell where they were, so it would seem the killer is just as clueless as we are."

"Probably. But I'll bet he hasn't stopped looking, either."

"And where does that leave us?"

Sam frowned and cut another piece of his rapidly dwindling lasagna. He shoved it into his mouth, chewed, and swallowed. "What if I can get into Morrow's former offices? As far as I know, they're vacant. I'll call the real estate office to see if I can make an appointment."

"There's not likely to be anything there in the way of furniture. The walls themselves may or may not have retained a sense of Morrow."

"Still, it's worth trying."

He'd told me not twenty minutes before that he was sorry he'd put me through all this psychic crap, and already he was trying to figure out another way to use me as his human Geiger counter. What are friends for?

"What other ideas do you have for tracking down the missing swag?' I asked, and polished off my last piece of toast.

"Morrow's wife and kids aren't around to talk. Even though he's dead, his lawyers are anything but cooperative, and Morrow doesn't seem to have had a friend left in the world. He swindled most of them. I'm sure more than a few of them cheered when they heard he'd been killed."

"It's hard to be sympathetic when you face an uncertain financial future." Boy, could I identify with that statement. Richard had once promised to leave me a million in his will, but I had a funny feeling he was going to outlive me. It was an intensely disquieting thought.

Sam toyed with the last of his salad and drained his beer. "I need to get back to work. Besides the Morrow story, I've got several others in various states of completion. I'd better hand in something today or my editor is going to explode." He signaled the waitress for the check, which was quickly delivered. Sam paid for the lunch with a corporate credit card, leaving a generous cash tip.

"So, can I count on you to come with me to visit Morrow's offices?" he asked as we waited for the credit card and slip to be returned.

I let out a breath, once again remembering the gun I'd never returned. "Sure."

"And now that you've got a better handle on the killer, try handling that chalk again. Maybe you'll get some new insight."

Now he was starting to piss me off. "Shall I try to cure cancer and impose world peace while I'm at it?"

He shrugged. "If you wouldn't mind."

I laughed in spite of myself.

We left the restaurant, which had filled up while we'd been otherwise occupied. The food—and the little blue pill—had quelled my headache. Sam dropped me off at my car and promised to call later that day or perhaps by morning to set up a time to see Morrow's offices.

I was glad I didn't have to work that night. It had been a rough couple of days. My schedule for the afternoon included a nap before I headed to Clarence to visit my neglected cat and equally neglected lady friend. Would she let me spend the night? I sure hoped so, but I was also ready to give her more space if she needed it.

Arriving home, I unlocked the door to my apartment, happy to see that no unwelcome visitors had trespassed during my absence. Maggie wouldn't be home from work for hours. Even longer if she intended to visit Lily at the rehab facility. That gave me hours and hours to kill.

I peeled off my jacket, hung it in the closet, and settled down on the couch. The chalk cube still sat on my coffee table. Sam wanted me to commune with it, but I wasn't exactly eager to revisit the emotions I'd experienced in the back of Morrow's leased Lexus.

Gathering my courage, I picked up the cube and held it in my fist. Again, I got the impression of a man rubbing the chalk on the end of a cue. Squeezing my eyes tighter seemed to bring the image into greater focus. Pale, white skin. Young hands. Hands unmarred by calluses— someone who didn't sully them with honest labor. Someone just as crooked as Jack Morrow?

I opened my eyes and set the chalk back down the on coffee table, sat back and folded my arms over my chest, quite content to leave connecting with Morrow's killer for yet another day. Knowing Sam, he'd be dragging me to Morrow's offices sooner rather than later.

And I wasn't looking forward to it.

EIGHTEEN

When the big furniture delivery van backed into the driveway, Brenda was all smiles. But when the merchandise came out of the truck in one very large cardboard carton, her eyes welled with tears. Big wet tears that silently cascaded down her cocoa brown cheeks. Tears that nearly broke Richard's heart.

"I think I may have forgotten to tell you that the crib was going to arrive unassembled," he apologized.

Brenda's lower lip trembled as the deliverymen brought the box into the kitchen and followed Evelyn to the nursery upstairs.

"Will they assemble it?" Brenda asked, her voice breaking. She was far more emotional than the situation warranted.

Richard placed what he hoped was a comforting arm around his wife's shoulders. "I'm afraid not."

Another big tear leaked from her left eye and she wiped it away. "I waited too long," she said and sniffed.

"What for?"

"To set up the nursery. We should have done this months ago. We should have—" Her voice broke again and she rested her head on his shoulder.

"We knew it was it was on backorder when we first saw it. And it's not like it's broken," Richard said and immediately felt like slapping himself upside the head. What if they opened the box and it was broken? He forged ahead. "I'm sure between us, Jeff and I can put it together by this evening. It's just a small setback, not a catastrophe."

Brenda nodded, cleared her throat, and straightened. "I'm sorry. I'm just—"

"Overwhelmed?" Richard suggested.

She nodded.

He kissed her. "Just a few more days; maybe a few more hours, and the baby will be here."

Brenda looked down at her belly and sighed. "She can't come soon enough for me."

"I'm going upstairs to make sure all the pieces are there before the movers leave."

"Good idea," she said, and sat down at the kitchen table once more.

Richard wasted no time heading up the stairs, but Evelyn had had the same idea and already had the deliverymen removing each of the crib pieces from the box so she could inspect them.

"Everything seems to be in order," she said, sounding satisfied.

"Sorry we can't assemble it for you, but we've got strict orders," said one of the burly deliverymen.

"I understand," Richard said, and reached for his wallet to tip them, but a glare from Evelyn stopped him.

"I'll show you out," she said in her no-nonsense principal's voice. The deliverymen followed her out of the nursery.

Richard found the assembly instructions sitting on the glider. He picked them up and examined them. There were so many slots and screws, rails and rods, that he shook his head. This was not his kind of thing. He'd be quite content to hold pieces together and hand Jeff the screwdriver, or hammer, or whatever else it took to build the damn thing.

Evelyn returned in record time. "Brenda is sitting at

the table and sniveling," she said acidly.

"She's just disappointed," Richard said, feigning interest in the assembly instructions. "She'll be okay once we put it together."

"We?" Evelyn asked.

"Jeff and me."

"I'll get Da-Marr to help."

"That's okay. Jeff and I can handle it."

He looked up to see Evelyn check her watch. "Where is that boy? I noticed he turned the TV off early last night. He should have been up hours ago."

Should Richard tell her that he had turned off the set and that Da-Marr had gone out and hadn't returned until after six that morning?

He decided not to—but he would have a word with Da-Marr.

Evelyn marched out of the room and Richard heard her knock on the guest room door. "Da-Marr? Da-Marr! It's long past time you got up. Do you hear me?"

Richard strained to listen, but couldn't made out what the kid was saying.

"I'll go fix you a late lunch. You be downstairs in five minutes or I'll be back with instant up."

Richard poked his head around the nursery's door. "Instant up?"

"Ice cubes," Evelyn said, trying, but not succeeding, to hide a smile.

Richard watched her as she headed down the stairs.

He waited, and it was nearly five minutes later when a still sleepy Da-Marr trudged out of the guest room, closing the door behind him.

"Da-Marr," Richard called.

The kid stopped dead and turned.

"Your Aunt Evelyn doesn't know you didn't spend the night in your room, but I do."

"Bullshit."

"Bullshit, nothing. I turned off the TV in your room last night, and I heard you come in this morning. Now, what are we going to do about this situation?"

Da-Marr eyed him coldly. "I'm a grown man. I can come and go as I please."

"Not in my house. You may be a guest, but right now, you're not a very welcome one. I don't know what you're up to, but if you step out of line one more time—"

"What are you going to do, tell my auntie on me?"

"Exactly. And then you'll have to face the consequences."

Tough guy though he wanted to be, the kid actually seemed to fear Evelyn's wrath. Without another word, he turned and hurried down the stairs, taking them two at a time.

Richard reentered the nursery and picked up the crib's assembly instructions once again. Now all he had to do was convince Jeff to come over and assemble the damn thing.

It took twenty minutes waiting on hold before the receptionist came back on the line and I finally got permission from my primary physician to contact a couple of allergists. As I suspected, I wasn't going to get an appointment for testing for at least two months. Well, in a couple of weeks all the bugs would be hibernating and I wouldn't have to worry about getting stung, so I wrote the appointment on the calendar and hung up the phone once again. Almost immediately, it rang.

"Hey, Jeff, it's me," Richard said, sounding rather sheepish. He wanted something.

"Hi." I said, drawing out the word.

"I thought I'd call to see how you were doing today."

"You could have walked across the driveway," I said.

"Yeah, I guess I could have. It's just—I feel like every move I make is being watched."

There was a way to remedy that situation, too, but I wasn't going to be the one to suggest it.

I let the silence lengthen.

"Uh, you said you'd help put the crib together."

Sure, I said I'd help, but that was before I'd had to experience a man's head exploding, communed with a killer, or been stuck on hold for what seemed like forever. "Don't you have a bassinette already stationed in your bedroom?"

"Yeah, but Brenda's got her heart set on having the nursery finished before the baby arrives. Do you think you could come over this afternoon and give me a hand?"

"You're going to build it?" I asked skeptically.

"We both know the answer to that."

I still had hours to kill before I could see Maggie, and I needed a distraction to keep from dwelling on the visions I'd seen in the leased Lexus. "Sure. But I don't want to run into your company."

"Thanks," he said, sounding relieved. "And don't worry, I'm working on that." Whatever he was going to say in further explanation never materialized because I heard Evelyn's voice in the background, although I couldn't understand what she said. "No problem," Richard said, his voice sounding muffled. When he came back to talk to me, his voice was back to regular volume. "I've got to take Evelyn to the store, but I should be back in an hour or so."

"We've got all afternoon," I said, but I'd already decided to scoot over there the minute he pulled out of the driveway.

"Thanks. I really appreciate it."

I knew he did. The poor schmuck was caught between a rock and a hard place, and despite the fact I was majorly pissed about dealing with Da-Marr, I wasn't going to make his life any more difficult than it already was.

"Richard!" Evelyn snapped somewhere in the background.

"Gotta go," he said.

"I'll see you later," I said and hung up the phone. I wandered over to the window, standing back far enough so that I could see the back door to Richard's house but not be seen, and waited. Within a minute, the door opened and Evelyn and Da-Marr marched out, with Richard dutifully following behind. He closed the door behind him.

I turned away and smiled, hoping he'd vastly under-estimated the time he and his guests would be gone.

I grabbed my keys from the breakfast bar, locked the door behind me, and headed down the stairs. I figured if I entered the house through the front door, I might be lucky enough to miss running into Brenda. Until things calmed down, I didn't feel like talking to her, either.

I made a stop in the garage and grabbed a couple screwdrivers from the big wooden toolbox some caretaker had left decades before and headed for the house.

The big oak door opened silently on well-oiled hinges, and I carefully closed it so that it wouldn't make a noise. I tracked across the polished marble floor and crept up the stairs. The door to Richard's and Brenda's bedroom was open, and I hurried past, grateful the floorboards under the carpet didn't creak.

The nursery door was closed and I carefully opened and closed it behind me, finding one hell of a mess scat-tered on the floor before me. Someone had emptied the huge rectangular box, tossing it and all the packaging aside, and had spread out all the parts across the carpet. I would have preferred to take everything out of the box myself, but what was done was done.

Except for the upholstered glider, all the furniture was

white and, except for the crib, was meant to be something little Betsy Ruth could grow into, instead of the room being stuck in infant mode for far too long. She'd like it, and I knew she'd be delighted with the matching mobile Maggie had chosen to hang over the crib. It wasn't infant specific, either, with fanciful bugs in various pastel shades—including a bumblebee. Since my recent unpleasant encounter with this particular insect, it was not something I cared to inspect too carefully.

The crib's assembly instructions sat on the top of the changing tray atop the dresser. I grabbed them and sat down in the glider in front of the window to study them.

I found the Allen wrench that came with the parts, and was just about to grab the first piece to attach it to the left end of the backside of the crib when the door opened. I looked up to find Da-Marr standing before me. What the hell? I'd thought he'd gone out with Richard and Evelyn.

"What in hell are *you* doing here?" he asked.

I swallowed, determined not to let the kid get to me. And yet my fists automatically clenched, my nails digging into my palms. "Excuse me, but I've got history with his house. You don't."

"And you think that makes you better than me?" he challenged, his anger deeper than the situation warranted.

"No. I'm just telling you that when it comes to family, I'm related by blood. You aren't. So bug off and leave me alone."

"To do what?"

"What does it look like I'm doing? I'm gonna build this crib."

"What do you know about building anything?" he demanded and stalked across the room, snatching the Allen wrench from my hand.

"Hey!" I protested and used the chair's arms to boost

me to a stand. Da-Marr reared back, his face screwed up in anger. He drew back his arm as though to hit me and …

Everything went black as a flashback overtook me.

The mugging.

The baseball bat arching toward my skull.

Skyrockets of pain overwhelmed me before I fell a million miles to the frozen pavement below me.

And then the heavens opened up, yawning miles above me.

A brilliant white light exploded and began to suck me upward, spiraling toward it—threatening to obviate all that I knew—all that I was.

Wrenching me from my most precious possession—my life!

It seemed eons later when once again I was able to absorb reality and found myself cowering in a corner of what had once been my own bedroom. Shouting voices registered somewhere behind me, but I couldn't make out the furious words. I was taken back to the screaming matches between my parents—the verbal and physical abuse that had been such a terrible part of my early childhood. A horrible place where I was sure that my world—my life—was about to end.

Then gentle hands grasped the balled fists that were pressed into my eye sockets so hard all I saw was that terrible, lethal white light.

"It's okay, it's okay," the voice crooned and pulled me into a fierce hug.

I knew that tears cascaded down my cheeks, but like all the tragedies from my past, I wouldn't allow a sound to issue from my throat—my sense of humiliation wouldn't allow it.

"What a wuss! He's a Goddamn wuss!" the terrible voice boomed.

"Get out—just get out!" a woman's voice shrieked.

Brenda. It was Brenda who held onto me tightly, and I realized I held her hand in a ferocious grip—scared to death to let go.

Somehow, I managed to get my breathing under control and opened my eyes, seeing only the intersecting walls, the corner molding, and carpet.

"It's okay. It's okay now," Brenda kept saying and kissed the top of my head.

I couldn't look at her. I was too ashamed. So ashamed I felt like puking.

"I'm sorry. I'm so sorry," she said and didn't let go. "I didn't know. I didn't understand...."

"What on earth is going on here?" asked a stern voice.

My eyes squeezed shut tighter yet and I felt myself pulling inward, trying to grow even smaller.

"Not now," Brenda said fiercely. "Go. Just go!"

I heard the door slam—really loud.

I turned my head so far to my right—trying to bury it in the corner—that I thought my neck might break, and the arm around my shoulder suddenly jerked back, pulling me with it.

"I'm sorry, Jeffy, but my center of gravity is so out of whack," Brenda apologized.

I forced myself to look behind me to find poor Brenda sitting on her backside in a terribly undignified state, with tears streaming down her cheeks.

"I'm sorry," I managed, awash with fresh humiliation.

"No, hon, I'm sorry. I shouldn't have—I didn't mean to—"

I reached out and pressed a couple of fingers against her lips to stop her from speaking. Suddenly I could breathe a lot easier. I reached out and grasped her hands, pulling her up and settling her onto the glider. Then I fell back on my bony ass on the carpeted floor, feeling a dozen different degrees of stupid.

"Did he hurt you?" Brenda asked at last, sounding frightened.

I shook my head. I wasn't sure I trusted myself to

speak without my voice cracking into a million pieces, but I had to at least try. "It was my fault," I said, not sure I believed it. At that moment, I wasn't at all sure what I believed.

The tears continued to stream down her face, and I knew that I had caused her this monumental, most terrible pain. "I don't know. I didn't—" I couldn't come up with any more detailed explanation for my abominable behavior.

This time she reached out to press her hand against my lips. "What a fine pair we make," Brenda said. "We've got so much baggage between us we might as well be porters." She laughed, but there was no mirth behind it. She reached for my hand and clasped it tightly. "You're so afraid of Da-Marr, and I'm just as afraid of Evelyn."

"Why does she scare you?" I asked, willing to do anything than admit my own failings.

"Because. In my parents' eyes, she could do no wrong. She did everything right. She married the right guy. She had great kids. She had a successful career...."

But that wasn't at all what she meant.

She seemed to be gulping great drafts of air. "I'm scared, Jeffy. I'm about to have a baby and all I want is my mama. She wouldn't come, but Evie said she would. But ... it's not the same. I knew it wouldn't be good, but I let her come anyway, and all she's done is try to destroy the family I have here. I'm sorry. I'm so sorry I let this happen."

And then it was her turn to completely lose it. Suddenly she was sobbing uncontrollably and I was scared to death her water would break and I'd be thrust into the role of midwife—something I wasn't at all prepared for. Instead, I struggled to my knees, threw my arms around her, and let her cry into my shoulder for what seemed like way too many minutes. Nobody should ever have to cry that hard. Her heart was breaking and I, too, was so swallowed up by her misery that tears leaked from my own eyes once again.

First Morrow's fear. Then Brenda's remorse and sorrow—it was a terrible, awful place to be, and yet I didn't let go. I held on to her. I tried my best to comfort her as I had with my mother. She who was too often drunk, who couldn't take care of herself, let alone me. It had been a terrible situation, and yet I'd loved her unconditionally. I loved Brenda the same way, and yet it was often she who took care of me. Now I had a chance to repay the favor.

Eventually Brenda's sobs quieted, but I could still feel the emotional pain that had a stranglehold on her heart. She pulled back and wiped a hand across her bloodshot eyes. "What're we going to do?"

I let out a shaky breath. "I guess there's nothing to do but get through it."

"I wish I could just send them home, but ... that isn't going to work. I just want to be with Richard, and you, and Maggie. You're my family here in Buffalo. We don't have anything to prove to each other."

I was glad she felt that way, but I also felt the tug of pain she felt for her missing twin. She'd lost a part of her soul when Ruth had died—and more than a decade later the wound was still a raw slash across her soul. I wished I could say something to comfort her, but at that moment, I was just as big a basket case.

An unopened box of baby wipes sat on the shelf below the changing table and I grabbed it, struggling to rip the plastic wrap from around it. Once open, I handed her a wipe and took one for myself, wiping that cool paper-cloth across my face and drinking in the baby-powder-like scent.

I sat back on my heels and looked around the messy room. We only had days—if that—to pull the nursery together, but at that moment I knew it was the farthest thing from Brenda's mind.

"Richard said you already know all about our girl."

Just the thought of little Betsy Ruth was like a balm to my soul. "She's gonna be one hell of a great kid."

"Oh my god, I'm going to have a daughter," Brenda said and looked down at her swollen abdomen and laughed.

"You sure are."

"You're going to be an uncle."

"Yeah," I said and laughed, and yet somewhere inside me I also knew that being Betsy Ruth's uncle was as close as I would ever get to parenthood. It was just never in the cards. When I was married to Shelley, I figured we'd eventually have a brood. Now I knew better and felt unaccountably sad.

"I need a drink," Brenda said wearily.

"It's another hour or so until happy hour," I told her.

"I haven't had a drink in almost nine months. I'm overdue."

"When Betsy arrives, I'll bring you a bottle of Dom Pérignon."

Her expression soured. "You will not."

"Who says?" I challenged.

She tried to hide a smile, but it peeked out anyway. "You will? But you can't afford it."

"Hey, I've got a generous landlord. He doesn't charge me an arm and a leg for my humble abode, so I can sometimes splurge."

Brenda shook her head, but her smile was beatific. "No, I guess he doesn't."

I sobered. "Hard as it is, I think we can get through the next week or so. At least, I'm willing to try."

She reached for and captured my hand. "It won't be easy for either of us."

"Yeah, but we're made of tough stuff."

"Not!" she said, and we both laughed.

That's when I knew we were going to be okay. Whatever shit had gone on since Evelyn and Da-Marr had arrived was not going to impact our lives in the long run. We were family once again, and it felt good.

And then I remembered that horrible yawning light that threatened to suck me into it and everything I'd just accepted as truth seemed to crumble.

The fact was that I might be dead in the not-too-distant future.

And the thought scared me shitless.

NINETEEN

Richard and Evelyn returned from the grocery store sooner than he'd expected. He followed her into the house, hands filled with plastic grocery bags, when Da-Marr stormed into the kitchen.

"She's crazy!" he hollered, absolutely livid.

"Who's crazy?" Evelyn demanded.

"And that brother of yours is an asshole," he railed, stabbing the air with his index finger. "A stupid, wuss of an asshole!"

"What's going on?" Richard, too, demanded.

"Aw, it ain't my fault," Da-Marr backpedaled. "I went in the baby's room and he was there. He picked a fight with me. And then he went berserk."

Richard's insides froze. "What did you do?" he asked, his voice low.

"I was just gonna give him a tap when—"

"Holy Christ," Richard grated, and practically tossed the groceries onto the kitchen table.

"Richard! Do not take the Lord's name in vain in my presence," Evelyn bellowed. She didn't wait for a further explanation, and took off in the direction of the stairs.

"Did you hit him?" Richard asked, finding it hard to keep his voice from rising.

"No!"

"Then what happened?"

"He made out like I did. And then Brenda showed up

and started screaming at me. She said some terrible things. She's crazy."

"What did she say?"

"I don't know. She was screaming so loud, nothing she said made sense and then she told me to get out." He pushed Richard. "And that's what I'm gonna do."

"Wait!" Richard called, and went after him.

Da-Marr grabbed his jacket from a peg in the butler's pantry, yanked open the door, and stormed out.

Richard felt no urge to follow, and instead he turned and started toward the stairs. Evelyn was on her way down, looking furious.

"She ordered me out! She wouldn't even tell me what had happened. I'm beginning to think Da-Marr's right. That girl *is* crazy!"

Richard took the stairs two at a time, but he stopped at the landing and listened. No sound came from the nursery where the door was closed. He walked softly and paused at the door, listening, but heard nothing. Quietly, he opened the door a crack and peeked inside. Brenda sat on the glider, and Jeff was on his knees—the two of them holding onto each other for dear life, while Brenda sobbed uncontrollably.

Richard hesitated for a long moment, fighting the urge to interrupt, and then closed the door softly.

He turned and slowly, quietly retraced his steps to the bottom of the stairs.

He saw Evelyn sitting on one of the living room chairs, her back to him, and ignored her. Once back in the kitchen, he put the groceries away. Glancing out the window, he noticed the garage door was open and that Brenda's car was missing. Da-Marr must have taken her keys.

Biting back anger, Richard resisted the temptation of a glass of Scotch. It was just too easy to pour himself a glass and sit and brood.

Instead, he went to his study, sat in what had long ago been his grandfather's big leather chair behind the desk, and stared out the window at the gloomy gray sky. The leaves on the maple tree out back had already started to fall.

Da-Marr had made two unforgivable mistakes. Threatening Jeff, and taking the car. God only knew where he was and what he was up to.

Richard wasn't sure how long he'd sat there, thinking of too much—and nothing—for far too long, but eventually he got up and wandered down the hall, passing the living room where Evelyn still sat, only now she was thumbing through a magazine.

In the kitchen, Richard pulled out a couple of glasses, filled them with ice, and then poured Scotch, neat, in one, and bourbon in the other. Then he took out a wine glass and filled it half way with Cabernet. Grabbing a tray from the cupboard, he tossed a clean tea towel over it and headed up the stairs.

Upon arriving at the nursery, he found the door still closed and knocked.

"Come in," came Brenda's muffled voice.

Richard turned the handle and stuck his head inside. Jeff was on the floor with the instructions beside him, while Brenda sat on the glider, holding up the partially assembled crib. "Can you use an extra pair of hands?" he asked.

"Yes," they said as one, and laughed.

Leaving the door open behind him, Richard entered.

"And what have we here?" Brenda asked, looking intrigued.

"Just what the doctor ordered," Richard said, whipping off the towel with a flourish. He passed out the glasses and set the tray on the changing table.

Brenda sniffed the contents of her glass. "Is this real?"

"As real as it gets," Richard assured her.

"But what about—?"

"One glass is not going to hurt the baby."

"It sure isn't going to hurt me," Jeff said, and took a good slug of bourbon.

"Hey, wait for the toast," Richard said. "To Betsy Ruth."

They clinked glasses and drank.

"To the crib!" Brenda proposed.

They clinked again.

"To us," Jeff chimed in.

"Let's not chug it," Richard admonished, and they all laughed. The icebreaker had worked, because the ensuing conversation was likely to be hard on all of them.

Richard eased himself down to the carpet, set his glass down, and picked up one of the errant crib pieces. "Now, where does this go?" he asked.

I'd arrived at Maggie's well before dark, and wasn't sure exactly when she was likely to return from visiting Lily at the rehab facility. I knew she'd be hungry and have no interest in cooking, so I stopped at the grocery store and bought a selection of ready-to-heat entrees and sides that would feed an army. She wouldn't have to make dinner for a couple of days. After putting everything in her nearly empty fridge, I went downstairs to visit my cat, who latched onto me like a leech. I hadn't realized how much we would miss each other when I'd dropped him off the day before.

"It won't be long before you can come home, buddy," I told him, and the cat's purr launched into overdrive.

I fed Herschel and read Lily's copy of the morning paper, keeping my cat company for more than an hour before I heard Maggie's car pull up the drive. Less than a minute later, she came through the communal door, where I met her and Holly, who whined with happiness to see me.

"Good girl," I said, petting the dog.

"How about me?" Maggie asked tiredly.

"You're better than good." I tried to give her a kiss, but Holly jumped up between us, trying to lick both our faces at once.

"Ugh! Dog germs!" Maggie squealed with delight.

"Let's go upstairs," I suggested. The cramped entryway could not accommodate the three of us.

"Upstairs!" Maggie said, and Holly raced up the steps for the apartment, while I turned off the lights and locked up Lily's apartment.

By the time I made it upstairs, Maggie had shed her coat and had wandered into the kitchen. She opened the fridge and whooped in surprise. "The dinner fairy has visited," she announced with joy—something I hadn't heard in her voice for a long, long time. She grabbed a beer for herself and one for me. "I've been waiting all day for this. Let's go sit down in the living room."

Holly tried to tell us she was near death from starvation, so before we could settle down Maggie fed the dog, and we finally sat down to the sound of happy slurping in the kitchen.

Once seated, I gave Maggie a proper kiss, and then we clinked beer bottles, not unlike what I'd done with Richard and Brenda several hours before. But this was different. The three of us had discussed what had happened in the nursery between Da-Marr and me—with Brenda coming to my rescue. I didn't want to rehash it with Maggie, but I did need to talk. Before I could unburden myself, I had to make sure that she was up to it, and if she wasn't ... then I would just have to keep the rest of the day to myself.

"I can't tell you how happy I was to see your car in the driveway when I pulled up."

"It's been a while," I said, and took a sip of my beer.

She sighed. "I know I haven't given you much attention lately, but I got good news today. Lily is making amazing progress. They say if she keeps improving, she might be home as early as next week. And I heard from Gary. He's coming up this weekend, and he's agreed to pay for home help until Lily is back in tip-top shape." She smiled. "It's been a really good day."

I looked away. There was no way I was going dump my load of shit on her.

"What's wrong?" she asked.

I took a long swallow of beer. "I'm glad you had a good day."

"But I can tell by your expression that you didn't. Do you want to talk about it?"

I shook my head. "It's not that important. Let's celebrate your day." I held my beer bottle up as though in a toast. We both took a sip, and I leaned back farther on the couch. After all that had happened that day, I was too numb to even feel disappointment.

"Most of the stuff in the fridge can be nuked," I said. "You should have enough for another dinner and maybe a lunch or two."

She gave me a sweet smile. "You got all my favorites. Thank you."

I shrugged.

The silence seemed to hover.

I got up and crossed to the stereo. A stack of CDs sat on top of the amplifier. I picked out a bunch I knew she enjoyed most and loaded the five-disk player, hitting the ON button. Soon southwest new age issued from the small speakers.

By the time I sat back down beside her, Holly had finished her dinner and was happily licking her chops. As usual, she pressed her warm body against my leg, settling her head on my thigh and looking at the two of us with adoring eyes.

"Are you going to tell me what's wrong, or are we going sit here all evening and make innocuous conversation?"

"That was kind of my plan."

"I can tell by your eyes that something is very, very wrong."

"I don't want to spoil your day."

"And I want to make your day better. Please, let me help—if only by listening."

I reached over to hold her hand and a warm wave of affection rolled over me.

"Tell me," she said softly.

I nodded. "I don't know what was worse—the crap with Sam or the crap with Da-Marr. I think I'll let Brenda explain the latter. I don't think I'm up to it. But the bottom line is they're going to ask him to leave."

She sighed and squeezed my hand. I don't envy Brenda for having that conversation."

"She's reached the end of her rope, too. If you've got time tomorrow, I think she'd appreciate a call."

"I'll make sure of it," Maggie promised. "So what's going on with you and Sam?"

"Have you heard the name Jack Morrow?" I asked.

She sighed. "Please don't tell me he has you looking for the guy's murderer."

"No, of course not," I sort of lied. "But Sam *is* interested in finding the guy's hidden assets."

"I read about Morrow's death in the paper. Don't tell me Sam made you relive it."

I let out a shaky breath.

"Oh, Jeff. Why do you let him pull this garbage on you?"

I wasn't going to mention the gun he'd loaned me. Firing that gun had saved Maggie's life, too, but it would just bring up all the bad memories of what we'd been through some four-and-a-half months before, and that wasn't a place I wanted to revisit.

"It doesn't matter why I agreed to help him, what matters is...." I frowned. What did matter? That I was freaked out by what I'd seen? Maybe I should talk to her about the white light that wanted to swallow me—sucking me into everlasting oblivion.

"Sam's taken me to see Morrow's home and the car where he was killed."

"Oh, Jeff," she admonished. "That had to be terribly gruesome."

"Yeah," I admitted. "It was. And tomorrow he wants to take me to Morrow's office to see if I can soak up any other vibes."

"Please don't do it."

"I don't know how to say no to him."

"You say ... no!"

I let out a long breath. "It's not that easy."

"What on earth can you possibly owe this guy that you'd take on this kind of obligation?"

I couldn't tell her: *your life; Richard's life. My own life.*

"It's a pretty big debt," I admitted.

She shook her head, exasperated with me.

We were quiet for a long few minutes, sipping our beers, listening to the quiet flute and percussion on the stereo. It was one I must have heard hundreds of times before, and yet I—and I knew for sure Maggie—had never grown tired of.

Maggie spoke first. "So what have you learned?"

I knew exactly what she was talking about. "Morrow didn't tell his killer where he hid his money. The guy shot him. But it's not the end of the story, because like us, the killer is looking for those assets."

"How close are you to finding them?"

"Not very," I admitted. "In fact, I think visiting Morrow's offices tomorrow will be a big waste of time, but I feel I have to go, if only to placate Sam."

"The guy is dead. His offices have been closed for more than a year. That means the place is probably empty. Goodness knows there aren't going to be any assets hidden there. Morrow would have moved them."

"But Sam thinks I might be able to pick up residual vibes." I told her about the billiards chalk and all the information I'd gathered from it.

She shook her head. "You're going about it from the wrong angle. Concentrating on the killer isn't going to find hidden treasure. You said yourself, he's still looking for it."

"I know, but I haven't been able to learn anything of relevance from touching any of Morrow's possessions, either. I get a sense of who he was and what he did—but it's like skimming the surface of the ocean. He was good at hiding things. About himself, mostly. And he apparently hid them from everyone he knew. For a scheme like the one he perpetrated, I guess that's the way it would have to be. I doubt he felt safe confiding in anyone."

Maggie was quiet for a long moment before she spoke again. "I don't like this. You have bad feelings about stuff—and I have a bad feeling about this." The lines around her eyes seemed to deepen. "Please don't go with Sam tomorrow, Jeff."

I shrugged. "I don't see how I can get out of it."

She wasn't going to beg. She never begged. Instead, she nodded. "Then I want you to be careful. Promise me you'll be very careful."

"I will."

She leaned over to kiss me, but once again Holly decided that it would be better if she was the center of attention, and she practically leaped into my lap to lick us both.

"Ugh! Dog germs!" Maggie wailed once again, and we both laughed.

We gave up, got up from the couch, and headed into

the kitchen where food awaited.

Maggie assembled the entrees while I set the table. It would be like going to one of those all-you-can eat buffets, but the truth was I had no appetite, and wouldn't until this little adventure with Sam was over.

I didn't like to think about it, because I had a feeling it would come to an abrupt and not-so-happy end ... but for whom?

TWENTY

Never had Richard suffered through such a painful meal. Evelyn had made enough food to feed a battalion, but since Da-Marr hadn't joined them for dinner yet again, there were tons of leftovers.

Retiring to the silent study for the evening had also proved a painful choice. Richard tried, but couldn't concentrate enough to read, while Brenda worked on her needlepoint. The click, click, click of Evelyn's knitting needles was about to drive him bonkers when Evelyn finally spoke.

"I'm very worried about Da-Marr. He's out there alone in a strange city. And he left here very angry."

"Well, whose fault is that?" Brenda said, challenging her sister for the first time since her arrival.

Evelyn glared at Richard. "We still don't know what your brother did to aggravate him."

"I don't think he had to do anything," Brenda muttered. "Da-Marr's presence was just more than Jeffy could take right now."

"Sounds to me like *your brother*," she kept saying the words as though they were an accusation, "could use the services of a good psychiatrist."

Richard was determined not to let her provoke him. He stared at the words on the page before him, worried about where this conversation was going to go.

"And Da-Marr could learn a thing or two about self-control. Let me guess, he was often in trouble in school for bullying," Brenda said.

Evelyn's lips tightened, but she didn't acknowledge the accusation.

"Tell, me, Evie, what is so special about that boy?" Brenda asked.

"He's not a boy, he's a man," she clarified.

"He certainly doesn't act it," Brenda said, and sorted through her skeins of yarn, choosing a different color. "And you still haven't answered my question. Why is he so important to you?"

"I've seen too many boys like Da-Marr go the wrong route. I wasn't going to have it happen in our family."

"Don't you mean Charlie's family?"

"Charles," she corrected. "My husband's name is Charles."

Brenda had told Richard long ago that the man had asked everyone in the family to call him Charlie. He hated being called Charles, and only Evelyn called him by that moniker.

"I know it's going to hurt for you to hear this, Evie, but things have got to change," Brenda said succinctly, sounding more like her real self—the person that Richard had known for the past nine years—the woman he'd grown to love with such an intensity that he couldn't imagine a life without her.

"What on earth are you saying?" Evelyn asked, sounding more than a trifle annoyed.

"Honestly, Evie, what were you thinking when you brought Da-Marr here?" Brenda demanded.

"The boy needed to see how the successful people live."

"Are you saying no one in his own family is successful?" Brenda demanded.

"Not at all. But none of them are millionaires," she said, leveling an accusatory glare at Richard.

"Is that my fault?" he asked, and instantly wished he'd kept the promise he'd made to himself to keep his mouth shut.

"You didn't earn it," Evelyn accused.

"No?" he asked, incredulous. "You'd be surprised."

"And what does that mean?" Evelyn demanded.

There was no way Richard was going to get into that subject with her.

"I'm sorry, Evie, but Da-Marr is no longer welcome in our home," Brenda said.

"Just because *his brother,*" she glared at Richard, "is some kind of a basket case?"

"He's a trauma victim," Richard clarified.

"Victimhood suits him," she said scornfully, "and you're both enablers."

"We're getting off the subject," Brenda said, keeping her voice level. "Da-Marr smoked marijuana in Jeff's apartment, *and* he vandalized it."

Evelyn turned her gaze to Richard. "I don't believe it."

"Worse, he let loose a couple of wasp's nests, knowing that Jeff is allergic."

Evelyn's eyes grew wide, but Richard wasn't sure if it was with anger or disbelief.

"He snuck out last night and didn't come home until early this morning," Brenda finished.

"Why would you say such terrible things?" Evelyn demanded.

"Because they're true. And now he's stolen my car."

"Borrowed it," Evelyn clarified.

"I'm sorry, but we," she looked at Richard for confirmation and he gave her a smile of reassurance, "can't go on like this." Her voice softened. "We'd be very happy to have you stay, but it's time for Da-Marr to go home."

"If he goes, I go!" Evelyn threatened.

"We're sorry you feel that way," Richard said.

Evelyn stood. "I'll go pack our things right now. I

won't inflict my company on you any further. As soon as Da-Marr returns, we'll take a cab to a motel near the airport and be out of your hair."

"Evie, don't be like that," Brenda admonished, but Evelyn strode out of the study without another word.

Richard and Brenda looked at each other for long moments and then Brenda seemed to deflate, sinking onto the couch. "Well, I guess now we'll never be invited to visit the folks back in Philly."

"I'm sorry."

"I'm not," she said, and strangely enough, she didn't sound it. "I mean I am, but I'm not—if that makes sense. I love my parents—I miss them terribly, but they cut me off. And now I have a new family here. This is my home, and I don't appreciate others abusing it or my family."

Richard got up from his desk and came to sit beside her. "What a terrible day—for all of us. Evelyn included." He picked up Brenda's hand and kissed it. Then she met him halfway for a pretty decent kiss.

They gave each other a smile and settled back against the couch, both staring ahead at nothing."

"What are we going to do about my car?" Brenda asked. "Sometimes I get funny feelings like Jeffy does. I don't think Da-Marr is going to bring it back."

"I'm willing to take a wait-and-see attitude. If we don't hear from him by morning, we might have to do something—like call the cops, if only to report him as missing."

"I don't want to get Da-Marr in any more trouble than he's already in."

"And that's the problem; we don't know what he's up to, or who he's with."

"What if we don't find him? What if—"

"Don't borrow trouble," Richard admonished, but he couldn't help but feel the same way. "He hasn't got any money—that we know of—and there wasn't much gas in the tank."

"He doesn't even know our phone numbers, so he can't call—he doesn't have a cell phone. We're not in the phone book, so he wouldn't know how to get in touch with us."

"He could call his parents, and they could contact us. In fact, if he doesn't show up by morning, we ought to insist that Evelyn call them."

"She may not want to. She may feel she's failed him, and I don't think failure comes easily to her."

"Let's just wait and see," Richard again suggested.

The sound of a throat being cleared behind them caused them to look over their shoulders. Evelyn stood in the doorway, her head hanging.

"Evie, what's wrong?" Brenda asked, concerned.

"I—I didn't want to believe you," she said, looking at Richard. "I may have made a hasty judgment. I thought perhaps .... Well, it doesn't matter what I thought. But—" She took several steps into the room. "I was packing Da-Marr's clothes and I found this." She held out a plastic snack bag that was full of dried green leaves and a packet of rolling papers. "It was tucked into a pair of socks. I don't know what to say," she admitted, sounding defeated. "I thought that boy was on the right road. I thought I'd caught him in time. I thought...." Evelyn plodded over to the wing chair and nearly fell into it. "I've failed him."

"Oh, Evie," Brenda said, and struggled to lean forward enough to touch her sister's arm. "For what it's worth, I don't think Da-Marr's a lost cause. How can he be with you on his side?"

"If he was capable of this," she proffered the bag of weed, "then perhaps he is capable of tormenting Richard's brother, and other things I don't even want to contemplate."

Richard and Brenda shared a pained look.

"You met that young man Da-Marr met at the marina. He must have been the one who gave him the marijuana. Da-Marr didn't have any money—at least not that I know of."

"Da-Marr said his name was Bobby—he never mentioned a last name. He drove a gray Infinity. His father owns a boat at the marina. That's all I know."

Evelyn shook her head. "I'm sorry, Richard—about everything's that happened since we arrived. It's occurred to me that I haven't considered the situation from your brother's perspective. As far as I can see, he never provoked Da-Marr. And if he was viciously mugged as you say, then I guess I can understand why someone of Da-Marr's stature might seem intimidating."

"Thank you, Evelyn," Richard said sincerely.

Evelyn's lower lip trembled. "How can we find Da-Marr before something terrible happens to him? My goal was to keep him out of trouble so that he wouldn't be just another statistic."

"Well, when he finally does surface, it might be a good idea to ask him what he'd like to do with his life."

"What do you mean?" Evelyn asked, clueless.

"Did you know that the idea of fixing jet engines appeals to him?"

"Manual labor?" Evelyn said, appalled.

"Not everyone is cut out for a white-collar job. It still takes a college degree, and the wages are extremely competitive. Then maybe one day, if he's interested, he could move into to a management position within the airline industry. The thing is he seems to like to work with his hands. And letting him choose the kind of collegiate experience that would be of interest to him could be the motivating factor he needs to find success."

"Airplane engines?" Evelyn repeated in amazement.

"I'll bet Da-Marr would be one hell of a mechanic. Look at the way he fixed our old broken down lawnmower. He has a knack for such things. When he shows up, instead of pouncing on him for what he's done wrong, why not ask him what he'd like to do that's right?"

Evelyn thought about it for a long moment, then let out a long breath and shook her head. "I must admit, when I first arrived, I didn't think either of you were ready for parenthood, but after this conversation, I'm pretty sure that you'll make a terrific mom and dad. And—" she gazed at Brenda. "I really don't think you need me here at all, Twinnie."

Richard cast a glance toward his wife, and saw her eyes brim with tears. She and her twin had been identical and when the family couldn't tell them apart, they'd both affectionately been called Twinnie.

"You'll always be welcome in our home, Evie," Brenda said.

Evelyn smiled. "I know. But I believe you're right; Da-Marr and I need to go home. He and I—and his parents—have a lot to talk about." She got up, kissed Brenda on the top of the head, and left the room without a backward glance.

They listened until they heard Evelyn mount the stairs and was long out of earshot.

"Well, that was unexpected," Brenda said softly.

"It sure was," Richard agreed. "I wouldn't mind giving the kid a hand to go to school."

"Your own personal scholarship?"

"We've taken our time thinking about what to do with some of my grandparents' money. Why not establish a few scholarships for kids in need?"

"Here, or in Philly?" Brenda asked, sounding hopeful.

"Why not both?"

Brenda nodded, with the barest hint of a smile on her lips.

"But Da-Marr is still a wild card," Richard said with

resignation. "The way he took off, the people he's met here—we don't know what kind of trouble he's courting. And we don't know if we can rescue him if he's gotten himself into something illegal. We just don't know."

Brenda's head drooped, and for a moment Richard was sure she was once again about to cry. But then she seemed to shake herself. "I can't let him be my problem. He has family—and especially Evie—he can fall back on. Right now, I have to concentrate on our family." She patted her belly and smiled. "We haven't talked about god-parents."

"I kind of thought that was a given."

"Jeffy and Maggie?" Brenda asked.

"Of course."

Brenda smiled. "That means a party."

"We don't have a lot of people to invite."

"Who do we need to invite besides Jeffy and Maggie?" Brenda asked.

"Not one other person," Richard agreed. "But, I think a few of the foundation board members might feel slighted if I didn't at least ask them. And what about the girls at the clinic?"

"You're right. We do have more friends than we think. And I like the idea of a party. Any excuse for cake. You cannot have a decent celebration without cake."

"We'll get a ten-tiered one, if that's what you want."

"Oh, don't be ridiculous. A five-tier cake will suffice," she said and laughed.

"Coconut?" he suggested.

"How about every layer a different flavor?"

"As long as one of them is bland white, Jeff will be happy."

Brenda gathered up the loose skeins of yarn and her project and stuffed them back into her workbag. "It's bed-time, at least for this tired girl."

"I'll be up in a few minutes," Richard said, helped

Brenda to her feet, and then watched her waddle off in the direction of the stairs. In the meantime, he wondered if he should track down and check Brenda's purse to see if all the credit cards were intact. And if they weren't … well, then it would be time to make another decision.

A much harder one.

TWENTY-ONE

Once again, I left a sleeping Maggie and headed for home. It was just a lot easier on her come morning. Too bad I had to work the next couple of nights. That meant we'd hardly see each other on the weekend when she would finally have some time to devote to us.

It was long after midnight and I braked as I approached the bakery with the big blue sign. As I'd hoped, the light was on in the back of the shop. My friend and mentor, Sophie Levin, was waiting for me.

By the time I parked the car on the side street and walked back to the bakery, she was standing behind the big plate glass door.

"It's cold," she scolded. "Hurry and get inside."

I knew the cold wasn't likely to bother her. She just liked to kvetch. Once I was inside and she'd locked the door behind me, she led me through the shop to the back room where cups were waiting on the rocky card table, along with a plate of macaroons and a pile of paper napkins.

"Coffee tonight," she said, and poured water into the mugs from the small saucepan she'd had heating on a hotplate.

I sat in my usual rickety chair and waited for her to sit.

"So, it's about time you came to see me." She shook her head as she pushed the creamer across the table toward me.

"I didn't want to bother you."

"Nonsense. You know I *live* for you to bother me." Then she laughed.

"Very funny."

"I'm sorry. You have been very unhappy. I only want to ease your pain. I thought the two of us could talk about anything."

"We can. But we've been over this ground so many times, it seems like we're beating a dead horse."

"It will take you a long time to recover from the mugging. Not just the physical injury, but the emotional one as well. I speak from experience when I say sometimes, no matter how hard we try to deny it, we never really recover from these things."

I knew she was talking about her time in the concentration camp.

"But the person who's been tormenting you must have some goodness in him," she went on, this time pushing the plate of cookies toward me. She always says I don't eat enough.

"Could've fooled me," I said, bypassing the cookies and spooning some powered creamer into my coffee.

"Everyone, even a man like Jack Morrow, has some goodness in them."

How did she know about Jack Morrow?

"Oh, yeah? Enlighten me."

"I believe the man gave a great deal of money toward cancer research."

"That's all well and good, except the money wasn't his to give."

"Will they make the charity give it back?"

"I've heard of instances where they do just that."

"That wouldn't be good. Some good should come from that man's thievery."

I sipped my coffee. I couldn't argue with her on that

account.

"You should be very careful tomorrow."

"When I go to Morrow's offices?"

She nodded. She always knew what I was up to. Sometimes I felt like she had me under surveillance 24/7.

"I think it's a big waste of time."

"You do?" she asked skeptically.

"You don't?"

"What do I know?" she said with a shrug.

"You always seem to know a lot more than I do."

"Like you. Some things I know; some things I don't know. But I think you will succeed in what you want to find."

"Can you give me a clue as to where? It would save me a lot of time."

She shook her head and picked up her cup. "It's like I said. Some things I know, some I don't. What you find will not repay the millions upon millions lost. It's just a trifle. But there's a chance all could be lost, too. You must be very, very careful tomorrow."

I frowned. Her vague threats were irritating to say the least, but I knew enough to pay attention to them. The problem was, she could never tell me exactly what it was I was supposed to be looking out for. I decided to ask, anyway.

"So, what do I need to beware of?"

"What looks the most innocent could be the most dangerous. And what seems too dangerous to tackle, might be where you most need to concentrate your efforts."

Talk about a confounding riddle.

"You're not helping me."

Again she shrugged. "I wish I knew more. I only know what I feel. And I feel strongly about this."

Great. She felt strongly about something she couldn't put into words, and I didn't know what the hell she was talking about. I decided to change the subject. "Care to guess when Brenda's baby will be born?"

She thought about it. "Maybe tomorrow night … Saturday morning at the latest." She smiled. "She will be adorable. I would love to see pictures of her," she said wistfully.

"I'll bring some the next time I visit."

She frowned. "If you are able."

"What does that mean?"

"It means what it means."

I didn't like the sound of that.

"Drink up," she urged me, sounding solemn. "And eat a macaroon. You're far too skinny and I worry about you so."

I sipped my coffee and did not take one of the offered cookies. If it made me look like a petulant child, then so be it. I drained my cup and stood. "I'd better get going. I'll come back and see you in a couple of days."

Her dark eyes looked terribly sad. "If you're able."

"Will you stop with all the negativity? You're scaring me."

"I'm sorry," she apologized and pulled a used tissue from her sweater pocket to dab at her nose. "Just promise me you will be very careful, because if you're not...."

Was that some kind of a threat? That the white light would suck me into it and....

Now I was angry. "Good night, Sophie."

I heard the rustle of paper behind me as I started for the shop. She caught up with me at the door, unlocked it, and thrust a white bakery bag into my hands. She'd dumped the plate of macaroons in it. "Give me a kiss before you go," she ordered.

When I leaned down to kiss her cheek, she grabbed me in a fierce hug. "Do everything you can so that we do not meet on an equal plane tomorrow night."

I pulled back, "What do you mean?"

She shook her head. "There are things I'm not permitted to tell you."

"*Who* says you can't tell me?" I demanded.

She shook her head. "Nobody. But there are rules. There are constraints. It's nothing you are able to know or believe. But one thing you can believe in is the love I have for you. The love your brother has for you. The love that Brenda and Maggie have for you. All of us have one wish, and that's for you to be safe. But you have to work at it, too. It's not God-given."

"I don't believe in God."

"Then why did you consult a priest?" she demanded, sounding as angry as I'd ever heard her.

She had me there.

Was this a test of faith? She was a Jew who'd been incarcerated in a fucking concentration camp. My mother had been a staunch Catholic, which had been abhorrent to that side of the family. They'd never accepted her ... but was it her faith or her mental illness that had caused the rift? I only know that I'd been caught somewhere in the middle.

"I had to talk to someone."

"Then why didn't you come to *me?*" she cried, sounding terribly wounded.

"Because I was afraid."

"Of what?"

"That you'd tell me to embrace the light. To join my parents and all my other dead relatives. And I don't want to die!" I actually shouted at her.

Sophie's eyes blazed, and for a moment, I thought she might slap me, but then she turned away. "Nothing is certain. Tomorrow could be a turning point for you. I thought you should know. I am telling you to be careful. There is nothing else I can do to help—to protect—you." She turned back to face me, her glare menacing. "Do you understand?"

No! I wanted to scream. *Tell me more!* I almost demanded, but then I didn't.

I didn't want her to tell me my future. I didn't want to follow somebody else's script.

Whatever happened tomorrow, I was determined that it wasn't destiny that would rule my path. It was *me. My* decisions. *My* experience that would guide me to make the right choices at the right time.

When it came down to it, I trusted me more than I trusted anybody else on the planet—living or dead.

"I have to go," I said.

Sophie nodded. "I love you. If and when we meet again, you will at least know that."

If and when?

"I love you, too."

Her lips quirked into a lopsided smile. "Go home. Get a good night's sleep. I have a feeling you're going to need it."

"I have a feeling you're right."

We stared at one another for a long moment, and then both of us burst into laughter.

"I'm scheduled to work tomorrow, Saturday, and Sunday. I'll plan to come here on Monday. You will be here, won't you?" I asked.

"I already told you. I am here for you. I am *only* here for you."

"Then I'll see you on Monday. And I will bring pictures of the baby."

Sophie tilted her head, but said nothing.

Man, that made me feel like shit. That she believed I just might die.

I was not going to let her fears sway me.

Whatever happened tomorrow—happened.

"Good night," I said.

"Sweet dreams," she wished me.

I strode through the door and heard her turn the deadbolt after me.

I didn't look back and headed straight for my car. I

knew that when I drove to the corner that the bakery would again be dark. That there'd be no sign that anyone had been there during the preceding half-hour.

That it would be devoid of all life.

I drove home in silence, and when I opened the garage door to park my car I found one of the three bays open. Brenda's car was missing.

I knew that wasn't a good thing, and I also knew that Sophie's wish for me to sleep well wouldn't come to pass.

I just didn't know how the missing car would affect my life in the coming hours.

TWENTY-TWO

Once again Richard sat alone at the breakfast table. He'd checked the guest room before heading to the garage where he'd found his own car—and Jeff's—but Brenda's car was still among the missing. He was pondering the option of calling the police to report it—or Da-Marr—as missing when the phone rang. He snatched it up on the first ring.

"Hello."

"This is Officer Walther of the Grand Island Police Department. Is Ms. Brenda Stanley available?"

It was barely eight o'clock. "No, she's not. But I'm her husband. Have you found her car?"

"Yes, that's why I'm calling. It was found sitting alongside East River Road. Apparently it's been there since late yesterday afternoon."

"Has it been damaged?" Richard asked.

"No, but it's about to be towed. I'm calling to let Ms. Stanley know where she can pick it up." He gave the address of the impound lot.

"Thank you. I'll try to get out there later this morning to get it."

"You will have to pay a fee for us to release it."

"I'm aware of that. My wife won't be able to accompany me. Should I bring the registration?"

"Yes.

"Thank you." Richard hung up the phone and looked

over to the doorway where Evelyn stood in her robe and slippers. "I take it the car was found?"

He nodded.

"But no Da-Marr?"

"They said it had been abandoned. My guess is it ran out of gas. It was found not far from the marina where our boat is parked. I'll pick it up later today."

"Why would Da-Marr go there?"

Richard shrugged. "Would you like some coffee? I just made a fresh pot."

Evelyn shook her head, her eyes brimming with tears. "What am I going to tell Da-Marr's parents? They trusted him to my care."

"I have a feeling he's all right," Richard said dryly. He stepped over to the cupboard, grabbed a clean cup, filled it with coffee, and handed it to Evelyn. "Sit down. Would you like some breakfast? I'm not much of a cook, but I make a mean slice of toast."

She shook her head. "I can't eat. I'm too worried, but thank you for the coffee." She sat down at the kitchen table.

Richard pulled out the toaster and no sooner had he pushed the lever on two slices of white bread when Brenda showed up as well. "No word yet?" she asked, eyeing her sister, who dabbed at her eyes with a balled-up tissue.

"The Grand Island police found your car, but no sign of Da-Marr."

Brenda nodded.

"Coffee?" Richard offered.

"Please."

Richard got another cup, poured, and handed it to her along with a spoon. She doctored it the way she liked it. The toast popped up, and he buttered it, then handed it, too, to Brenda, who smiled gratefully.

"I had better call Da-Marr's parents."

"Why don't you wait until after I go to the marina? He said he made a friend there. I'm willing to bet he stayed with that friend, or maybe on his boat, since ours is..." he didn't want to admit to Evelyn it had been vandalized. "...not ready for an overnight stay."

"Very well. But if you can't find him, then I will have to call his parents. I just don't know what I'll say to them."

"Evie, Da-Marr may have already called them," Brenda said, and took a bite of toast.

Evelyn shook her head. "Florence would have called me if he had. She didn't want him to make this trip with me, but Martin thought it would be good for the boy." Again she shook her head, and wiped at the tears that had formed in her eyes once more.

"I'll see if Jeff will drive me to pick up the car. That way you'll have mine in case—" In case Brenda needed Evelyn to drive her to the hospital to give birth. This was not the way he'd intended to spend the day.

Brenda nodded.

"I'll call him from my study," he said, and left the sisters to sit in awkward silence.

Thanks to blackout blinds, I was usually able to sleep in after late-night shifts at the bar. That is if I wasn't awakened by the bloody phone ringing at way too early o'clock.

It rang, waking me with a start. I let it ring until voice mail took the call. I rolled over, intending to go back to sleep, when it rang again. Again, I let it roll over to voice mail, and cursed whoever was on the other end of the line.

When it rang for a third time, I figured I had better pick up. "Yeah?"

"We're good to go to visit Morrow's office. Can you meet me there about nine forty-five?"

It took a few moments for me to realize it was Sam speaking.

"What?"

"Can you meet me there?"

Sophie's warning came back to me. "I guess," I said without enthusiasm.

"Great. There's a ramp garage nearby. It's within walking distance from my office, so I'll meet you in the lobby."

"Fine." I already knew we weren't going to find Morrow's treasure at that locale, but I had a feeling we might learn something pertinent, and anything that brought us closer to finishing this unsatisfying romp would be welcome.

"And the address is?"

He gave it to me. "See you there." Sam sounded enthusiastic, and I felt anything but.

I put the phone down, determined to put in another hour of shuteye when it rang again. I felt like tossing the wireless receiver across the room, but instead hit the talk button once again.

"Jeff, it's Richard."

"I kind of figured as much. Why are *you* calling at the crack of dawn?" I squinted at my clock. "Okay, the hour *after* the crack of dawn."

"Da-Marr took Brenda's car and didn't come home."

"I knew that."

"Yeah, well, the cops found it abandoned near the marina. I need to pick it up. Can you drive me?"

"I guess," I said, and rolled onto my back. So much for going back to sleep.

"Da-Marr might be at the marina. If he isn't—we've got one last shot at playing with the boat before it's mothballed for the winter. Are you game?" Richard said.

I didn't want to appear too eager so merely replied, "Okay."

"The thing is," Richard began. "What if we find him there?"

"Then I'll leave and he can drive home with you," I groused.

"I know he threatened you. I know he's been a real bastard to you, but I think the talks we've had since he arrived might have made a difference." He let out a breath. "Maybe I'm living in a fantasy world, but I *want* to believe they might have made a difference to him."

I can't read Richard in a psychic sense, but I could hear by the timbre of his voice that he fervently believed what he'd said.

In the grand scheme of things, Da-Marr was a nonentity ... at least in Richard's and Brenda's lives. The yawning white hole of death was still a specter that haunted my dreams and waking hours. I already knew my unborn niece ... I knew so much about her and who she would become in a future yet to unfold ... but I wasn't at all sure I'd be there to witness and share her life. The thought left me bereft.

Damn this erratic psychic ability I seemed to be cursed with!

Richard still waited for me to respond.

The thought of going out on the boat with that loose cannon of a kid made my chest constrict. And yet ... I knew it meant a lot to Richard. He had reached out to the kid—like he'd done for me. Had he made a difference in the kid's life? He wanted to believe so, and I guess I could at least give Richard that.

I felt myself giving in. "What the hell."

"Thank you."

"I just got off the phone with Sam. He wants me to check out an office."

"What for?" he asked, annoyed.

"He's looking for treasure—in all the wrong places. I'll probably be back by noon. Is that soon enough?"

"Yeah. You can tell me what you're up to on the way there." He didn't sound pleased.

"Fine." Why did I keep saying that when I felt anything but fine about the demands other people were making of my time?

"Talk to you later," he said and hung up.

There was no reason for me to stay in bed, since I was never going to get back to sleep. I got up and headed for the kitchen to make a pot of coffee when I caught sight of the bag of macaroons on the counter. Breakfast. Thank you, Sophie.

I frowned as I measured the coffee into the filter basket. Why had Sophie been so damned enigmatic hours before—hinting I wasn't going to be around to bring her pictures of the baby? But then I remembered I'd broken my camera. Was that what she'd meant? I preferred to think so, but wasn't going to pin my hopes on it, either.

Her words came back to me: *What looks the most innocent could be the most dangerous. And what seems too dangerous to tackle, might be where you most need to concentrate your efforts.*

What was the more innocent destination—Morrow's office or Richard's boat? But she'd also implied that it was the evening that held danger.

I grabbed a mug from the cabinet and poured the coffee. I had a whole day in front of me that would be danger free and therefore was determined not to worry about it, hoping it wouldn't be a fatal mistake.

TWENTY-THREE

The Banyon Building had been built back in the 1920s and was one of Buffalo's Art Deco gems. The lobby had never been stripped of its architectural features, nor had it ever fallen into disrepair. Sam had plunked himself on one of the velvet upholstered chairs and was checking his emails as I approached. It took him a few moments to realize I stood before him.

"Right on time," he said with a smile. "Are you up for this?"

"I'm just peachy. Are we meeting the real estate agent upstairs?"

He stood. "Yeah."

We started for the bank of elevators with their elaborate bronze doors etched with geometric lines and scrollwork. "What's our cover story?" I asked.

"None. When it comes to high-priced real estate, they do a pretty thorough background check. They don't want to waste time with jokers who can't pay the freight."

"How are you going to explain me?" I asked and pushed the UP button.

"I'm not. If pressed, you're either a colleague or a consultant. Take your pick."

The doors opened and two women got off before we could get on. Sam pressed the button for the tenth floor and the doors closed.

"Are you using your brother's season tickets for the

Bills game on Sunday?" he asked.

"Can't." *I might be dead,* I thought sadly. "The baby's coming tonight or early tomorrow. It would be hard for Rich to leave Brenda the day after."

"I've got nothing going on. It would be a shame to let them go unused," he said wistfully.

"It sure would," I said non-committedly.

The doors opened and we stepped out. It looked like Morrow Securities had leased the entire floor. Double frosted-glass doors bore no mention of its last occupants. We could see the silhouette of someone standing behind them. Sam pulled on the handle and it opened.

A well-dressed man in his late twenties turned to face us.

"Sam Nielsen. And you must be Eric Armstrong?" Sam asked, offering his hand.

The man held out his hand. "No. Eric couldn't make it. He asked me to talk to you and show you around. My name is Harry Morrow."

"Jack Morrow's son?" I asked, taken aback.

"The same."

It was his picture in one of the frames at the auction. Had he been the one who'd held the chalk? I stuck out my hand to shake hands. "Jeff Resnick, I'm a colleague of Sam's."

Harry Morrow briefly clasped my hand. I held on a little too long and he pulled away, looking uncomfortable.

Nothing. I got absolutely nothing from him.

"So, what are you doing here—just background for a story?"

Sam nodded. "We didn't expect to find anything here in the office, but I had an idea that maybe we could soak up the vibes in what used to be your father's offices." He shot an amused look at me.

"My dad was responsible for the Ponzi scheme. He took the blame, denying anyone else was involved, but he couldn't have done it alone. He had to have had help. Whoever killed him probably figured he'd eventually crack. Maybe for a plea bargain—or the possibility of parole somewhere down the line for naming names."

"You think?" I asked.

Harry shrugged. "It doesn't really matter. Dad's dead, and the police say they have no leads." He eyed Sam. "Do you?"

"Sorry. Not yet. But it can't hurt to keep digging. Sometimes the truth manifests itself in unexpected ways." Again, he looked at me.

"Several people have come around to inspect the place looking for buried treasure—as if the bank and IRS haven't already grabbed everything."

"How are you making out?" Sam asked.

"They can't take my education away from me, but I had to leave my last job because of the scandal. I'm lucky to have a few friends—and their parents—who didn't invest with my dad's company."

"Do you mind if we walk around and look the place over while we talk?" I asked Harry. This was probably a wasted trip and I didn't want to spend more time than I needed to. Richard would probably prefer me to show up sooner rather than later.

"Sure," he agreed. He was being awfully nice to us. I would have expected some belligerence. Of course, he could be feeding us a line of bullshit, too. Since I'd gotten nothing from him, it was impossible to tell.

We wandered from what must have been the reception area to a conference room. Sam and Harry hung back, while I entered it. A few sheets of paper littered the floor. I picked one up and glanced at it; a printed handout from the real estate company handling the property someone had discarded. I folded it and stuck it in my pocket to study later.

"So you never worked for your father?" Sam asked.

"No. He was adamant about it. I guess he always knew the scheme would fail and he didn't want me tainted by—" He left the sentence hanging.

I sidled past them and continued down the corridor, looking into an empty, glassed-in office, so much nicer—and bigger—than the cell I'd occupied when I'd worked in Manhattan.

Walking through the office made me feel itchy, like I'd suddenly developed a rash, but I pulled up my left sleeve and didn't see anything. It had to be the place. But what was it that was trying to get under my skin?

I entered another of the empty offices. There were no windows; nothing but marks on the carpet where the furniture had stood and a flattened area where a sheet of plastic had protected the rug from the office chair's rollers.

I left the office and tried several more. It seemed the farther I went along the corridor, the more I wanted to scratch. Invisible fleas?

I looked back. Sam and Harry still stood outside the conference room, conversing. I went back to snooping.

When I came to an intersecting corridor, I turned left. At the end of the hall was a large wooden door—cherry?—buffed to perfection. It had to have been Morrow's office.

The door handle turned easily and I entered. Like all the rest of the offices, it was empty, but since I was already familiar with Jack Morrow's presence—aura, whatever—the place practically buzzed. A bank of windows faced west. In the distance, I could see the harbor, and I wondered if Richard should have chosen to rent a boat slip there instead of on Grand Island. A wide slab of marble sat atop the long sill. I plunked my ass down. Morrow had sat there on many occasions, looking down on Franklin Street while he'd talked on the phone. Had he ever conversed with his killer from that vantage point? I reached into my pocket and extracted the billiards chalk, holding it tight in my right hand, but got no sense of Morrow.

Something flashed. I looked out the window, confused. It wasn't even noon. The sun wouldn't swing around until later in the afternoon.

The flash came again, and I realized it wasn't physical light that had burst before my mind's eye.

A bright, white light.

Light. Like in my out-of-body experience.

It freaked me, so much so that I dropped the chalk.

I bent to pick it up, and the light flashed again. But different this time—more a sparkle.

Great. Was I going to start having flashbacks—or were they flash forwards?—on a regular basis? I could crash my car if it happened while driving. Just what I needed.

I thought back to what Sophie had told me much earlier that morning. *What looks the most innocent could be the most dangerous. And what seems too dangerous to tackle, might be where you most need to concentrate your efforts.*

I looked around the empty office. It seemed innocent enough. Well, depending on your point of view. Morrow had cheated thousands of people from this very room. Did that make the space as guilty as he'd been?

I looked out the office window and watched the traffic crawl along Franklin Street. For all the time we'd spent together these past few days, Sam and I hadn't talked about the missing assets all that much. He'd mentioned stamps, or bank accounts in foreign countries, but I got the feeling Morrow, who had filled his home with artwork and other beautiful items, would have wanted to have his booty nearby so he could admire it.

Could he have accumulated gold coins? Outside of Fort Knox with its gold bars, did people keep gold ingots? Would Sam know? If not, I supposed a Google search would fill me in. Would I have time to do so before I had to drive Richard to pick up Brenda's car?

"There you are," Sam said.

I looked up to find the two of them standing in front of the open door.

"Here I am," I agreed.

"I take it this was your father's office?" Sam asked.

Harry nodded. "I came here to visit many times. We'd have lunch by the window. He said he didn't have time to go out. He said his work was too important to waste on frivolous matters."

Did that include spending time with his son?

"So how did he relax?" Sam asked.

"He took vacations with Bonnie—my stepmother—usually at the Cayman house. But he always took his work with him. All of his residences had fully functional offices. They entertained clients a lot back in the days when they all loved him. He'd take them to a variety of venues—some he owned and some he rented. It depended on the audience and how much he wanted to impress them."

"You loved your father and miss him," I guessed.

A blush colored the younger man's cheeks. "Yes, I do. I never had a clue about his illegal business practices. To me he was just dad, and even though he wasn't the best father in the world, he tried to carve out time for my sister and me. I think he wanted the best for us, and I know when his empire came crashing down he was ashamed for us—for how we might be judged for his actions."

"Do you believe the feds have found all his assets?" Sam asked.

Harry shrugged. "Who knows? If they're out there, I certainly don't know about them, and neither does my sister," he added pointedly.

I studied Harry's expression. I didn't get a psychic signature from him, but I believed him.

"We should get going," I told Sam.

He nodded.

I left my perch and followed them back to the reception area. Harry locked up the office and the three of us headed for the elevator. "How 'bout those Bills?" Sam asked.

"My Dad had a box at the stadium," Harry said wistfully. "That's gone, too."

"Jeff's brother has season tickets. We might go to the game on Sunday, right Jeff?"

I ignored his second hint for the tickets.

The elevator brought us back to the lobby.

"Nice meeting you, Harry. Thanks for talking to us," Sam said and shook his hand.

I did likewise, and once again got no sense of who this guy was. He gave us both a smile before he turned and headed for the exit. I made to follow when Sam's voice stopped me.

"So what do you get from him?"

"Absolutely nothing. Why do you think he showed up instead of the real estate agent?"

"Probably to get a feel for how I'd portray his father. He'd prefer a sympathetic angle."

"Can you blame him?"

Sam frowned. "Hang on a minute while I call the real estate agent. We have no clue if that guy actually was Morrow's son or if he was blowing smoke up our asses." He pulled out his phone and walked a few steps away. I moved to the big plate glass windows at the front of the lobby and looked for Harry Morrow. There weren't many people on the sidewalk, but he was already out of sight.

Sam's call didn't take long, and he soon rejoined me. "He was the real thing," he said, which I already knew. "Armstrong described him to a T. It just seems odd that he was so willing to talk." He shook his head. "You said you got nothing from him?"

"Not a thing. But I'm also sure he wasn't the one who

held that billiards chalk when playing pool with Jack Morrow."

"I asked him about it. He said he hates the game, but his father would snag anyone who came in the door—guests, friends, relatives—to play. Morrow liked to make it more interesting with a side wager—and he usually won."

"Do you think the person who killed him was a disgruntled pool player?" I asked skeptically.

Sam shook his head. "But say the topic of hidden assets came up while they played. Did Morrow brag about how he'd outfoxed his creditors and the IRS? Everyone I've spoken to said the guy had a big personality, that he liked to brag. It wouldn't be the first time a tall tale got a guy killed."

"Maybe."

"Did you learn anything from coming here today?" Sam asked, sounding a little desperate.

"What do you know about diamonds?"

"Diamonds?" he asked, his eye growing wide.

"I'm not saying I got anything solid, but when I was in Morrow's office I got a couple of flashes of—" It wasn't really insight. "Of something. And when I thought about it, I thought of diamonds."

"Hidden in the office somewhere?"

"No, definitely not. And I get the feeling they weren't in his home, either. They'd be somewhere he considered safe, but he never got a chance to retrieve them, and I haven't got a clue where that could be, either."

"You're not being all that helpful."

I shrugged. "Sorry. It's the best I can do. But maybe if we go to enough places I'll soak up something else and figure it out."

"I'm running out of ideas," Sam admitted. He let out a long breath. "I'll do some more digging and get back to you by Monday at the latest. That is, of course, unless you want to call me to join you at the game on Sunday."

"Don't push it," I warned him.

He shrugged. "It isn't sold out, so it won't be on TV. You can't blame a guy for trying."

"What's your next line of inquiry?" I asked.

"I'll spend the weekend rereading my notes. I've got a hunch there's something we've overlooked."

"I'm the one who's supposed to have hunches."

"Then reconsider everything we've looked at. Maybe you'll come up with something."

"Okay. But right now I've got another errand to attend to."

"Anything interesting?"

I shook my head. "Just something my brother needs help with."

"Remember, I'm free all day Sunday if you want to contact me," he said with another not-so-subtle hint for Richard's Bills tickets.

"I'll keep that in mind."

We headed for the exit.

"Later," I called, and Sam gave me a wave before we separated. I had a lot to consider that weekend, but was determined to put Jack Morrow and his hidden assets at the bottom of my list. I was supposed to work on Sunday evening. I might be able to fudge an hour so and go to the game, but I hated to even mention the tickets that would probably go unused. Then again, Richard would probably rather see them used. I'd wait until Sunday morning to ask him about it.

I stopped dead on the sidewalk as Sophie's warning once again bombarded my thoughts. I might not be alive on Sunday.

Thanks, Sophie. Thanks a lot.

I'd barely been home a minute—and hadn't had time to change into my grungies—when Richard showed up at my door. I let him in. "Ready to go?" he asked.

"No. Give me a minute, will you?"

I went into my bedroom and he waited in the living room. "I've got two worried women on my hands," he called out.

"What?"

"Brenda is about ready to jump out of her skin. If this baby doesn't come this weekend, she wants to be induced."

"I have it on good authority that the baby will be here before the game on Sunday."

"Damn. We're going to miss it. Why couldn't the team be on the road this week?" he groused.

"Sam has already begged me for the tickets."

"Do you want them?"

"I wouldn't mind going. Maybe I can get Sam to buy the beer." Of course, that was supposing I was still alive come game time. Damn you, Sophie, for being so enigmatic.

"Then they're yours," he said as I came back into living room, carrying my sneakers. I sat down on the couch and put them on. He'd already grabbed my denim jacket from the coat closet and held it out for me. "Let's go."

The sunny weather was holding when, a minute later, we were pulling out of the driveway and heading for the marina. Richard spent the next twenty minutes giving me a blow-by-blow description of his discussions with Evelyn about Da-Marr. I wanted to hear that like I wanted a tooth pulled and barely paid attention, thinking about what I'd learned that morning and hoping I didn't experience any more of those annoying flashes of light.

Our first stop was the Grand Island police impound lot. The tow job had cost a hell of a lot more than if Richard had been given the option of a Triple A tow and, as he expected, he found Brenda's gas tank dry. The sky seemed to darken as I drove to the nearest gas station, paid an outrageous deposit on a five-gallon jug, and then returned to the lot to dump the gas in Brenda's tank. Richard followed me back to the station where my credit card was refunded and then he filled the tank. By that time, it was nearly two.

"Did you eat breakfast?" Richard asked.

"A couple of cookies."

"That's more than I had. I'm starved. I think there's a diner down the road. Are you up for it?"

"Why not?"

I followed him to the diner. It was busy, and obviously filled with the local retired population. The young skinny waitress, dressed in dark pants and a white shirt, brought us some menus and upended the coffee cups before us on the paper placemats, pouring before I had a chance to stop her. I would have preferred a beer.

"I'll be back to take your order in a couple of minutes," she promised and commenced to pour more coffee for the people at the next table.

We perused the menu for less than thirty seconds before we both set them aside, and then Richard and I sat and looked at each other. It reminded me of the time we'd hit a diner before we went to spill our guts to the investigating detective in the Matt Sumner murder. But this was different. Thank God, this time we weren't going on a mission to reveal a killer. But then Sophie's warning came back to haunt me once again.

Damn her.

I needed to distract myself. I added a container of half-and-half to my coffee and took a sip. "You're a rich guy. Have you got any hidden assets?"

"Only in my underwear," he said with a wry smile.

"Seriously, have you ever thought about hiding assets?"

"What for? I have more money than I can possibly ever use. I've been giving it away and intend to do more of it in the near future."

"Okay, but say you did want to hide it. What would you do?"

He shrugged and picked up his cup. "I might buy gold coins, or jewelry. But then I'd have to worry about it being stolen. Insurance might be a nightmare."

He thought too practically. I needed a little creativity here. I thought about the flashing light. How it had sparkled. "What about diamonds?"

He shrugged. "The diamond market has changed since DeBeers lost the worldwide monopoly."

"Who did what? And how do you know about it?"

He frowned. "I read. DeBeers used to control nearly all the diamonds sold in the world. That was before lucrative mines were discovered in Russia, Australia, and even Canada. Still, the bigger the uncut diamond, the more it might be worth when it comes time to shape it. Big uncut stones are becoming a rare commodity, you know."

"No, I didn't." And I wasn't sure I wanted to know it. "What about cut stones?"

He shrugged. "It depends on their size and clarity. Why are you so interested in all of this?"

"It's something Sam and I have been looking into."

"Yeah, you were going to tell me all about it."

I took another sip of coffee. He wasn't going to like this. "Sam's doing a story on Jack Morrow."

"The racketeer who was shot to death?" he asked, his voice rising. He definitely didn't like this. "Please tell me you're not looking for his killer."

"We're not looking for his killer. Although if we found him, Sam would probably dance a jig. We're actually looking for his missing assets."

"And you think they might be diamonds?"

"No. Well, not really. I was thinking maybe gold. But we haven't found anything concrete."

"I wish you'd stop looking. It's dangerous. You've had a rotten week and you deserve some peace." He lowered his voice. "We both know that invoking this psychic crap really takes a toll on you. Please drop it."

I wasn't sure I could. Not with the debt I still owed Sam.

The waitress arrived, giving me the out I needed.

"Grilled cheese and tomato soup," I said.

"A Reuben," Richard said.

She collected our menus. "They'll be out in a couple minutes."

Richard nodded, and picked up his cup once more. "I didn't think to check the boat's fuel tank the last time we used it. We might have to top it up, but I don't want to get too much diesel. I'm not even sure if they drain the tank before they put the boat in storage. We've got so much to learn."

"You said this was our last chance to run it."

"Everything's got to be out of the marina before the end of next week. The baby will be here any minute, so after we're done with our ride today, I'm going to tell them to do whatever it is they do. I've seen a lot of boats with shrink wrap. I guess I'll go for it, even though it'll be stored in a building off-site."

"You went for that? What did Brenda say?"

"I didn't bother her with the details."

And probably for good reason.

As promised, our food arrived quickly and we dug in. For someone who had wanted to take one last boat ride of the season, Richard seemed antsy—as though he wanted to get this over with. This was going to be my first and last chance of the year to drive the thing and I intended to milk it for all I could. After all, if Sophie's rather vague but dire prediction came true, it might be the last fun thing I got to do.

Had she seen a boating accident in my future?

Surely, she would have said.

I chewed my sandwich a little slower.

Richard finished long before me, and in fact, I just gave up and pushed my untouched soup away. He paid the tab and we started off for the marina once again.

We got separated at the next traffic light, and I arrived at the marina before Richard did. I got out of the car and planted my butt against the warm metal of the driver's side door. The wan sun ducked behind yet another cloud, one of many that seemed to be gathering in the west and north.

As I waited, I wondered again about the life jackets. I hadn't seen them the last time we'd been onboard. I remembered Sophie's worried face and I wondered if we ought to pick up a couple before we took off. As soon as Richard arrived, I asked him about it.

"Good idea," he said. "You go on ahead and I'll get some from the marine store."

"Okay."

We split up. As I walked along the wide dock, I noted that there were only four other boats left in their slips, including the one Da-Marr had been aboard several days earlier.

A cold wind blew off the water, and I found myself walking slower as I approached Richard's boat. Sophie's warning buzzed through my mind like an angry insect— a bee or a wasp—just as deadly.

The smoky glass doors made it difficult to see into the salon, so I backed up a few feet until I was in line with the starboard side window and definitely saw movement within. Damn that Da-Marr. He turned, saw me, and I could see rage unfold across his features. He charged for the sliding glass door to the deck, shoving it back with such force I was sure it would shatter.

"What are you doing here?" he demanded.

"I could ask you the same thing."

"Go!"

"Who the hell do you think you are ordering me around? First you steal Brenda's car—that's grand theft auto—and now you're trespassing."

"Get the fuck away from here!" he hollered even louder.

Although I was sick of letting this petty thug intimidate me, I backed up a few paces. For such a big guy, Da-Marr was fast. In one fantastic leap, he made it over the side of the boat and onto the dock.

I flashed back to the mugging.

The baseball bat came arcing toward me.

I raised my arm to stave off the blow.

Da-Marr grabbed hold of my jacket, knocking me off balance, and hauled me back toward the boat. Stunned, I had no time to offer resistance as he tossed me onto the deck. I smacked my head so hard I saw stars and time seemed to stop. I was vaguely aware of him rifling through my pockets until he'd fleeced me of my keys.

"Don't move!" he shouted.

I could barely think, let alone move.

I heard a noise that took me far too long to identify.

Rolling over on my side, I managed to pull myself into a sitting position, and realized the boat was bobbing. The powerful diesel engines fired up, and suddenly we were moving away from the dock.

What the hell?

I looked up to the bridge deck to see Da-Marr at the boat's controls.

"Da-Marr!"

I looked back at the rapidly retreating dock where Richard stood holding onto a couple of orange life jackets. "Da-Marr, wait!" he hollered, panic-stricken. He tossed the life jackets onto the dock and started running. "Jeff! Jump—jump!" he hollered, but my head was still spinning. He was gaining on us, and when he got to the end of the dock he dove in—just as Da-Marr hit the throt-tle. The momentum knocked me over. By the time I crawled to my knees to look over the back of the boat, all I could see was the top of Richard's head in the water as we sped away.

TWENTY-FOUR

"What the fuck are you doing?" an unfamiliar voice shouted.

The engines cut back, but Da-Marr stayed at the controls. "We almost got caught."

I looked at the open door to the salon and saw a vaguely familiar figure—a skinny white guy, older than Da-Marr by a few years—step onto the deck. I'd seen him somewhere but couldn't place him, and yet I knew who he was—but not his name. Clutched in his hand was a large Philips screwdriver. He looked down at me in anger. "Who the hell are you?"

I swallowed—didn't answer. Understanding dawned as I realized that Easy Breezin' had to have been Jack Morrow's boat—one of three that the IRS had confiscated. One of three sold at auction. Why the hell did Richard have to pick this damn boat?

The engines began to idle, and Da-Marr trundled down the stairs from the bridge deck.

"He's the asshole brother of the dude that owns this boat."

"What's he doing here?"

"I figured if he was at the marina, so was the brother and we'd get caught. I ain't goin' to jail for this."

"For what? What are you looking for, boys? Something shiny?" I asked.

Whitey turned abruptly. "What do you mean?"

"Diamonds. Isn't that what you're searching for? Isn't that what you were searching for when you ruined the salon's upholstery the other day?"

Da-Marr looked scared; despite the stiff wind, his upper lip had beaded with sweat. "Shit. How did you know about that?"

"I know a lot of things—especially about Jack Morrow." I turned to Whitey. "About how you two used to play pool at his house. How you let him beat you every time."

"Who the hell are you?" he demanded again, growing angrier.

"I told you," Da-Marr said. "And he don't know nothing."

"Don't give me that shit. You squealed. Who'd you tell?" Whitey demanded.

"I swear, Bobby, I told nobody." He glared down at me. "Especially not this pussy."

Bobby glared at me, convulsively clenching the screwdriver, thinking things over.

The boat began to drift north with the current, waves smacking the sides as it bobbed.

Finally, Bobby nodded at me. "Get up."

"What you gonna do?" Da-Marr asked, fear creeping into his voice.

Bobby ignored him. "I said get up!"

Holding onto the end of the boat, I struggled to my feet.

"If you know so much, you can lead us to the diamonds."

"That's one secret Jack Morrow never shared with me."

"He's lying," Da-Marr said. "He never knew the guy. Richard said they didn't know who owned the boat before him."

"I'm not taking any chances," Bobby said. He stood

back and motioned me to enter the salon.

Richard was right. I should have jumped overboard. Bobby could easily stab me with the screwdriver and toss me over the side anyway. It made sense to bide my time.

I hoped.

I stepped forward and Bobby grabbed my jacket.

The baseball bat arced toward me, and I raised my arm to protect my head.

Bobby shoved me into the salon that bore no resemblance to the peaceful sanctuary of leather and cherry wood I had known only days before. Everything had been dismantled. Holes had been punched into the walls and ceiling, and I saw the baby sledgehammer that had been responsible for the destruction lying on the floor.

The microwave had been ripped from its housing, its case removed. The two-burner ceramic range had been smashed, no doubt another victim of baby sledge. The Corian counters were gone, and I had a feeling they lay at the bottom of the marina, too bulky to throw into the dumpster, and too heavy to have to move, they'd probably slid into the water the night before, on the port side and out of range of the dockside security cameras.

Now that I knew about the diamonds, and that this was Morrow's boat, I thought I knew where they might be hidden—in the tidy engine room. But there was no way I wanted to go down there. It would be too easy for them to kill me once the stones were found. Then what would they do?

The boat continued to drift north, and I knew what lay ahead if we didn't stop moving in that direction; something enormously big, with a very long drop.

"Da-Marr, get this boat out of the middle of the river and find us a place to hide," Bobby ordered.

Da-Marr looked uncertain, but nodded, and headed up the stairs once again for the bridge deck. Bobby shoved me toward the master stateroom. "Get moving."

As I started to move, the Slipstream's engines thrummed to life below us once more.

My heart sank at the sight of what had once been a sumptuous respite. The queen-size bed took up ninety-percent of the tiny bedroom, or at least it had. That was before the mattress had been reduced to the consistency of shredded wheat. The platform had been reduced to tinder—out of spite, no doubt. As in the salon, there were holes punched in all the walls and Fiberglass ceiling, and even the flat-screen TV attached to the wall opposite the bed had been smashed in what was probably frustration at not finding Morrow's treasure.

"So where is Jack's stash?" Bobby demanded.

"It's not in here," I said, and turned to face him. For a moment, I thought he might hit me, but then his lips turned up into a smarmy smile.

"Are the diamonds here on the boat?" Bobby asked, his tone menacing.

"What made you think they were?"

"Because Easy Breezin' was the thing Jack loved most. Even more than that whore he married ten years ago. Crap, that bitch couldn't wait to leave the country with everything she could lay her hands on. She never took to heart the phrase stand by your man. But Jack was arrested before he could get the stones. The feds took the boats the next day."

"Are you a friend of Harry's?" I asked. Bobby looked to be about the same age as Harry, but not nearly as sophisticated. Had he been a schoolmate who hadn't been privy to the money and status Harry had enjoyed and resented him for it—enough to kill because of it?

"Friend?" he repeated in disgust. "Harry wouldn't know the meaning of the word."

That wasn't the impression I'd received from the younger Mr. Morrow. He'd seemed like a decent enough guy who'd been shamed by his unrepentant father, and yet … when I thought about him, I got the impression he'd loved his father unconditionally. My mother was a drunk and the worst excuse for motherhood to set foot on the planet, and yet I'd felt the same way about her. I hadn't always liked her, but I had loved her. The more I looked at Bobby, things I'd been feeling when touching the chalk seemed to coalesce within my mind. He'd been jealous of the Morrows' wealth. He hadn't been Harry's friend—more like a hanger-on. He'd shown up at the Morrow home even after his friendship with Harry had waned, after high school or college—I wasn't quite sure which.

"Da-Marr thinks you're Morrow's son," I said, as I bent down to look through the litter on the floor.

"So what?"

I straightened. "What will happen when he finds out you aren't?"

"It doesn't matter. He's going to have a mysterious accident."

My stomach did a flip-flip. "You don't leave witnesses," I stated.

Bobby smiled. "No, I don't."

Was he underestimating Da-Marr? Or had he brought along the gun he'd used to splatter Morrow's brains across the Lexus?

"What you're looking for obviously isn't in here," I said, keeping my voice level.

"I've spent the last eighteen hours tearing this boat apart. They're here, I just haven't found them yet."

"What if you're wrong?"

"You'd better hope I'm right."

I shook my head. "You already said you don't leave witnesses."

The smarmy smile returned. "Get to work."

"Doing what? How are you going to find the diamonds when you can't move around in here?"

"Then you can start dropping the stuff into the river

to give us room."

That wasn't a bad idea. If someone on shore saw us dumping junk overboard, they could call the Niagara County Sheriff's Office marine patrol. Then again, what awaited us north of Grand Island could be lethal.

I grabbed an abundant armful of what had once been mattress stuffing and shuffled out the stateroom, into the salon and out onto the deck. As I tossed it overboard, I scanned both shores.

Not a boat in sight.

The engines below my feet stopped dead.

Bobby looked up to the bridge deck. "What the hell are you doing?"

"Nothing." Then Da-Marr let loose with a blue cloud of profanity. "We're out of gas."

"Are you shitting me?" Bobby asked.

"No!"

Bobby left me, taking the steps to the bridge deck two at a time.

I looked back to the salon. Unfortunately, the radio was upstairs on the bridge deck. Would it even be intact, or had they already destroyed some of the dashboard looking for the diamonds? We were caught in the current, drifting north again. I reached into my pocket and pulled out my cell phone. There were cell towers along the shore, but was I close enough to get a signal? Yes! I punched in 911, and seconds later a dispatcher came on the line.

"Please state the nature of your emergency."

"I'm on a boat in the Niagara River and—"

A hard shove nearly sent me overboard. My phone went straight into the drink.

"What the hell are you doing?" Bobby demanded. I hadn't heard him come back down the stairs.

"What did it look like I was doing?"

Bobby punched me hard in the gut and I fell to my

knees. Then he kicked me, his heavy boot smashing into my left knee.

"Hey!" Da-Marr hollered. "Stop it. Stop it!" He grabbed the back of Bobby's shirt and hauled him away from me.

Bobby turned on him. "Don't you touch me!"

Da-Marr backed up a step, looking scared. "What in hell is with you?"

"Drop the anchor. We've got to stop the boat and figure out what we're going to do next."

"Anchor?" Da-Marr repeated stupidly. "I don't know where the control is."

Bobby shoved him aside and started up the steps to the bridge once more. Da-Marr watched him go up, then turned for me.

The thug came at me with the baseball bat, this time with intent to kill.

I ducked my head for the blow, but instead Da-Marr grabbed me by the front of my jacket and helped me to my feet. "That fucker's crazy," he grated and looked back to the bridge deck. "We gotta do something, man." He turned back to face me. "You got any ideas?"

Could I trust him? He'd threatened me. Terrorized my cat. Filled my apartment with deadly wasps.

I took a chance. "Does he have a phone?"

"I don't know."

I bit my lip and looked toward the north, where the sky was growing darker over Lake Ontario.

"Do you know where the diamonds are?" Da-Marr asked.

"No," I said, not sure if I was telling the truth.

"Holy Christ!" Bobby nearly screamed from the helm. "Da-Marr, bring that fuckhead up here."

"You know any more about running this boat than me?" Da-Marr asked.

I shook my head. "You never let me have a chance at

the wheel, remember?"

"We better get up there. And don't you let on that I don't wanna kill your ass."

"Thanks."

Holding onto my throbbing knee, I struggled up the steps first and found Bobby in a rage, pushing buttons and pounding on the helm when nothing seemed to work. "Where's the goddamn anchor control?" he bellowed.

"I have no idea."

Bobby turned to Da-Marr. "Is he lying?"

"He's too chicken shit to lie." He gave me a shove, but there wasn't any heft behind it. He was on my side.

"We have got to find those fucking diamonds and get the hell off this boat fast or we're going over the falls!" Bobby ranted.

"Falls?" Da-Marr asked with what sounded like panic.

"Don't you know what's up ahead? Niagara fucking Falls! You have heard of them, haven't you? Or didn't they teach you anything in your fucking ghetto school?"

Bobby did not know how to win friends and influence people—and if Da-Marr still had any doubts about his character, they'd been wiped out by that last statement.

Da-Marr lowered his head, his eyes blazing, reminding me of a bull about to charge.

"We have got to find those diamonds!" Bobby bellowed.

He grabbed me by the jacket and shook me. "Where are they?"

"I don't know."

"You're lying. Where. Are. They?"

Da-Marr was right. This guy was a nutcase. His blue eyes bore into me, but I answered truthfully. "I. Don't. Know!"

He shoved me backward with savage force that sent

me crashing against the fiberglass bistro table; then he pushed Da-Marr out of his way and nearly fell down the stairs in his haste to get below.

Da-Marr and I looked at each other; his eyes were filled with terror and I wondered if he could see the same emotion in mine. "What do we do now?" he asked.

"The life jackets are gone. Can you swim?"

Da-Marr shook his head. I'd had swimming class in high school, but all these years later could I do much more than tread water or dog paddle? The shore—either east or west—was a long way away.

The billiards chalk was still in my pocket. I took it out and rubbed it between my right thumb and forefinger, hoping it would give me some insight into Bobby.

"What are you doing with your hand?" Da-Marr asked.

"Don't ask."

The impression that burst upon my mind was different this time. It was a reversed image of Bobby, as he'd seen himself in a mirror in Jack Morrow's game room. His expression was bland, but it was his eyes that consumed me. Inquisitive? No, calculating, As Morrow's world had collapsed around him, Bobby had made a greater and greater effort to ingratiate himself with the older man. They'd sparred as they'd knocked colored and striped balls into the pockets of Morrow's vintage billiards table, and Bobby's admiration had fed Morrow's faltering ego, something he'd badly needed at that time. And when Bobby had shown up on Morrow's last night alive, the old man had never suspected that his last remaining sycophant had homicide in mind.

"What did Bobby tell you, that he was Morrow's son and deserved a portion of what his father had worked for all his life?"

Da-Marr nodded vigorously.

"He lied. I met his son. His name is Harry—he's nice

guy. This jerk is a psychotic opportunist. He shot Jack Morrow execution style. And you know what? He won't hesitate to do the same to us."

Da-Marr looked confused and hurt. "But he said—"

I actually felt sorry for the poor schmuck. Da-Marr had thought of me as an asshole worth dismissing, but he was, after all, just a kid without a lot of experience. He was just figuring out that he'd been lied to—taken advantage of—and that he might actually go to jail for the acts of vandalism he'd performed at Bobby's behest.

"It's a tough world, kid. You can't just take people at face value."

Da-Marr said nothing, but looked shaken, and for a moment I thought he might actually burst into tears. Then he straightened, finding some inner resolve. "We got to do something. We can't let him kill us."

"Hey, I'm not advocating murder, but the truth is—it's us, or him. We've got to subdue him—tie him up—something. And then we've got to contact someone—cops, sheriff's office, somebody—to come and intercept this boat before we go over the falls. You said you can't swim, and though I barely can, the current gets faster and faster the farther north we go. If we go into the water—there's no way we can survive."

Da-Marr pivoted and, frustrated, slammed his fist into the fiberglass wall. It didn't budge, and he shook his hand, wincing.

"We have to decide—right now—how we're going to approach this." Da-Marr's expression was filled with indecision. "I know we aren't related by blood, but we are family," I said, hoping to God he would buy my next line of bullshit. "Your father's brother married Evelyn. Brenda is Evelyn's sister. She's married to my brother. That's a family line. We have to stick together. Are you with me?" I held out my fist.

After a long moment of indecision, Da-Marr clenched

his own fist and bumped mine. "Family," he said, and nodded gravely, but still looked scared shitless.

"Okay," I said, trying to fill my voice with a confidence I didn't actually feel. "You've got to make Bobby believe you still have me intimidated." And, man, that wasn't going to be a hard act for me to perform. "But if any opportunity presents itself, we've got to act. We've got to get his cell phone, because if we don't—we're all going to die."

Again, Da-Marr nodded. He took a deep breath, schooled his features, and straightened. "You go down the steps first and show him you're a goddamn wimp. If we can get him inside the salon, the two of us can smack that sucker down and get his phone."

I hoped.

"We have to do it in the next couple of minutes, or there's no way the authorities can get a boat out to intercept us. Once we go past the Grand Island Bridge, we're dead.

Da-Marr was so scared he nodded like a bobble head.

The choppy water seemed to get rougher the farther north the current took us and with a bum knee, it was hard to get down the steps. Both sides of the shore were dotted with houses and businesses. I had no idea how far we'd gone up the river or how long we had before we got closer to the end of the island.

I looked into the salon, but didn't see Bobby. Da-Marr pushed past me and entered the boat's interior. I hobbled over to look toward the bow and saw Bobby trying to access the anchor locker. Fat lot of good that would do us— the river's current ran about one-and-a-half miles an hour and it was about twelve miles from the marina to Buckhorn Island State Park. That gave us a little time. But I'd lost track of when we'd left the dock and how far Da-Marr had taken the boat before we'd run out of fuel. But the more time we had, the better. If we could keep Bobby searching for the diamonds and dropping trash into the water, we'd have a better chance of being intercepted by a police patrol boat.

Bobby hauled the anchor out of its locker and tossed it overboard, the momentum nearly sending him into the river, but he grabbed onto the chrome rail that ran along the bow and I watched in disappointment as he pulled himself back onboard.

"What the hell are you looking at?" he shouted at me.

I backed off and dug the chalk out of my pocket once more, rubbing it like a lucky rabbit's foot, only, it wasn't luck I was looking for, but insight.

I already knew what this joker was capable of doing, and I didn't want him doing it to me.

TWENTY-FIVE

The first thing Richard did when he got out of the water was try to find a phone, since his own had been ruined by its dip in the Niagara River.

"Mr. Alpert, what happened?" Frank, the marina manager, asked, springing up from behind his desk as a dripping Richard entered his office.

"No time to explain. Can I borrow your phone and maybe a towel?"

"Sure."

"I could use a phone book, too."

After coming up with the white pages, the marina manager left Richard in privacy. But, instead of calling the police to report a stolen boat, Richard called the *Buffalo News,* hoping to find Sam Nielsen at his desk. He answered on the second ring.

"Sam, it's Richard Alpert—Jeff's brother. What the hell are you two up to? Why are you looking for diamonds?"

"Did Jeff find some?" he asked eagerly.

"I don't know. But someone has just stolen my boat and I was wondering if the two were related."

"Holy shit." Sam was silent for a moment. "I asked a friend of mine to look up the registration on the boat. Let me put you on hold to see if he ever came up with the info."

The line went silent.

Frank returned with a couple of faded beach towels and a dry jacket. Richard toweled off his hair and then peeled off his wet jacket and shirt, drying off before he put on the borrowed jacket, which was a little snug, but its warmth was welcome.

Sam came back on the line. "Damn, I could kick myself for not following through with this when Jeff first mentioned it. The boat, it's called Easy Breezin', right?"

"That's right."

"It was registered in Jack Morrow's company name. You know who he was, right?"

"I know," Richard said grimly.

"Man, if I'd known this we could have saved a lot of time. And you say Jeff's found diamonds?"

"No. But someone must think there's diamonds on board. The boat's been stolen, with Jeff on it."

"Damn. Have you tried calling his cell phone?"

"No."

"Hang on." The line went silent once more. It was at least thirty seconds of standing in squashy shoes before Sam came back. "I get a message that the call can't be completed. Is the marina manager around?"

"I'm calling from his office."

"Better get him to call the cops—they're more likely to listen to him than you. What marina are you at?"

"Sundowners."

"I know the place. My boat's parked just down the way. I'll get there as soon as I can."

He hung up; Richard did likewise. He looked up to see Frank waiting for an explanation.

"Are you sure the boat's been stolen? The young black man who's been with you on several occasions was on it earlier today. He said he had your permission to be there."

Richard let out a long breath. "He neglected to ask me."

"Are you sure they didn't just leave without you?"

"I had the life jackets. And neither of them know

what they're doing when it comes to boats—and I should know, because I have no idea, either."

The two men looked at each other for a long moment before Richard spoke again. "My friend seems to think the police would pay greater attention if the call to report the theft came from you. The young man driving the boat did not have my permission to take it, and I'm afraid he may have obtained the keys by assaulting my brother."

Frank's expression darkened. "I'd be glad to talk to the police—but I think it should be you who reports it."

"Whose jurisdiction is it?"

"Call 911 and I'm sure they'll figure it out."

Richard nodded, picked up the receiver, and punched in 911. He listened to the dispatcher for a moment and then said, "I'd like to report a stolen boat."

I'm sure if I'd tossed out even a tenth of the trash from my car that we tossed over the side of Easy Breezin' that I'd have been arrested in a heartbeat, but nobody seemed to notice as we jettisoned more and more of the debris that had once been the interior of Richard's beautiful boat. All that infrastructure gone, and still we hadn't come across the diamonds Bobby sought.

Da-Marr had been stationed at the helm, trying to keep the boat heading in a forward position in the middle of the river, but it swerved with the waves, rolling and turning, and I was sure I wasn't the only one who felt vaguely nauseous.

We'd dumped all the detritus from the salon and the staterooms without finding anything that resembled hidden treasure and Bobby's temper was growing shorter by the minute.

"Do you even know what uncut diamonds look like?" I asked him.

"Uncut? What does that mean?"

Holy crap. The kid was clueless. Then again, I'd been just as uneducated on the subject only a few hours before.

"I haven't actually seen any, but I was told they don't look like the rocks in a ring. They can look like pebbles—from clear, to yellow, to gray lumps of stone."

"Are you shitting me?" he asked angrily.

"No."

Bobby's expression darkened with anger. "My God, did we toss anything away that looked like that?"

"I don't know what you guys tossed overboard before this afternoon. Do you even remember?"

"Shit! That fuckhead Da-Marr might have thrown them away in the marina's Dumpster or over the side. We were looking for sparkling stones."

"Google can be your best friend."

"And how the hell was I supposed to know Jack might have uncut stones?" Bobby demanded angrily.

"You made assumptions. You *both* made assumptions without any basis in fact. Not smart. Not smart at all."

Bobby's lip curled. "Do you want me to kill you where you stand?"

Sophie's warning came back to me. Well, she'd said it would seem that the innocent was dangerous. Yeah, approaching the boat had seemed innocent, so I guess she'd been right about that. But she'd been so vague about everything else. One thing was for sure, being inside the boat was too dangerous. I needed to get back out on the back of the boat in the open air if things were to tip in my favor. Oddly enough, Bobby hadn't seemed too interested in searching the engine room, but if I was going to hide something, it might be there, where it was hard to maneuver and with lots of potential hiding places. Had I gotten that feeling from touching Jack Morrow's stuff, or from what was left of him on the boat?

The thing was, Morrow had probably spent the most time either in the master stateroom's bed, or holding the boat's steering wheel, which I'd never had a chance to touch. Bobby had no idea that I could connect with the living—and the dead—via that sense, and I wasn't about to tell him, either. And I was pretty sure that if I was going to find those diamonds, I would have to get to the bridge deck and wrap my fingers around the steering wheel.

"We should look up top," I said, keeping my voice even. "If Jack had to make a fast escape, he'd have hidden the stones where they'd be easily accessible."

Bobby eyed me coldly. "Why are you cooperating?"

"Because I don't want you to kill me."

He laughed. "I thought we already settled that."

I swallowed.

Bobby's lip curled. "Da-Marr's right. You are a pussy."

I said nothing.

He nodded toward the salon. "Get outside."

I hobbled onto the outside deck feeling Bobby's gaze burning my back as I went.

It had started to rain—big, cold wet drops that immediately soaked into my denim jacket. The waves were bigger now, too. I looked around at both shores, but didn't have a clue how far we'd gone along the east side of the island—or how much farther it would be until the point of no return.

It was a struggle to get up the stairs to the bridge deck. What kind of damage had Bobby inflicted on my knee? A torn tendon or ligament? Crushed cartilage? If I wasn't going to get off this boat alive, did it even matter?

Da-Marr still sat in the driver's seat and looked up from the controls. "This bitch is hard to drive without the engines."

"Pussy here thinks the diamonds might be up here. Have you had a chance to look?" Bobby asked.

"I've been trying to steer this sucker while you guys

have been diddling around downstairs. And if you're up here, it means you ain't found jack shit."

Bobby glared at me. "Well, what are you waiting for? Start looking."

I turned to the left and opened the small fridge. Of course, there was nothing in it. It had been switched off, so there was no ice in the icemaker, either, which would have been a perfect place to hide cut diamonds—but I was pretty sure we were looking for them in their natural state.

"The stones might be hidden in back. Take it out of there," Bobby ordered.

I tried to pry the fridge from its cabinet, but it was wedged in tight. I yanked and yanked, and it finally budged, flying forward, sending me crashing onto the deck. Bobby laughed at me and it took all my self-control not to punch him in the knee. Of course there was nothing hidden in the gaping hole in the cabinet.

There wasn't enough room for the three of us and the fridge. "It's getting tight in here," I said.

Bobby grabbed the fridge and wrestled it to the top of the stairs, then gave it a shove that sent it toppling end over end, making one hell of a racket. He looked over at me. "Get down there and throw it over the side."

"I don't think I can lift it—not with this bum knee."

"Da-Marr, go toss it overboard."

"You toss it," Da-Marr challenged.

"Hey, I gave you an order."

"I ain't gonna get ruptured throwing that hunk a metal around. I got my manhood to protect."

"Give me a break," Bobby groused.

I scooted over to open the cabinet under the wet bar and found a sponge, some liquid hand soap, and nothing else. I closed the doors. "Why don't you help Bobby toss that fridge in the drink?" I said to Da-Marr.

"I don't take orders from you," he said, and I wasn't sure if he was bluffing.

"Why do you want him to go? Is it because you know where the diamonds are and you think you can get them for yourself?" Bobby asked.

I let out a breath, unwilling to answer.

Bobby eyed the boat's controls. "We should take this whole console apart."

Da-Marr turned on him. "Are you crazy? I'm having a hard enough time keeping us goin' straight. We let the river take this baby and she'll be spinning or floating backwards, and ain't that gonna attract a lot of attention?"

"Well what you do you suggest?" Bobby challenged Da-Marr.

Da-Marr glanced over at me. "Maybe he's right. Maybe I ought to help you toss the fridge in the river. I already looked around the bridge. There ain't no secret hiding places. Everything's made of molded plastic."

"Fiberglass," Bobby corrected him.

Da-Marr's eyes blazed. "I'm gettin' sick of you insinuating I ain't got no education."

"Talking like that, you've proved it."

"I'm going to college in January," Da-Marr said, his voice almost a growl.

"Wanna bet?" Bobby said and laughed.

"Say somethin' else," Da-Marr threatened and straightened to his full six-foot plus height.

Bobby seemed to realize that he might have pushed his partner in crime too far. He backed down. "Come on; help me toss that fridge over the side."

Da-Marr glared at him, and Bobby turned for the stairs, hurrying down them. "Try to keep the boat going straight," Da-Marr told me without rancor.

I nodded, and moved to stand behind the steering wheel as Da-Marr went down the steps.

Rain spattered the windshield that overlooked the bow and the river before us. I wrapped my fingers around the wheel. Da-Marr had been right; without power to the rudder—or whatever it was that steered the forty-six foot boat, it was damned hard to keep it going in a straight line. But I had something else to do besides steer the boat. I closed my eyes and tightened my grip, concentrating, straining to sense Jack Morrow, to absorb the secret he'd died to protect.

A lot of people had stood in my place—more than Da-Marr, more than Richard. How many people had climbed all over the boat before the auction? How many cops and feds had searched it, albeit not with the destructive intensity Bobby and Da-Marr had given the job. Mostly men, but a few women, had held onto the steering wheel, wondering what it would feel like to cruise along the river at twenty knots on a gorgeous sunny day, the wind buffeting them while the diesel engines thrummed down below.

I had to get past all that crap. Somehow, I had to wade through others' excitement, trepidation, and discouragement.

I thought about the Rolex.

I thought about the Lexus's steering wheel, and the sensations I'd felt.

I opened my eyes. It wasn't working.

Maybe I was going about this the wrong way.

I concentrated on what I'd seen—or thought I'd seen—while in Morrow's office. The sparkling flashes of light. It didn't make sense. Somehow, I knew the diamonds he'd hidden were uncut, so why had I seen the glint from polished cuts?

I pondered that thought for a long moment.

Morrow had bought the stones for cash. He'd seen them as an investment. Was the flash of light what he anticipated the stones would look like when cut and sold on the open market? Would he have known how to get the work done and how to unload the stones without drawing attention to himself?

Then again, why not draw attention to himself? He'd been a successful businessman before his downfall. Why shouldn't he have planned to sell the stones at a great profit—that's what he'd been famous for; turning a little money into a lot. Of course, it had all been a sham, but perhaps at one point even he believed his own hype.

It wasn't an image that filled me—more a feeling of what I'd already surmised. The stones were in the engine room somewhere. Yeah, *somewhere.*

"What the fuck?" Da-Marr yelled from below, his angry voice shattering my deliberation.

I abandoned the wheel to look out through the zip-up plastic cover that enclosed the back end of the bridge deck to see Da-Marr and Bobby wrestling on the deck below. Cursing, I hurried to reach the steps, slick with rain, and nearly tumbled down to the deck below.

"You're crazy!" Da-Marr shouted.

They were both on their feet. Da-Marr, clutching at his neck, while Bobby stood behind him with a piece of rope, pulling it taut.

Too horrified to move, it took the sounds of Da-Marr coughing and choking to finally penetrate the fog around my mind before I pounced on Bobby.

I launched at the bastard. "Get your hands off him!"

Bobby hadn't expected me to help Da-Marr. Startled, he fell to one side, and in that instant Da-Marr turned, knocking Bobby off-balance. He stumbled backward and fell over the back end of the boat.

Except for the sound of the wind and the river, all was quiet.

Still clutching his throat, Da-Marr stared at me, and then it seemed like we both slogged through cement to reach the rail. I searched the choppy water, but couldn't see any sign of Bobby. I turned to face Da-Marr.

"What happened?"

The poor kid was actually shaking. "I don't know. We picked up the fridge and tossed it over the side and I turned to watch it sink, and then the next thing I knew the guy came at me with a rope. He tried to kill me!" he cried incredulously.

I looked back to the water and saw Bobby's head bobbing in the water. It had only been seconds, but already we had traveled too far away to save him—we had nothing to toss him—not a rope, not a life jacket—nothing. Bobby had destroyed or gotten rid of every piece of safety equipment on the boat.

"Oh, man," Da-Marr breathed, "what an asshole." Then he turned to me, his face still filled with fear. "Look ahead."

I craned my neck to look around the starboard side. Up ahead were the supports for the Grand Island Bridge.

"Holy shit," I mouthed.

"What the fuck we gonna do now?" De-Marr demanded.

"We've got a couple of options. First, we could jump overboard—"

"I told you—I can't swim," he shouted.

"Or we could try to crash the boat into the supports. It may or may not sink."

"Tell me you've got some kinda better idea than that," he said on the verge of panic.

"Sorry. If only we had some fuel in the tank, we could head back to the marina."

"Fuel? Hey, we still got something."

"What are you saying?"

"I turned the motor off when I figured Bobby was a crazy ass lunatic."

"But I saw the fuel indicator. It was on empty."

Da-Marr smiled. "Hey, when I drive my dad's car the indicator says empty but I can always get a couple of miles out of it before it runs dry."

"You better hope you're right about this sucker."

"What about those diamonds?" he asked.

"What about them?" I asked.

"You know where they are."

Should I be honest with the kid? Our lives were on the line—maybe I should.

"I think so."

"Then go get 'em."

"And what do we do with them? You know we can't keep them. A lot of people lost their life savings and deserve to get even a nickel on the dollar."

Da-Marr frowned. "Shit, I guess I knew I was never gonna see a penny from them."

"Just so we're clear on that," I said, and studied his eyes. I wasn't at all sure I could trust him on that.

"Sure," he said almost casually, and I wondered if I might be the next thing tossed overboard.

"I think they're in the engine room. I'll have a look. You see if you can get the engines to come back online. We might be able to save ourselves yet."

Da-Marr nodded. Not a second later, he pivoted and headed up the stairs to the bridge deck, and I ducked into the salon and headed for the hatch to the engine room.

Thank God, we still had battery power, because I knew there were no flashlights aboard. Once inside the cramped space that housed the engines, I had to shuffle around using my good knee and elbows to scramble across the cramped space. Until that moment, I wouldn't have thought I was claustrophobic, but inching my way toward the front of the engine room made me long for the cold fresh air above. Da-Marr hadn't managed to start the twin car engines, but I could hear clicks and other noises as he tried to coax the fuel-starved motors back to life.

It was obvious that Bobby had already been down here and searched. The covers were off the various modules and the main battery unit that that was big enough to power a house in an electrical outage.

I looked around me and had no clue where to start my search. And unless Da-Marr got those engines started, I only had minutes to do it.

Closing my eyes, I opened my mind and hoped whatever link I'd forged with the late Jack Morrow would lead me to the diamonds. But as I waited for inspiration to hit, I suddenly wondered why I gave a flying fig about the damn stones. They wouldn't benefit me. They wouldn't benefit anyone I knew. The people who'd lost their money by trusting Morrow were probably all greedy bastards who deserved to lose their cash. But not their futures. The mugger who'd cracked me over the head with a baseball bat deserved the worst in life. I guess I'd wished that on Da-Marr, too, just because he reminded me of the bastard who'd ruined my life. Well, maybe not ruined—but had changed it in ways that could never be recovered. And Da-Marr wasn't entirely innocent, either.

I shook those thoughts away. *Diamonds, idiot, diamonds.*

Opening my eyes, my gaze focused on a small red fire extinguisher clamped to the room's silver-backed insulation. If there were a fire, it would be totally inadequate to douse all but the smallest of flames.

I can't say why, but something about it called to me. My elbows scraped against the fabric of my denim jacket as I pulled myself through the narrow well between the twin engines. Unclamping the extinguisher from the wall, I noticed how light it felt—as though it was empty. I examined it from all angles but saw nothing out of the ordinary. Why would Morrow have left an empty fire extinguisher in his boat? It didn't make sense.

I was about to replace the bottle when I noticed a slight ripple in the insulation. I peered closer. Not a ripple—a cut. I poked at it, but the imperfection appeared to have been mended. I ran a fingernail around the edges of it, hoping to poke through the thin silver skin, but it was tougher than it looked. I patted the insulation and felt a slight bulge. The beginnings of a shit-eating grin tugged at my mouth.

Resting the bulk of my weight on my left forearm, I reached up and fumbled with the insulation where it met the room's low ceiling until I found a breach, then I ripped it downward and out popped a bundle wrapped in a soft purple cloth bag—the kind that used to come with a bottle of Crown Royal. I opened the gold drawstring and dumped out a jeweler's chamois, unfolded the cloth and found pay dirt—a handful of gray and yellow hunks of stone.

Rewrapping the bundle, I replaced it in the bag, stuffed it in my jacket pocket and extricated myself from that damnably small space. A minute later, I entered the salon to find Da-Marr standing in the center of the room. I hadn't noticed that the noises in the engine room had abated.

"I thought you were trying to start the engines."

"They're not going to start."

"Are you sure?" I asked, growing uneasy at the menacing look on his face.

"I'm sure." He held out his hand. "Give 'em to me."

"Give you what?"

"The diamonds."

"What makes you think I found them?"

"Give them to me, or I'm at yo head," he threatened.

"What?"

He snorted an angry breath. "I'll knock the shit out of you like that brother did back in the city."

I swallowed. I believed him. But he didn't have to beat me up. If we couldn't get the engines started again, we were already dead men.

TWENTY-SIX

Da-Marr lowered his head, back in his raging bull stance.

I reached into my pocket and handed him the purple bag. "Okay, now let's see what we can do about those engines."

He pocketed the stones. "I told you, I couldn't get it started."

"So, let me try."

Maybe it was because I handed him the diamonds without an argument, or maybe he figured he had me cowed once again, but he stood aside and let me pass.

It was raining harder now. The low clouds seem to boil as they churned over the river. Easy Breezin' was moving at a sideways angle. I looked to the left shore and saw an expanse of parkland. Not a happy sight. I hurried up the steps as fast as I could, squinted through the droplet-covered windshield and swallowed convulsively. Looming up ahead were the twin spans of the North Grand Island Bridge.

Da-Marr was suddenly beside me. "Jesus," he breathed.

"Yeah. We've got a choice here. If we smash the boat into the pylons, we might get stuck. Someone's sure to notice us and come find us."

"What if I don't want to get found?" he asked.

"If your plan is to take the boat over the falls, then

good luck. It's a hundred-and-sixty foot drop."

"You're shitting me."

"No, I'm not."

Da-Marr pursed his lips, not looking quite so confident. "Then I guess we'd better ram this sucker." He pushed me aside, and took the wheel, resting one knee on the captain's chair to brace himself as he fought to straighten the boat.

We said nothing as the rain continued to pound the bridge deck's roof. Da-Marr aimed for one of the cement supports.

My knee was killing me, so I flopped onto the end of the leather couch and watched in horrified silence as we came nearer and nearer the bridge. Despite his best efforts to ram it, the boat seemed to want no part of what appeared to be our death wish. Instead of crashing head on, we grazed the side of the concrete abutment with the ear-splitting sound of scraped and breaking fiberglass.

Easy Breezin' seemed to do a pirouette, the back end slamming against the concrete abutment of the southbound span. But that didn't stop our momentum as the boat slowly danced back into the river's main channel.

"Da-Marr turned to glower at me. "Got any other bright ideas?"

"Let me have a go at those controls."

"You get this sucker moving and you can have those diamonds back." He stepped away from the controls. I pressed all the right buttons. I did everything according to spec, and nothing happened.

The scenery seemed to be going by faster. Had we picked up speed? I knew it wasn't far until we hit the rapids, just a half mile from the falls. That was the point of no return. Hell, we'd already reached it when we'd gone under the damn bridges.

Da-Marr stood there, shaking his head, a self-satisfied grin plastered across his face. "I told you."

In fury, I kicked the front of the console then turned the key so hard I thought it might break. Amazingly enough, at least one of the engines sputtered to life.

"Ha-ha!" I whooped in triumph.

"Fucking good luck," Da-Marr groused.

"Your aunt would not approve of your potty mouth," I said and laughed.

For a moment I thought Da-Marr might say, *Fuck her,* but then his lips turned down in a classic pout. I kept turning the wheel until the boat came around and we faced the bridge once more. "I believe you owe me one package of diamonds."

In that instant, I thought the kid might clock me, but then, incredibly, he reached into his pocket and pulled out the purple pouch, slapping it into my outstretched hand. "Fuck you. But if you don't get us out of here, I want 'em back."

I pocketed the diamonds, feeling smug.

That feeling was short-lived, however. For it soon became apparent that though the engine below us was thrumming once again, it didn't have the power to overcome the current's awesome force. We'd probably destroyed at least one of the propellers, and probably damaged the second when we'd hit the bridge abutment. Everything inside me started to tense as Easy Breezin' began to lose ground.

And then the engine died once more and the boat started floating backward.

"You can give me back those diamonds," Da-Marr said, his voice devoid of emotion.

I reached into my pocket and handed them back to him. Fat lot of good they were going to do him.

"What the hell do we do now?" he asked, his voice tight.

I let out a long breath. "Did I mention there are rapids ahead? That means shallow water. There's a miniscule chance the boat could get caught up on the rocks."

"And if it doesn't?" he asked.

It occurred to me that Da-Marr had lost the ghetto slur he'd so often used. "It's a long shot, but there are a couple of small islands right before we hit the falls. If we can crash the boat into one of them, we might be able to jump off. And then...."

"Wait for rescue?" he asked skeptically.

I nodded. "Rich saw us take off. He knows I wasn't a willing participant. He's a real law and order fanatic. My guess is he marched right into the marina manager's office and called the cops. It's been a couple of hours, but law-enforcement is often slow to react. But believe me, he isn't going to give up on us."

"On you," he said, which sounded like an accusation. "Is he gonna have me arrested?"

"I wouldn't worry about that now. See, I was told by someone I trust that I just might die tonight, and you're here with me."

Da-Marr looked through the windshield. Up ahead the water was a frothy white. We were approaching the rapids. "This person ever bullshit you?"

"Nope."

"Then let's hope he or she is wrong," he said, grasping the wheel once more.

Neither of us spoke, staring ahead where we could already see a misty cloud obliterating the sky: the spray from Niagara Falls—the second-tallest waterfall in all of North America.

We hit the rapids with a staggering jolt that knocked us both off our feet. Da-Marr recovered first, struggling upright and grabbing the wheel in a death grip.

The sound was the worst. How could the river have been so deep and then suddenly so shallow, filled with jagged rocks that ripped the keel like it was made of tissue paper? Da-Marr had far more physical strength, so while he struggled to keep Easy Breezin' under some kind of control, I went down to the into the engine room to find it quickly filling with water. But we weren't going to sink, not in this current. We might be clinging to wreckage when Easy Breezin' went over the falls, but there was no stopping the inevitable now.

I held on to my throbbing knee as I struggled up to the bridge deck once more. My heart pounding so hard I wasn't sure I could speak.

"You said islands. How big—how many?" Da-Marr demanded.

I didn't know—couldn't remember the lessons I'd learned in school far too many years before.

"Aim for anything that stands between us and the falls. It's our only chance."

Da-Marr nodded, and I looked down at his fingers clutching the wheel, straining to keep the boat on some kind of course,

"If I get us to crash on some little island, you don't say a word to the cops about any diamonds," he said.

"You got a deal," I replied in earnest.

The shadow of a smile crossed his lips.

The rain that had already been hard seemed to pound on us as we broke free from the rapids.

We. Were. Doomed.

Thank you, Sophie, for warning me in advance. A warning with no real details. If she'd said, "Don't get on a boat," I would have listened to her. When we met in the afterlife, I was going to give her one fucking big piece of my mind.

Up ahead we could see the vague outlines of trees and rocks.

"There," I pointed to the right. There's an island over there. Try to steer toward it.

Already the tendons in Da-Marr's arms were distended as he struggled to keep the boat under his control, but the mighty river had other ideas. Easy Breezin' seemed to have a mind of her own as we progressed ever forward toward our deaths.

TWENTY-SEVEN

Parked at the pull off by the Robert Moses power plant intakes, Richard held the binoculars pressed hard against his eyes, watching in horrified fascination as the boat he'd so recently acquired and had so little time to appreciate floated past him on the river. There was no sign of life. There didn't appear to be anyone on the bridge deck. No one, and the boat was obviously under no one's control.

"Do you think Jeffy and Da-Marr could be inside it?" Brenda asked, her voice sounding small and tired. She'd insisted on joining him when he'd called to tell her what had happened, and had brought him some dry clothes— not that they were going to stay that way standing in the rain as he was.

Evelyn had driven her, and though she hadn't said more than two words, he could see she was upset and angry that he'd accused Da-Marr of stealing the boat.

"I don't know," Richard said tersely, his mind racing. How much further could they go and still keep the boat in view? There wasn't much time before....

The police hadn't come soon enough, didn't seem to understand the urgency of the situation. And now the boat was being carried away by the current. More than a quarter of a million bucks down the drain, and along with it something far more precious: his brother.

He lowered the binoculars, got back in the car, started

it, and rolled up the window.

"Now what?" Brenda asked.

Richard let out a breath. "We head for Niagara Falls State Park. The cops said they would send a patrol car there to wait to see if it—when it...." He couldn't finish the sentence.

"I blame myself for all this," Evelyn said from the backseat. "If I hadn't come here—if I hadn't brought Da-Marr with me, he wouldn't have been tempted by the things he could never have."

Richard looked over at Brenda. Her lower lip quivered, and her eyes were beginning to fill with tears. He didn't have a psychic connection with her the way Jeff did, but he did know her soul—as if it was a part of his own.

I'm sorry, she mouthed.

He shook his head, reached over and squeezed her hand.

A single tear cascaded down her cheek. He clasped her face, and with his thumb wiped it away. Then the turned to look at the review mirror.

"Evie," he said in preamble. He had never called the woman by her sister's more familiar name. "We don't know what the circumstances were. Why Da-Marr took the boat. I think it's premature to assume the worst. He did it, but we don't know why." And Christ, they would probably never know. Except the idea of diamonds and their fantastic worth could have—*must have*—been the impetus. Richard hadn't told the sisters about them—or the possibility that that was what lay at the heart of the entire situation. He couldn't—not now, not when Brenda was about to give birth to their child.

To lose a brother and gain a daughter in the span of a day or so would be Dickensian to the max: the best and worst of times.

But Jeff was nothing if not resourceful. He'd proven it far too many times to assume the absolute worst.

Richard started the car. "I'm not giving up on either of them. Not yet. They're two very smart guys."

"You're a fool, Richard Alpert," Evelyn said, her voice grave.

Maybe he was. But Richard was a doctor, and far too many times he'd witnessed life-saving miracles. Right now he was counting on one—or maybe two—to happen.

"We're skunked," I told Da-Marr.

He peered through the windshield. "What's with all the fog ahead?"

I managed a mirthless laugh. "That's not fog—that's spray from the Canadian falls."

Da-Marr stared ahead, his expression grim. "Aunt Evelyn will kill me if I don't live to go to college in January."

"How can she kill you if you're already dead?"

Da-Marr looked down his nose at me. "That woman would find a way."

I couldn't help but smile. I had no doubt he was right. But the smile was short-lived. Was there a chance in hell we could hit an island and then have time to jump off the boat to relative safety? Had we been observed from the shore? Maybe. I sure as hell hoped so, but we couldn't count on it—at least not until the wreckage appeared below the falls. It was late in the day. Would Easy Breezin' hit one of the last Maid of the Mist forays of the day? I sure as hell hoped not. Bobby was probably already dead. We were doomed as well. I didn't want us to take out, or injure, anybody else.

The mist ahead grew thicker. The end was near.

I felt like I should say something profound, but when facing the end, it wasn't a stranger I wanted to be with. I kind of thought I'd be talking to Richard or Brenda or Maggie. Then again, wasn't this as final as a random traffic accident or getting hit by a bus? Except then the end would be fast—like I'd have never seen it coming. I could see the end of the world coming at us with terrible speed.

I looked down at Da-Marr's hands on the wheel. The skin over his knuckles was stretched taut—it was taking all his strength to keep Easy Breezin' on a forward trajectory. Crap. A trajectory that was going to turn us and the boat into paste.

The terrible sound of the roaring river filled my ears. If not for the enclosed bridge deck, I was sure we both would soon be deaf.

This wasn't the way I thought I'd die.

"Do you have any regrets?" Da-Marr asked.

I caught his gaze. "About a million of them. You?"

He shrugged. "I had a kid," he said, and I could have sworn his lower lip trembled. "He died. Now I ain't got no one to carry on for me."

"What was his name?"

He laughed. "Da-Marr."

"Wow, that's original."

"Hey, it's a great name."

"If you say so."

"And what would you name your kid?" he asked, sounding belligerent.

I shook my head. "It was never in the cards for me."

When I was dead, Richard would live on, and he'd have little Betsy Ruth to carry on our mother's genes. And maybe my half-sister Patty would one day have a child to carry on my father's line. But I was a biological dead end. I'd never given it much thought before now. How sad was it that nothing of me would go on?

I felt a lump rise in my throat. Pretty damn sad.

The mist grew higher and thicker.

"Where the fuck are those islands you mentioned?" Da-Marr demanded.

"They should be to the right," I somehow managed. God, my voice sounded so damn calm considering how panicked I felt.

Despite Da-Marr's best efforts, Easy Breezin' started veering to the right. Holy crap—this was it.

And then out of the mist came a large and terrible brown object—we slammed into it with such force that the two of us flew through the air and crashed in a heap on the deck.

"What the fuck was that?" Da-Marr hollered.

"The old scow."

"The what?"

"Come on, we've only got seconds if we're going to live."

TWENTY-EIGHT

I practically fell down the fiberglass steps from the bridge deck onto the stern. Easy Breezin' was lodged against the rusty old barge that had been caught near the brink of the falls for almost a hundred years—but it wasn't likely to be here for long.

"Are you crazy?" Da-Marr hollered over the incredible roar of the Canadian Horseshoe Falls only some eight hundred yards from the precipice.

"This boat ain't gonna stay here for long. I'd rather take my chances on something that hasn't moved in decades," I hollered.

Da-Marr studied the old rust bucket and winced. It was at least four feet higher than Easy Breezin', so climbing aboard wasn't a sure thing. God, how I wish Richard had tossed those life jackets aboard the boat before Da-Marr had taken off from the dock at breakneck speed.

The scow was made of steel—and obviously not the stainless type. It was rusty and ragged and we were likely to be torn to pieces before our ordeal was over. Da-Marr was a lot stronger than me. He yelped as he grabbed onto the edge and pulled himself over the back of the scow, then he disappeared.

My knee screamed as I jumped—once, twice—trying to grab onto the back end of the old barge, both times cutting my hands on jagged metal.

Easy Breezin' bucked in the turbulent water. I had

only a minute, maybe seconds before she would break loose and then it—and I—would be over the falls.

Panicked, I tried again, and this time threw my left arm around the edge just as Easy Breezin' broke away, leaving me hanging onto the old scow's stern. I kicked, trying to walk up the side, but my sneakers kept slipping. My arm and shoulder protested. I was losing my grip. About to fall—

Suddenly, the world's strongest arms grabbed me by the shoulders of my jacket and yanked and yanked and yanked, hauling me over the edge and pulling me onto a short, flat deck pocked with rust holes.

"Thanks," I managed, feeling like I might never catch my breath again.

I shut my eyes and thanked God, and Sophie, and Zeus, and all the gods on Mount Olympus. But I also knew that we were a hell of a long way from being safe. Earlier the temperature had been in the low sixties. It was a lot colder than that and we were both soaked.

I looked up at Da-Marr. "Where the hell were you?" I hollered once I could speak once more.

"Lookin' around. Man, this boat is one big piece of shit. Half of it's missing!" Da-Marr yelled.

I studied his face. His left cheek bore a jagged cut, still oozing with blood, and his hands were just as bloodied as mine. How long had it been since I'd had a tetanus shot?

I sat up and looked around. Since childhood, I'd seen many pictures of the old scow, but never an aerial view, and never in my wildest fantasies did I think I'd ever board her. She'd originally carried sand and rocks after a dredging operation, but the rusty cargo compartment before us was empty. I'd heard that the guys who'd originally been stranded on the barge had shifted more than a ton of their cargo to help stabilize the craft. They'd been rescued without any loss of life. Would we be as lucky?

"What the hell do we do now?" Da-Marr demanded.

I shrugged. "Wait."

"For what?"

"Rescue. It's been done before."

"How?"

I thought about what I'd learned in school about the barge's last passengers. It had been a long time ago. "Some soldiers shot a rope from a cannon and then saved the two guys who were stranded in a breeches buoy."

"A what?"

"It's like a pulley on a rope. They hauled them along on a line over the river."

"Ain't nobody hauling me over this damn river," Da-Marr cried.

That only left one other way of rescue.

I looked up at the darkening sky, but couldn't really tell if it was raining or if it was just the thick mist from the thundering cataract ahead of us.

Da-Marr followed my gaze. "A helicopter?"

I nodded, but the thought sickened me, especially if the weather worsened.

Da-Marr shook his head. "I don't think so. I don't like flying."

"But you flew here from Philadelphia."

"That was a on a plane with big engines. And I Googled the safety record of the airline before I said I'd come. Helicopters crash—a lot. Uh-uh, I ain't gonna get rescued by no fucking helicopter."

If I recalled correctly, the guys who'd crashed the barge on the rocks had had to spend a long day and night onboard before they were rescued. That had been during the summer. This was fall, and the temperature might fall to the forties overnight.

"Do you want to die of hypothermia?" I hollered.

"Hypo what?"

"Hypothermia. Where your body temperature drops low enough to kill you."

Da-Marr's brow wrinkled. "Didn't you say you had that and lived?"

"Yeah, but it wasn't fun."

"How'd you do it?"

I grimaced. "Some guy tried to kill me. I managed to tie him up and then … I hugged him all night."

Da-Marr pulled away, his mouth dropping open in horror. "That's sick."

I shrugged. "It saved my life. I saved both our lives."

He shook his head again. "I'd rather die."

"Suit yourself."

I looked around us. To our left was the old Canadian power plant that had been shut down for decades. Small islands with a few scrub trees about to lose their leaves were to the right. I couldn't see the American shore through the mist.

Someone must have seen Easy Breezin' travel down the river. Someone must have reported it to the authorities—both American and Canadian.

Please, God, please let someone have reported it.

Crowds of frustrated rubberneckers had gathered in Niagara Falls State Park, hoping for a glimpse of the men stranded on the old scow. "We should have brought our passports," Richard groused and checked the Twitter feed on his phone once more. The car radio had been useless when it came to finding news on what had happened, but at least the online community (#strandedNiagaraFalls) had been active for the past hour or so.

"I didn't bring my passport," Evelyn said, her voice catching.

"I don't want to go to Canada," Brenda said. "I mean not today. Not now. Take me to Niagara on the Lake and the Oban Inn any other time, but no adventure to Canada today, please."

Richard glanced over at her, noting her pinched expression. "Are you okay?"

She nodded. If he had to include an adverb, he would have said, bravely. Hadn't Jeff said the baby would come today or tonight? *Please—not now!*

Two men were stranded on the old scow—but who? Da-Marr and his cohort in crime, Bobby? Jeff and Da-Marr? Jeff and Bobby? There'd been a report of someone going over the falls, but the body hadn't surfaced—might not for several agonizing days, and so far there'd been no description of the stranded men.

Richard swallowed down his rising panic, staring through the windshield at the darkening landscape. It would be full dark in only minutes.

His cell phone chimed, startling him. "Hello?"

"Mr. Alpert? This is Captain Gainer from the Niagara Falls Police Department. I wanted to give you an update on our plan to rescue the stranded men."

"Yes, please do."

"All you have to do is look out the window to see the weather isn't good. It may not be possible to rescue them until the morning."

"Captain, I'm a doctor. I'm pretty sure I know what these men are up against. They've been stranded for hours in the rain, let alone subject to the mist from the falls. The temperature is dropping. That's a pretty lethal combination."

"I understand that, sir, and I don't mean to sound unfeeling, but we can't sacrifice four people trying to rescue two. We also have no idea if one of the stranded men is your brother."

"I don't care who's out there, Captain. I just want them to be rescued."

"I understand that, sir. I invite you to come to the Niagara helicopter tours site up on Main Street by the big hotel—not far from the Rainbow Bridge."

"I know the place."

"I'll meet you there. And sir, I hope your brother can be brought home safely."

"Thank you, Captain."

Richard ended the call.

"Well?" Brenda asked.

"They want us to wait at the commercial helicopter site, but they're saying the weather might not guarantee they'll attempt a rescue until tomorrow morning."

"But aren't they worried about them suffering from hypothermia?" Brenda cried.

From the backseat came a strangled cry. "Oh, my Lord, Da-Marr ... what have I done by bringing you here?"

"Evie," Brenda admonished. "You just hush. If there's one person on this earth who knows how to survive, it's our Jeffy. He's got a knack for escaping death."

"But you don't know who's out there—maybe it's not Da-Marr. Maybe it's that terrible man who led him astray."

Brenda closed her eyes and breathed deeply for a few moments. "Jeffy isn't dead. I would know it if he was."

"Don't you give me that crap that Grammie used to spew."

"You don't believe?" Brenda asked, her voice tinged with surprise.

"Not for a moment," Evelyn practically spat. "Second sight? There's no such thing."

Brenda looked at Richard, and they both managed to produce the shadow of a smile.

"You'd be surprised what we believe," Richard said.

"Nonsense," Evelyn declared.

Richard started the car. "If you ladies don't mind, I think we should follow the Captain's advice and go wait at the commercial helicopter site."

"I agree," Brenda said, but her voice sounded strained.

"But can we make a pit stop. I really have to pee."

"There's a big hotel right near the helicopter site. We'll stop there first."

"Bless you," Brenda said.

Blessed. They'd have to be to survive this terrible night—or maybe for Jeff to survive this terrible night. But who was he stuck with out in the middle of the Niagara River—in the cold and the dark? Da-Marr had tormented him, and if it wasn't Da-Marr, how safe would he be with the other person who'd been on the boat when it had taken off from the marina?

Richard shifted the car into drive and hit the accelerator. It was going to be a long, long evening—maybe night. And what if Brenda went into labor? Where was his loyalty? To his brother or to his wife?

He was pretty sure he knew, and yet he also knew that no matter what choice he made there'd be guilt that would follow him for years and years to come.

TWENTY-NINE

I was pretty sure that, despite my previous experience out on Mount Mansfield, I'd never been quite as cold as I was at that very moment. The rain, the wind, and the spray all conspired to kill me—us. When the light evaporated, we'd retreated to the empty cargo area. Even though we sloshed in icy water, it was better than falling into the treacherous river. Da-Marr stood defiantly with his back to me several feet away, his arms clutching his chest. Even in the almost nonexistent light I could see he was shivering just as badly as I was. Shivering was good. It meant that our bodies were still trying to make heat. When we stopped shivering—it was time to worry.

Talking was almost out of the question. We were both hoarse from shouting to be heard over the roar of the river and the falls, and what did we have to talk about, anyway?

My fallback in times of terrible stress had always been reciting the times tables. Two times two, three times three, all the way to twelve times twelve. But instead I dwelled on thoughts of Maggie and her mother-in-law. Would her ex keep his promise and come back to take care of his mother this weekend? If Rich knew about what had happened, would he call her when he didn't know the outcome, or wait until he had the worst to report? Would she cry for me? Would she be sad for a few days and then carry on? It bothered me that she might get over me a lot faster than she would have if this had happened a year before. In fact, she'd been frantic with worry when I'd faced hypothermia back in Vermont. But a lot had happened since then. We'd only really reconnected in the previous few days after months of awkward attempts.

Moving on to another subject, I worried about Herschel. What would he do without me? Carry on. That's what he'd done when my father died and I acquired him rather than see him go to a kill shelter. In retrospect, it was one of my better decisions. Maggie was fond of him; I was fairly certain she'd find him a good home, although I would much rather she kept him—if only to remember me by.

You're not dead yet.

I wasn't about to think about Betsy Ruth. If so, I was sure I'd lose it and then Da-Marr would be ragging on me and calling me Pussy once again.

Okay, two times two is four. Three times two is six ....

"Hey!" Da-Marr shouted.

I turned to look at him, not that I could see more than just a silhouette.

"I'm frozen down to my soul. Can you really die from being this cold?"

"Yeah."

"What?"

"Yeah!" I shouted.

"I ain't hugging no other man, but maybe if we could stand back to back, then at least one part of me would be warmer."

I shrugged, realized he probably hadn't seen it, and agreed aloud.

We moved closer until our wet backs touched. He was taller than I was by six or seven inches, so I was more likely to benefit from this new arrangement than he was.

He groused about something, but I wasn't sure what

he'd said.

I turned and shouted in the direction of his left ear. "What?"

He turned his head, too. "I said where's the damn helicopter?"

"Delayed by weather."

"Nah, they just don't care 'cause I'm black."

"Bullshit. For all they know, it could be me and Bobby here. That is, if they even *know* about him."

"What do you know?" he asked sourly.

"I lot more than you, apparently."

"Sure. Spoiled little pussy white boy. You had all the advantages. Not like a black kid like me."

"Excuse me, but from what I understand, you ain't from da hood. You're just a middle class kid with a 'tude."

He ignored my comment and went on. "You had everything handed to you; living in a rich house and all."

"Like hell. I grew up in the hood."

"Did not."

"Did too."

"No shit?"

"No shit."

"But what about Richard?" he asked,

"He didn't even know I existed until I was fourteen."

"I thought he was your bro."

"Half-brothers. He didn't live with our mother."

"But you went to college," he asserted.

"Two years, thanks to the GI Bill."

"Pussy boy like you was in the Army?"

"Worst four years of my life."

"Then you came home and lived high," he said with contempt.

"No, then I moved to a shitty, roach-infested, studio apartment in Manhattan, where I lived until I got married."

"You got no wife now," Da-Marr sneered.

"No. Thanks to her cocaine habit, she had the top of her head blown off from her supplier when she couldn't pay."

It was a long few moments before Da-Marr replied. "That's tough." The words weren't right, but his tone held far more compassion than I thought him capable of. "So then you got mugged," he said.

"Yeah. A little over eighteen months ago. Ruined my career. I'm grateful Richard was willing to help me out."

"And now you're a bartender?"

"Hey, I'm lucky to have that job. I had my head caved in. There's not a lot I'm qualified to do these days."

"And the guys who did it looked like me?" he asked.

"Yeah."

"Sorry, man."

"That's okay," I said, but I wasn't sure I meant it.

"No, really. I'm sorry. I'm sorry I been messing with you. I figured you were just some asshole. I should have asked more questions. I should have been nicer. That's the way my mama brought me up."

Once again, the ghetto slur had disappeared from his voice.

"I accept your apology."

He was quiet for long few minutes; minutes filled with the roar of the falls, and the icy raging river not more than a couple of feet away.

"I've had a lot of time to think these past couple of hours," Da-Marr said.

"Yeah?"

"And ... I've got lots more to think about."

I couldn't help but smile. "Yeah, me, too."

After that, we didn't talk much. What was there to say? The old scow had sat in the Niagara River for almost a hundred years. Chances were it wasn't going to go anywhere that night, either. And the chances were that if the weather cleared enough there was a good shot we might get rescued.

If we didn't die of hypothermia first.

Our situation was bad. Worse than when I'd been stranded in Vermont.

It sucked that I'd had to face the same possible end in just over a year.

I was tired of a life that sucked.

Puddles the size of ponds riddled the large expanse of asphalt in the parking lot of Niagara's Wonders Air Tours. Instead of being filled with the cars of eager tourists, it was filled with police cars from three different jurisdictions, state trooper cruisers, and a couple of ambulances. Outside of the police perimeter, every Buffalo TV station had positioned a van with a satellite uplink, ready to report the daring rescue of the stranded men on the old scow.

The problem was ... there didn't seem to be a rescue at hand.

Sam had never caught up with Richard. Was he out there, too?

"What's the holdup?" Brenda cried, her voice filled with strain.

Richard couldn't do anything but shrug. He reached out his hand to her and she grabbed it, holding on far too tight. "Hey, are you okay?"

"No, I'm not. And neither are you or Evie."

Evelyn had left the car to stand under an umbrella some ten feet away. She kept staring at her shoes and seemed unwilling to commiserate with them. It was obvious she blamed herself for the situation, which was totally ridiculous. Well, maybe she was a little bit responsible, but it was nothing Richard felt he was ever going to speak of.

A Niagara Falls patrol officer approached the Mercedes

and Richard hit the button to roll down the window. "I'm sorry to disturb you, Dr. Alpert, but there's a woman at the perimeter who claims she's a family member and wants to be let in. A Ms. Maggie Brennan."

"Of course she's family," Brenda cried.

"Yes," Richard agreed. "She's family."

The cop nodded, tipped his hat, and soon disappeared into the gloom beyond the big mercury vapor lights that lit the lot as though it was day.

Richard turned to Brenda for an explanation.

"I called her a while back when you were talking to one of the cops," she admitted. "Would you have wanted to risk her wrath if I hadn't?"

He shook his head. "I just didn't want to worry her."

Brenda leveled the evil eye on him.

"I'm sorry. And you're right. She'd never forgive us."

Seconds later the blue Hyundai pulled up alongside Richard's car and Maggie got out. Brenda opened the passenger door and practically jumped out of the car, shuffle-hop-running as fast as she could move in her advanced state of pregnancy. Richard got out of the car as the women collided in a fierce hug. By the time he reached them, they were both sobbing hysterically.

"Hey, hey, hey," he chided, and drew them both into a far more gentle hug; they clung to him like lichen on a brick wall. He looked up to see Evelyn standing apart from them, tears streaming down her own cheeks. He reached out a hand to usher her to join them and was surprised when she hesitantly approached.

"Evie," he said, again waving her nearer, and then suddenly she'd attached herself to Brenda and they stood there like a pile of gerbils, just hanging onto one another. It was disconcerting and yet somehow comforting to share so much misery.

It was Maggie who finally drew back, wiping her eyes. "Tell me what's happening."

"Nothing," Brenda cried. "And they won't tell us why."

"It's on a need-to-know basis, and obviously the family doesn't need to know," Evelyn piped up.

"I'm sorry. We haven't met," Maggie said, holding out her hand. "I'm Maggie, Jeff's girlfriend."

"How do you do. I'm Evelyn Mason, Da-Marr's aunt."

"She's my sister," Brenda said acidly, with a sideling glance at Evelyn.

"Yes, that, too," Evelyn agreed rather sheepishly.

"Why is nothing happening?" Maggie asked, looking at Richard for answers.

He shrugged. "The weather. The availability of a rescue helicopter. Apparently, some sailboat was in trouble on Lake Ontario. They can't be in two places at once. We're all getting wet," he observed. "Let's go sit in the car where we can stay warm."

"Da-Marr won't be warm out on that terrible river in the dark," Evelyn said.

"No, he won't, but I can't take the cold—not right now," Brenda said, sounding exhausted. "I must sit down."

"You go right ahead, dear," Evelyn said, "but if you don't mind, I want to stay outside, near the command center. Just in case."

Brenda reached for her sister's hand. "If that's what you need to do, then do it."

Evelyn nodded, and when Brenda leaned close to kiss her cheek, Evelyn allowed it but didn't reciprocate, standing as stoic as a totem pole once more. The poor woman just didn't know how to accept love, and for that, Richard felt sorry.

Richard followed Brenda to the passenger side of his car, opened the door, and helped her in, while Maggie piled in the back behind the driver's seat. No one spoke until he'd resumed his seat behind the wheel.

"Thanks for calling me, Brenda. I want to be here when Jeff gets off that helicopter."

"If it ever arrives," Brenda said tartly.

"Jeff and I have been through some rough times. He stuck by me when I didn't deserve it. I want him to know I'm there for him, too."

"Will Lily be all right without you?" Richard asked.

"Gary and Brian arrived on the five-thirty flight from Lauderdale. I'm free for the weekend and I intend to spoil Jeff … if he's okay and up to it," she amended, with just the trace of a catch in her voice. Her gaze shifted to Brenda. "Have you gotten any vibes in that direction?" she asked almost timidly.

Brenda shook her head. "Not lately, and it's scaring the hell out of me."

Richard looked out the window to see Evelyn speaking with a uniformed officer. "I'll be right back," he told the women, opened his door, got out, and jogged over to join his sister-in-law.

"Richard!" she called, her voice filled with hope and trepidation. "The helicopter is on its way. It should be here in only a few minutes."

"Thank God."

"Once they arrive, a team member will be lowered down to evaluate the situation before making a decision if a rescue can be made tonight," said Captain Gainer.

"If?" Evelyn repeated, her voice breaking.

"I'm afraid so, ma'am."

"Thank you, Captain. Please keep us advised," Richard said.

The officer nodded and turned back to the command center.

Evelyn looked up at Richard, her eyes brimming with tears. "You're a doctor. Please tell me they can survive the cold until morning."

"Jeff's done it before. He knows what to do to keep

warm—at least as warm as is possible under the circumstances."

Evelyn's frown deepened. "I'm sorry, but I don't have a lot of faith in your brother."

Richard straightened to his full height, but spoke kindly. "Then it's lucky I have enough faith for both of us."

Chapter 30

I was losing it. I'd been chanting twelve times twelve for who knew how long and the answer would not come to me. I couldn't remember eleven times twelve, either.

I went back to the tens. They were easy.

"What are you mumbling about?" Da-Marr complained. He hadn't spoken in quite some time. I thought maybe he'd fallen asleep—which could be deadly. Despite the constant noise of the river and the cataract ahead, I was having a hard enough time fighting the urge to lapse into what could be my final slumber.

"We're gonna die," Da-Marr said. "Either that or we're already dead and in hell. My mama told me if I didn't straighten up, I was going to hell in a hand basket. And what the fuck's a hand basket?"

"Beats me. Do you know what twelve times twelve is?"

"Are you crazy?"

"No, I just can't remember. And it's important," I told him with conviction.

Oh, man I was losing it. Lost it. It—whatever it was—was gone.

Everybody knows what twelve times twelve is.

Everybody except me.

I could be in serious trouble for this.

"I cannot feel my feet. They are gone. They have fallen off and how will I walk on stumps?" Da-Marr demanded.

"Fake feet. They have them you know. They don't

look like feet, they look like flippers, but you can run with them."

"I can't run with real feet, how in hell am I gonna run in flippers?"

"Someone will teach you."

"I don't want flippers. I want feet with toes!" Da-Marr yelled.

"You're getting all pissed off for nothing. If we live, they'd probably amputate our legs from the knee down."

"What?" he demanded, horrified.

"Well, maybe not. What do I know? Richard's the doctor—not me."

"Does he cut people's feet off?"

"Not as far as I know, but there's always a first time."

Holy shit! What was coming out of my mouth?

"Hey, look, there's a UFO," Da-Marr said, pointing to the north.

"There's no such thing."

"I saw a show on TV that positively proved there are aliens."

"Oh, and you believe everything you read on the Internet, too, I suppose."

"Mostly. Why shouldn't I?"

I opened my mouth to answer, but couldn't think of a reason why he shouldn't.

"Damn, that UFO is getting bigger. I think it's gonna get us. You know what they do to humans they capture?" he asked.

"Eat them?"

"No! Well, maybe that, too. They do experiments on them—like that Nazi guy in Germany."

"Mengele?"

"Bless you," he said.

"Where did you learn about that?"

"In school, where do you think?"

"I thought you dropped out."

"I did. But I got my GED. I'm going to college—but maybe not where Aunt Evelyn wants me to go. I don't have to do what she says, you know."

"I never said you did."

"I'm gonna fix airplane engines. Richard said I could."

"If he said it, you probably can."

I watched the UFO get bigger and bigger above us. It began to hover right over us, and then the sky opened up—a burning white light that shared none of its heat.

"Oh, shit—they're gonna cut us open, rip out our guts, and eat the rest of us," Da-Marr wailed.

"I don't think so," I said, but I wasn't sure if he could even hear me.

This was my nightmare. This was what I'd feared.

This was the end.

We were going to be sucked into the light.

Forever. Gone.

And then something obscured the light—a black speck that grew bigger and bigger until it hit the back of the scow and bounced back into the air several feet before landing. I squinted up at the figure towering over us. "Gentlemen, I'm Deputy Joe Williams of the Erie County Sheriff's Office; are you ready to get out of here?"

"You better believe it," Da-Marr hollered.

"Which of you wants to go first?"

Da-Marr and I looked at one another before answering at the same time, "Take him."

"How about you first?" Williams said, looking at me.

I looked to Da-Marr, who nodded.

Seconds later, I was hooked into a rescue harness alongside Williams and with a mighty jerk that scrambled my insides, we started our assent.

My nightmare had come to life. The glaring white light obliterated everything. I looked below to the yawning abyss, like the darkness before creation—ebony so dense, no light could penetrate it. No light, no warmth, no love.

The wind, the noise of the falls, the chopper's engine, nearly deafened me as a treacherous gale blew through my hair, stinging my eyes.

We spiraled higher and higher as the wind worked to suck at my soul. I squinted, desperate to block the piercing light as we spun 'round and 'round—as through gravity held no power over us. The cold air seeped into my sopping shoes and socks like thousands of needles while a powerful winch, and that magnetic light, pulled us ever higher, ever closer. The light was so white, so pure, it burned like a hundred suns.

We came to the end of our ride with a sudden jolt, then other arms pulled us into the cabin. Still blinded, I couldn't make out my surroundings as I was released from the harness. Someone slapped a pair of earphones over my head that blocked out the worst of the noise.

Williams gave me a thumbs-up before he disappeared out the open side of the chopper.

"Hey, guy—want to tell me your name?" some deputy asked.

"Resnick. Jeff Resnick. The other guy is Da-Marr … God, I don't even know his last name."

"That's okay. You've got worried family waiting for you," he said.

Sweeter words were never spoken.

He spoke to someone up front, who no doubt would relay to the ground who we were.

Family was waiting. And what did that consist of? Richard and Evelyn? Or was it just Evelyn waiting? And what about Brenda? She was supposed to pop that baby at any minute. Surely, she wasn't with them.

I was supplied with a blanket, and the guy I'd spoken with must have been a paramedic, for he stripped off my shoes and my socks and was examining my feet. I didn't pay much attention. My gaze kept straying to the hole in the side of the copter and the deputy—who looked out for his comrade who'd fallen like a stone into the inky blackness. And suddenly I realized I was worried about Da-Marr. He'd been freaked by the idea of riding in a helicopter. How scared would he be? He was just a snot-nosed kid. Okay, he was older than I was when I'd left home, but for all his tough talk, he really wasn't as worldwise as he wanted everyone to think.

The chopper hovered for what seemed like forever, but I wasn't jostled nearly as much as I thought. The guy at the controls was good—very good. Thank God! After all we'd been through, did we want the chopper to crash into the river and kill us all? But that's where my head was at. I'd faced death too many times and one of these days, my good luck would run out.

Then suddenly Williams reappeared at the copter's open door with Da-Marr in harness.

"Hey, you made it," I said into the microphone just beyond my lips, but of course he didn't hear me and indicated so by smacking his left ear.

Da-Marr was pulled inside and given a blanket. The cabin door shut and the copter took off with a swoop, banking to the right. Like me, he was given a headset. His eyes were dilatcd, looking wild, and his first words were, "That was some fine ride!"

I laughed and held out my clenched fist. He clenched his, and we bumped hands. But then his face seemed to crumple. He reached into the pocket of his soaked jacket and pulled out the purple bag with the diamonds. "I figure you know where these need to go. I got no use for them."

I nodded, and pocketed the diamonds once again.

Then the paramedic between us got serious and started asking way too many questions, assessing our mental states I'd guess. My feet hurt. Bad. Pins and needles. I wasn't sure if that was good or bad, but it was what it was. If I'd been loopy down on the old scow, I'd regained my senses in no time flat, feeling better—more se-cure—with every second that passed.

"Hey, we got family waiting for us," I told Da-Marr.

"Oh, yeah?"

I nodded.

"Who's that?"

"I have no idea."

He laughed. "Bet they've been shitting themselves."

"You mean you didn't?" I asked, straight faced.

His mouth dropped open in horror. God, he was such a kid.

"No, I didn't."

"Me, neither."

"I want something to eat. A couple of burgers. Fries. A pizza."

"Screw that. I want a bottle of Mr. Jack."

He laughed.

Only seconds later, the copter seemed to slowly sink and the night blackness eased into a sea of bright lights.

"Can you walk?" the paramedic asked us.

"Hell, yes," Da-Marr said. He looked at me, his ex-pression sincere. "If you can't, I'll carry you."

"I can walk," I said, and we both removed our head-phones. I shook hands with the crew, thanking them, and then let the deputy help me from the chopper. The rotor wash was incredibly strong, and an ambulance crew instantly descended on us.

"Wait for a wheelchair," one of the paramedics en-couraged, but Da-Marr and I brushed them aside.

I won't say we walked with dignity across that park-ing lot—more like we stumbled—but at least we were up-right. And up ahead was the sweetest sight I'd ever seen: Richard, Brenda, and even Maggie. They ran toward me and we collided in a tangle of arms and necks and kisses and tears.

"God, I love you guys," I said, savoring the sensation

of six arms encircling me.

"You scared the shit out of us," Richard admonished in my ear.

"Oh, man—if you think *you* were scared."

"You're safe, and that's all that matters," Maggie said, and kissed me hard on the lips. Too bad we were standing in a parking lot, because a kiss like that warranted a whole lot more than the situation allowed. I pulled back, and looked Maggie in the eye, felt the tug of our connection back to where it had been a year ago and grabbed her in a fierce hug. "I've missed you, babe," I whispered in her ear.

"Me, too," she breathed.

We pulled apart and I looked behind me to see Evelyn and Da-Marr walking arm in arm, smiling.

A uniformed paramedic appeared at my side. "Sir, we'd like to check you out, if you'll step this way."

"Sorry, guy, but I really don't need your services," I said rather smugly, with euphoria or stupidity—I wasn't sure which.

"Me, neither," Da-Marr echoed. "But where the hell are my shoes? My feet are gettin' dirty."

"Sorry, guys, I'm afraid I *do* need some help," Brenda said with desperation in her voice.

We all turned to look at her, but her gaze was on Richard. "I'm sorry I didn't tell you, but my water broke a couple of hours ago."

"Oh, Brenda," Richard chided.

"The baby is on her way—right now!" she cried.

Suddenly the attention turned from us to her and a couple of paramedics swooped to her side, lifting her up by the elbows and carrying her to the nearest ambulance, with Richard running after them.

Dumbstruck, the rest of us followed, clustering around the outside of the ambulance.

The paramedics donned clean latex gloves, ready to

help with the delivery, but Brenda shook her head. "No, please, I want my husband to deliver our baby."

"Are you sure?" Richard asked.

Brenda looked at him with absolute trust. "I've never been so sure in my life."

I looked away as the paramedics removed her underwear.

"Oh, my God," Maggie breathed next me. "I can see the baby's head."

"Maggie!" Brenda cried. "Evie!"

Both women practically jumped into the ambulance, and somehow positioned themselves behind her so that they could each hold one of Brenda's hands

"Oh, shit," Da-Marr muttered and looked away.

"Push," Richard demanded.

Brenda wailed; a sound that scorched my soul.

"She's coming, she's coming!" Richard cried.

I focused my eyes on Richard's outstretched hands, poised like a quarterback waiting for the center to snap the ball, but instead, Richard stood ready to catch a much more precious payload.

"Ohmygod, ohmygod," Brenda wailed, and I could see her fingers clutching both Evelyn's and Maggie's hands.

"You can do this, you can do this," Maggie encouraged.

"Push!" Richard encouraged.

"Oh...my...God!" Brenda screamed.

Suddenly an extremely bloody and slimy baby girl popped into Richard's waiting hands. A second or two later, the baby began to wail.

The paramedics stepped forward, grabbed the baby, and did whatever it was that newborns needed, while everybody else whooped with joy—including Da-Marr and me.

Brenda was crying. Maggie was crying. Evelyn was

crying. It seemed like all of us had tears in our eyes as we listened to little Betsy Ruth scream her tiny lungs out.

A minute or so later, Maggie and Evelyn retreated and Richard took their place as the paramedics laid the tiny, blanket-wrapped girl onto Brenda's chest.

"Oh my God, look what we've done," Brenda said and kissed the top of the baby's head.

"She's beautiful," Richard said, his voice breaking. "Just like her mom."

Brenda laughed. "Oh my God, I'm a mom."

"You sure are," Maggie echoed.

The paramedics asserted themselves. "We've got to take this new mom to the hospital," they said, shooing the rest of us away.

Just before they closed the ambulance doors, Richard tossed his keys my way.

I caught them, not sure I was up to driving.

Maggie looped her arm around mine and we watched as the ambulance took off.

"Sir, we really need to check you out," a uniformed paramedic said.

"Don't give them a hard time," Maggie chided, and I could see the concern in her eyes.

"I won't."

"You, too, Da-Marr," Evelyn ordered.

"No, ma'am, I won't."

But before I let the paramedics lead me away, I handed Evelyn the keys. "You should have these. I have a feeling I'll be going home with Maggie."

Evelyn nodded. "Thank you." She leaned in close and spoke into my ear. "Thank you. I have no doubt that if you hadn't been there, Da-Marr wouldn't be here with me right now."

I shrugged and turned away. Was that true? I didn't know or care.

Maggie dragged me toward one of the other ambulances. Now came the part that I didn't like. Strangers touching me, prying into my personal life. Then again, it was a small price to pay for being alive.

THIRTY-ONE

The ball danced around the rim and went in. Two points for me.

"Cheater," Da-Marr accused, grabbing the basketball.

"Liar," I responded.

He dribbled the basketball some more, but I only half-heartedly went after him. We'd been playing for nearly an hour and despite the tight elastic brace, my knee was killing me. Besides, I was pooped.

He aimed, threw—slam-dunk! "Ha!"

I held my hands up in surrender. "I'm done."

"Loser!"

"Hey, I gotta shower and get ready if we're going to the game."

"Shit, I almost forget," Da-Marr said, bouncing the ball a few more times. He took aim one last time, threw, and missed.

"Sucker," I said and laughed.

Richard's Mercedes pulled into the driveway, followed by Maggie's blue Hyundai, and Da-Marr let the ball roll away. We stood watching as multiple car doors opened. Richard had driven Evelyn, Brenda, and the baby home from the hospital, while Maggie had brought back the flowers, balloons, and gifts that had accumulated in only a day—mostly from Richard's and Brenda's California friends.

"I could use some help here," Maggie called.

"You can do it," Da-Marr muttered.

"You can do it."

"Who's going to make me?"

"I will," Richard said, sounding just a little annoyed.

"Yes, sir," Da-Marr said, lowered his head, and walked toward Maggie's car. The kid's behavior had done a one-eighty since our ordeal on the Niagara River two days before. He seemed to have lost most of his swagger after a day being interrogated by various police jurisdictions.

I'd surrendered the bag of uncut diamonds with the assurance they'd be given to the proper authorities—as soon as someone figured that out.

Bobby's body had been found the previous day near the river's whirlpool. And of course, wreckage from Easy Breezin' had been scattered along the shores of the gorge. What a mess—for us, for Bobby's family, and the impact on the environment. At least the boat's fuel tanks had run dry before it went over the falls.

Richard helped Brenda from the car before he bent down to retrieve Betsy Ruth, who was bundled up in pink jammies decorated with little bunnies, a blanket, and the knitted cap her Aunt Evelyn had made for her. I paused to admire her. Friday night she'd looked a goopy mess; on that warm, bright Sunday morning, she looked positively gorgeous.

I tweaked her cheek and she smiled.

"See, she already knows her Uncle Jeff," I said.

Evelyn frowned. "That's gas."

I shook my head. "No, this little girl and I are already old friends."

"You've held her exactly once," Evelyn reminded me.

Richard gave me a knowing look, but said nothing.

Da-Marr walked up to join us, balancing several floral arrangements on a teetering pile of gift boxes, with the ribbons from several pink balloons wrapped around each arm. "Someone gonna open the door for me?"

"I'll take the baby," Brenda said in a rather proprietary manner.

"I can carry her," Richard said, cradling his daughter as though she was a delicate soap bubble.

"I think I should carry her in," Evelyn said. "I've had more experience with babies than all of you put together."

"Tell you what, Evie, since you are the most experienced among us, I'm going to let you change her diaper," Brenda said, smiling.

Evelyn looked about to make a withering reply, but then seemed to think better of it. "I'd be happy to."

Maggie brought up the rear, her arms filled with yet more vases of flowers. "Well, will somebody open the door or are we going to stand around in the driveway all day?"

Richard was not about to surrender the baby to any of them. "The keys are in my jacket pocket."

"I'll get the door," I said. It wasn't locked.

"Hey, take one of these flowers," Da-Marr demanded. So I grabbed one of the vases and led the assembled up to the back door, holding it open for everyone to enter.

They all trudged through the house and into the living room, where Richard finally surrendered the baby to her mother, who sat down in one of the wing chairs.

We all looked at each other.

"Now what do we do?" Brenda asked.

I shrugged. "I guess we figure out the new normal."

Betsy Ruth yawned and moved her pudgy hands up to rub her eyes.

"Awww," all three women chorused.

Da-Marr rolled his eyes. "We should get ready for the game."

"Don't fill up on beer and junk food," Maggie warned, "I've got a pan of lasagna all ready to go in the oven about five—it'll be ready at six. That should give you plenty of time to get home from the stadium."

"Da-Marr is underage. He can't drink," I pointed out.

"The hell I can't!" he protested.

"You will not drink," Evelyn said in a tone that broached no argument.

"I will not drink," Da-Marr said meekly.

I smiled. "Guess who's the designated driver?"

"Don't celebrate yet. The Eagles are gonna trounce the Bills."

"Won't."

"Will."

"Won't."

"Will you please stop that," Maggie snapped.

I put the flowers down on the coffee table, and then bent down to kiss the top of the baby's head. "I'll see you later, Princess Betsy."

"See you later, Jeffy," Brenda called to my back, as she and Richard turned back to admire the baby.

Evelyn reached over to take more flowers from Da-Marr's pile of stuff.

I paused at the doorway and looked back at the people in the room. It had been one hell of a week. Like Dickens said: the best of times and the worst of times.

And as I'd told Da-Marr out on the river, Betsy Ruth wasn't the only new member of my family.

ABOUT THE AUTHOR

The immensely popular Booktown Mystery series is what put Lorraine Bartlett's pen name Lorna Barrett on the New York Times Bestseller list, but it's her talent -- whether writing as Lorna, or L.L. Bartlett, or Lorraine Bartlett -- that keeps her there. This multi-published, Agatha-nominated author pens the exciting Jeff Resnick Mysteries as well as the acclaimed Victoria Square Mystery series, and now the Tales of Telenia fantasy saga, and has many short stories and novellas to her name(s). Check out the links to all her works here: http://www.lorrainebartlett.com

If you enjoyed **Dark Waters**, please consider leaving a review on your favorite review site.

Thank you so much.